ALSO BY JOHN DRAKE

Fletcher and the Flying Machine

JOHN DRAKE

LUME BOOKS

LUME BOOKS

This edition published in 2022 by Lume Books

ISBN 978-1-83901-458-1

Typeset using Atomik ePublisher from Easypress Technologies

www.lumebooks.co.uk

In fond memory of
David Burkhill Howarth

----------- *DBH* ------------

1946–2009

PATRIFAMILIAS AMATISSIMO
MAGISTRO DOCTISSIMO
INGENIOSISSIMO TECHNITAE
OPTIMO AMICO

INTRODUCTION

This book is the seventh in a series of the memoirs of Admiral Sir Jacob Fletcher, 1775–1875. I hope that readers who come first to this book will accept that Fletcher's full story is covered in earlier books, such that by 1803 he was notorious to the newspaper-reading public of England and America.

Note that he was a bastard: the illegitimate son of Sir Henry Coignwood, the industrialist, and press-ganged into the Navy by the machinations of his stepmother, Lady Sarah Coignwood. He rose to high rank and was involved with extremes of contemporary high technology, incorporating steam engines and early submarine boats: even sinking a British frigate with a submarine mine in Boston Harbour in 1795.

He was furthermore unique in being the only naval hero who never wanted to be in the Navy, wishing only for a career in trade because of his formidable business skills. But Fletcher was a fine seaman and man of action, being huge in bulk, enormous in strength, and instantly recognisable by the thin white streak in his black hair.

Whatever his inclinations, he had an extraordinary career of seafaring adventures which, in later life, he recorded as memoirs dictated to his secretary, the Rev. Dr Samuel Pettit who transcribed them into twenty-five volumes. Poor Pettit was horrified by the content of Fletcher's dictation and, after Fletcher's death, he added chastising notes to the memoirs, which I have included:

[**inside square brackets in this different font and signed: S.P.**]

Thus, my main role is to edit Fletcher's own story, having acquired the twenty-five volumes at auction in 2012 plus a large trunk of papers and memorabilia. But I have used this archive to construct third-person chapters to give a rounded account of Fletcher's adventures. These chapters are merely my invention but I have tried hard to reflect reality.

Finally, note that Fletcher was adored by women and was chivalrous towards them. But there was one exception: his stepmother, Lady Sarah Coignwood, a woman of extraordinary beauty but vindictive character.

Since she appears in this book, here is Fletcher's opinion of her, given in a letter of June 5th 1876, from Dr Pettit to his brother Ignatius:

*"On my referring to the Coignwood woman in his presence, the Admiral fell into appalling rage and bellowed the following words, which I have cleansed of hideous oaths: 'God * * ** her for the nasty, spiteful, * * * * * that she is, and may the * * * * * * * devil come down the * * * * * * * chimney and carry her off to hell! And as for you, Pettit, you long thin streak of * * **, I'll gut and fillet you should ever you speak of that * * * * * * * * * * again!'"*

John Drake, Cheshire, England. 12/8 /21

—1798—

PROLOGUE

The Atlantic Ocean,
Three miles north-west of Dursey Island,
Near the southern tip of Ireland.
(Early morning, Tuesday February 13th 1798)

"My good and beautiful ship was close to rounding the island and passing clear from all perils."

(Translated from a letter of Wednesday February 21st 1798, written in Bantry, Ireland by Capitaine de Vaisseau Gwilherm Madec and addressed to his wife.)

Madec stood by the binnacle and the ship's wheel where four men were needed to hold a course. All hands were hanging on to hand-lines to keep footing on a deck swilling with water as the ship struggled to save the eleven hundred souls aboard: seamen, infantrymen, artillerymen as well as women Cantinières.

"The ship's doing her best!" said Madec, though 'said' meant shouting with all his strength into the ears of his First Lieutenant, with heads touching and the sleet hammering their oilskins like musket balls. It was the only way to be heard, with the sea and the wind so loud that a seaman's shout was the squeak of a mouse.

The First Lieutenant nodded and hoped – and Madec hoped – that their ship would save them. Everyone hoped: the afterguard hauling lines on deck, the elite topmen aloft, and the troops crammed down below. For them it was horribly worse, with hatches battened over them and their tight wooden world heaving and groaning and dripping and leaking. They barely had light: just dim lanterns and deep shadows. They barely had air:

they were packed together half-suffocated, with each one clutching the next for fear of being thrown over by the violent motion and slammed against the bulkheads.

Out came the rosaries, however much the Revolution despised them, as these trapped and terrified land-folk begged God and the Virgin for salvation, and begged every saint in the calendar to intercede. They begged as good Catholics, just as their mothers had taught them and just as the village priest had hammered into them before he was got rid of by the Enlightenment. They just prayed and prayed, because they could do nothing themselves and depended entirely on the seamen and the ship.

Up above, Madec raised his telescope and focussed on the mass of the island that was reaching out for *Fructidor*. It was black and it was wet: black and white wet. Everything was black and white: the huge seas with vicious caps, and the black clouds with a great hole where the white moon shone through. Madec looked at the island and cursed. He knew that everything possible had been done. The yards were braced round, the ship under the minimum of sail, preventer-stays rigged, and hand-lines for the deck people so nobody got washed overboard. And he had a good crew and a good ship: *Fructidor*, a frigate built for thirty-eight guns, fresh out of of Le Havre, and as fine as any afloat. But a ship was small and the ocean vast, and its power without limit.

"Is it Dursey Island, Mon Capitaine?" the First Lieutenant shrieked into Madec's ear.

"Who the hell knows?" said Madec shrieking in reply. If it *was* Dursey Island, then *Fructidor* was right on the south-west tip of Ireland, blown there at high speed by winds that couldn't be resisted, and which had scattered the Fleet of Ireland, ruining all attempts to land men and guns in support of the Irish rebels. But how could any seaman be sure where he was after days like this? And given old charts that couldn't be relied on? Madec sighed. Whatever damned island it was, it was waiting in hunger for his ship, and he could see the God-almighty enormous waves smashing the rocks that jutted out from the island, and throwing up spray in sheets that flew a hundred feet into the air: thirty *metres* if Madec must use the ludicrous new measures that all decent seamen despised, or at least they did if they were Bretons like Madec, born to the sea, and born three hundred miles from Paris.

"Bah!" thought Madec, and left off all nonsense of politics, just hoping his ship would clear the rocks ahead.

"Steer small!" he yelled at the helmsmen. "Close as you can get!" Which was stupid because they already knew that, because their lives were on it, and they couldn't hear him anyway. But they guessed what their captain had said, nodded, and looked up at the sails. They made the futile effort to bring *Fructidor* closer to the wind in the hope of clearing the ruin and destruction ahead that was beckoning the entire massive eight hundred tons of their ship, like a magnet pulling a pin.

Madec kept his glass on the island, and so did the First Lieutenant, and so did everyone with a glass from the Boatswain to the young Aspirants, who were officers in training. Everyone looked, and *Fructidor* – God bless her – didn't lose a spar, or a line, or any stitch of canvas even with the Devil's own personal wind trying to tear her apart. She was doing her absolute best, and all the mariners on board were looking at the island, judging and judging.

"Mary, Joseph and Jesus!" said Madec. "She's going to do it! She's coming clear!" He turned to shout that at the First Lieutenant, but he didn't get the chance because, in that same moment, there was a *WHOOOOSH* and a splintering crash, as something came over the ship like a fiend of hell. It hit the mizzen-top, smashed timbers and threw men overboard, to be gone forever and gone in an instant, and gone beyond all hope of saving. The thud of a gun came seconds after. A double thud of two guns, in fact, but only one shot came anywhere near *Fructidor*.

Every glass now turned to look astern, and there was communal groan that nobody heard for the noise of the storm.

"No!" thought Madec. "Not now!" It was the English. A week ago, the Fleet of Ireland had got past them completely. It had got round their self-satisfied Channel Fleet that was supposed to be so superior and so wonderful. The English had failed to intercept the French expedition and, if it hadn't been for the weather, they'd have lost Ireland because of it and serve them damn well right! He put his glass on the enemy and saw an English frigate with banners flying, and the wind snatching white clouds of powder smoke away from her bow. But the First Lieutenant was yelling.

"Shall we beat to quarters, Mon Capitaine?" he cried.

"How can we?" screamed Madec. How could they indeed? *Fructidor* wasn't really a fighting ship: not any more. Not with most of her guns removed, and everything below decks turned into a floating barracks. Not with a whole regiment aboard, and field pieces and gunners, and women.

WHOOOSH! WHOOOSH!

The English fired again but scored no hits. Madec saw the powder smoke, then heard thud-thud! He looked at the ruin of the main-top.

"Clear that away!" he cried, "before it fouls the sails! Clear it or we're done for." He had to say that. He couldn't help it, even though it was impossible to give commands to the men aloft, and even though they would use their seaman's initiative without thinking and without needing any order. And yes, yes, they were busy! They were cutting and splicing and doing what they could.

Then the First Lieutenant was yelling again. Madec listened. He heard some of it.

"Frigate … bow-chasers … 9-pounders … taking the same risk as us … same rocks." Madec nodded and looked at the Englishman. Where the hell had he come from? Was it chance? What else could it be? Wherever he came from the Englishman couldn't chase *Fructidor* much longer or he'd be in the same peril as her. The First Lieutenant seized Madec's arm and shook it shouting, "Stern chasers? Rig stern chasers?" Madec sighed. The First Lieutenant was young. He wanted to bring forward one of the broadside guns that was still aboard, haul it astern, and fire on the English from a stern-port.

"Yes!" said Madec. "Try! Make the attempt!" The First Lieutenant saluted and ran off to attempt the impossible: to haul an 18-pounder plus carriage and tackles through the mass of bodies crammed in down below. He got a hatch prized open and went below, and he really tried, but even with the help of the artillerymen, it couldn't be done.

WHOOOSH! WHOOOSH! Thud-thud! The English tried again and were lucky. They were lucky because they were on the extreme limit of any ability of any gun to hit anything whatsoever, when fired from a moving deck at a moving target. But the bastards were lucky. Another crash came from aloft and the main topsail yard was blown away ten feet in from its larboard side, causing the topsail to shudder and spill, and causing the ship to lose way, and lose the safe course that she had been steering.

Another groan from all who saw it. More desperate work aloft to make good the damage and get the sail drawing again. But the English were too lucky for *Fructidor*. The English had fired just six times, miraculously scoring two hits that could only be by pure chance. But the two hits ruined the narrow balance by which *Fructidor* would have been saved. After that, whether by luck or judgement, the English captain – whoever he was – came about and got clear of Bantry Bay before it caught him too, just as now it caught *Fructidor*.

The ship had done her best. It wasn't her fault, and now Madec had to do *his* best. He struck sail to give steerage way only. He tried to find a gap in the rocks as the ship was driven on to them. But there was no gap. He did his best when she groaned, rumbled and died on jagged stone, barely a cable's length from the shore. She was so close, but she was broken and ruined and could do no more. Madec did his best to control the panic when hatches were opened and those below poured out in their misery and ignorant terror, and onto a canting, slippery, sleet-battered deck. He did his best even when the seamen's courage failed.

He did his best as the ship rolled over on her beam ends, and showers of human bodies went into the sea. When she settled, with her masts over the side and rigging and splinters everywhere, but miraculously upright, Madec got the boats away and the women aboard. When all the boats were gone, he had rafts made and lines taken ashore for the benefit of those who followed, by those rafts which grounded safely. By these and other feats of seamanship – and under the most appalling conditions – Madec did every last thing that ingenuity and courage could contrive for the salvation of those in peril on the sea.

Despite this, over eight hundred men were lost, though even this was not the worst disaster of France's failed attempt to raise rebellion in Ireland, since there were greater horrors on land. But Madec saved one hundred and eighty lives and was the last to quit the ship: refusing to go until he knew for sure that nobody was left behind.

He was a hero by the traditions of any service that ever flew a flag, and by the fortunes of war he survived.

But the French Nation was deeply scarred by the appalling losses of 1798 and vowed never again to make such an attempt upon Ireland.

Unless of course, something should change.

—1803—

CHAPTER 1

I blame my sister, Mary. If it wasn't for her, I'd never have been heaved off the ramparts of a Baltic castle, with only some silk and bamboo between me and death. But that came later. At first a new interest came upon me and it was all consuming fascination. You youngsters should take note that when you're innocently happy you might never know what's creeping up behind you.

In June of 1803, I was back from adventures in Africa, and suffering from a severe falling-out with the Admiralty. It was all about diamonds such that, while I was now an exceedingly wealthy man, the Admiralty wouldn't employ me even though we were at war with the French.

As regards *employment* remember that in those days, even if you were a full captain as I was, you weren't really in the Navy unless you had a commission which sent you to serve aboard a specific ship with a specific rank. If you hadn't got that, then you were in a limbo of emptiness, with nothing to do, and many poor devils went mad with the despair of it.

Fortunately, I was different. I was press-ganged *into* the bloody Navy and spent half my life trying to get *out* of it, because I was never meant for the sea. The sea knows this only too well, which is why it's always tried to kill me, because the sea is vicious, cruel and spiteful and it takes joy in breaking the hearts of those who sail upon it, or do I fail to make myself clear?

[Nonsense and affectation! Even as he spoke the above, Fletcher grew emotional in fondness for the seafaring life. Moreover, he was deeply proud of his seamanship and would discourse at length about it given the slightest opportunity. It was his lifelong vanity to pretend otherwise. S.P.]

In truth, all I ever wanted was to be left in peace to make my name as a man of commerce, and I could have done it too. But I give blessing to small mercies that I had a sister and brother-in-law, Mary and Josiah Hyde, who were active at the top end of the carriage-building trade, and just as soon as I came ashore, they welcomed me as a partner in business to live with them in their home, Hyde House, near Canterbury.

But there was more to it than that because I came home wounded from Africa, where there was a princess of the Zulu people who I had fallen for deep. She affected me as no woman ever did before or since. But she was another man's wife, and things happened that are painful to recall. So I sought comfort and peace, which meant my sister's house and my nephews and nieces. I spent many hours with these youngsters, taking them boating and teaching them how to knot and splice.

I should have been jolly at Hyde House, with a flourishing business, and new ventures constantly planned. There was no drink though, since Josiah was of the Methodist temperance persuasion and there wasn't a bottle in the house. But it's a wicked world, and you can't have everything this side of paradise. There weren't any women either but just for once I did without, since there couldn't be anyone to compare with my princess. So I was content rather than jolly.

The trouble was that while I had always wanted to get out of the Navy, now that I was really out, I kept thinking about the sea!

[**My point is made. S.P.**]

My sister sent me out to walk off my misery and I don't blame her because – aside from myself – I never met anyone to equal her as regards consuming diligence for business. It was her, not Josiah, that was the driving force in the carriage business, and she was a steam-powered calculating engine when it came to figures. It's in the blood. We get it from our father. So she sent me out soon after I got back from Africa.

We were sitting in the counting house, in one of the big sheds in the grounds of Hyde House, and we were supposed to be considering investment in the beds of coal beneath a gentleman's estate near Wigan. But I was looking out of the window.

"Jacky!" says she, which is what she always called me. "Jacky!" and she rapped the desk with her knuckles. "You are not paying attention! What's the matter?" I looked round: bright windows, high desks, clerks, ledgers and everything I loved. But I didn't know what Mary was talking about. She looked at me and sighed. She was thirteen years older than me, and still thought of me as a baby. "It's ships, isn't it?" says she, and I nodded.

"Go for a walk. Go for a walk and make up your mind. Out! Out! Out!" So I got my hat and coat, and went out.

I went out and wandered, trying to decide what to do with myself. Hyde House was in the countryside; it was a beautiful summer's day, and there were hedges and cottages, and green grass and round hills. It was the England you dream of, but I don't remember much else because I was deep inside my head and thinking hard. Then I came over the crest of a hill and saw the most amazing sight. In front of me there was a slope like a green lawn. Beyond that there were fields and oaks, while below me – charging away down the slope – there was a team of two horses, with a man riding one and other men running alongside. The horses had a weird contraption under tow. It was a tiny, canoe-shaped carriage on two light-built wheels. It was about six feet long, and a young lad was aboard. He was hanging on to a great tiller that ran out astern, ending in fins like the flights of an arrow. Meanwhile, above the carriage held on by thin poles and braced lines, there was a huge kite, with a pointed nose and trailing tail, and the kite was filling with wind as the horses galloped.

Then – most amazing of all, and I gasped at the sight of it – all the men ahead of me cheered, and the carriage jumped, and bloody well flew into the air! Then the tow was cast off, and the carriage and kite soared upward. It covered some two hundred yards, with the lad working his tiller, trying to control the beast, but it swerved and bucked, and the kite sail flapped, and spilled, and down came the whole lot in a scraping and ripping.

It had left everyone behind, so we all ran forward to the lad in the carriage now covered in the wreck of the kite. There was quite a crowd of us: dozens at least. Some were persons connected with the device, while others were locals out for fun. Some of these were yelling mockery.

"Another one down, sir!" says a cheeky fellow.

"Will you aim for the moon next time?" says another.

"Why don't you try pulling it with geese?"

"No, *swans* is what he wants!"

"Ha, ha, ha, ha!"

I pushed through, and not gently because I didn't like the mockery of boldness. So some of those who'd shouted loud got knocked over hard. I then helped pull the kite clear of the carriage because the kite was awkward and flopping with its bracing lines gone. There were three men working besides me dressed in servants' livery and they were most polite.

21

"Thank 'ee, sir!" says they.

"Thank 'ee indeed!"

Then an elderly man came up, who'd been left behind, and he was yelling and gasping. He was bald with a fringe of white hair; he was red-faced, stocky and broad, and had the speech of a gentleman. He had a gentleman's clothes too, complete with gloves and top-boots, and a round hat.

"Arthur!" says he. "Arthur! Pray God you are unharmed!"

"Here, Grandpa!" says the lad in the carriage, grinning furiously. He was about fifteen, and reminded me of the mids aboard ship, because he was small and young yet full of confidence. He was knocked about, but no bones broken. He just sat in the wreck, merry as can be.

"Oh Arthur!" says the gentleman. "I should never have let you do this."

"Mind your wife don't find out, Sir David!" says a voice, to much laughter.

"Mustn't risk the heir apparent!" says another.

"She'll have your guts for garters!"

"Ha, ha, ha, ha!"

Once again I was annoyed. So I turned on them.

"Shut your blasted traps," says I, "or I'll come among you." After my threat they did shut their traps but looked on, muttering to each other. Meanwhile, the young lad was stuck in the canoe-carriage.

"Can you get me out, Grandpa?" says the lad. "This thing's bent and squashing me." We all looked down, and there was an iron rod, bent out of shape and bearing on the lad's leg. One of the servants tried to shift it but couldn't. Reaching down, I took hold and hauled it clear without effort, because it's what you can do if you're my size and strength.

"Ah!" says the lad and climbed out. He laughed, clapped hands and skipped around to show he was fit. He made me smile.

"Thank you, sir!" says the elderly gent. He considered me and added, "Would you be Captain Fletcher, sir? Brother to Mrs Hyde?"

"I'm Fletcher," says I, well used to being recognised.

"Captain Fletcher," says he, "I've heard of you." He held out his hand. "David Bayley, Baronet. And this is my grandson, Arthur."

"Captain Fletcher?" says young Arthur. "Fletcher of the submarine boats? And the steam engines?" He obviously knew of my past adventures, and was pleased to meet me. So was Sir David. He was as wide-eyed as the boy, because he was old in years but young in mind. It was hero worship, and it was embarrassing and unwanted by myself.

[**Rubbish! Fletcher revelled in his reputation as the navigator of a submarine boat off Boston, Massachusetts, and with steamboat engineering in France. S.P.**]

"My house is a short walk that way," says he, pointing. "And I'd be honoured if you'd take a glass with myself and Arthur."

"And we can talk about steam!" says the lad. I couldn't help but smile. I liked them. I liked them both. How could I not?

"It's me that would be honoured," says I, pointing to the wreck. "Did I not see this aerial carriage in flight just minutes ago? And this young gentleman aboard of her? Surely this is a new thing on the face of the earth?"

"Not at all, sir," says Sir David. "The Montgolfier brothers were aloft, twenty years ago."

"Very modest of you, sir," says I. "Because they had a balloon!"

So off we went, discussing the navigation of the air, and leaving the servants to clear up the wreck and load it into a handcart. As we went, we passed the locals and I'm afraid they were awestruck too, and they weren't peasants with dung on their boots, but farmers and tradesmen.

"Cap'n Fletcher!" says one, raising his hat, and the rest joined in.

"Cap'n Fletcher!"

"Cap'n Fletcher!"

You youngsters should note that the Bible says if God be for us, who can be against us? But your Uncle Jacob says that if the newspapers be for us, who can be against us? Meanwhile, the 'taking of a glass' turned into several glasses, and an invitation to dinner from Lady Patience, Sir David's wife, and a rider sent to Hyde House to invite Mary and Josiah besides. But all that afternoon, before dinner, I was in Sir David's workshop – a barn-sized outbuilding – with him and his grandson, looking at plans, designs and models for flying machines. It was wonderful and I give but one example.

"Show Sir Jacob the ornithopter," says Sir David.

"Ornithopter?" says I.

"The flapper!" says Arthur, and he ran over to a corner where an untidy collection of discarded models lay in heaps. "Here, Sir Jacob!" says he, coming back with the oddest model, near six feet long but with not the least weight to it. It was another carriage but with a seat for a man to haul on levers like oars that would cause wings to flap: light, butterfly-looking wings of silk and spindly wood that stuck out on either side, and one wing broken.

"Ornithopter," says Sir David, "a machine to fly by flapping wings, which is a dead end and useless because no man has the strength to flap wings big enough to lift him." "How do you know that?" says I.

"By mathematics," says he, and off he went into the most wonderful exposition of thrust, and speed, and weight, and the design of sails of great spread but little weight in order to catch the lift of the wind. "Flapping is useless," says he, finally, "so for the present we must look to gliding like a seagull, until such time as we may propel the carriage with air-screw turned by steam."

"But steam engines are heavy," says I, "and isn't weight a great problem?"

"Quite so, Sir Jacob!" says he, and off he went again, down the track of steam-engine design, and how to make them small and light. It was wonderful. I've seldom enjoyed a conversation so much.

Later, when Mary and Josiah arrived, we all sat down to dinner and talked of aerial navigation most of the evening. I enjoyed every word of it, which Mary and Josiah did not, and if I'd known where it would lead me, then I'd have changed the subject. But I didn't. So I suppose it served me right for being selfish.

CHAPTER 2

14 Dulwich Square,
West London.
(Morning, Friday June 17th 1803)

*"What she said was cruel beyond believing, since the lady was so wonderful
lovely."*
(From a letter of 19th June 1803, from Miss Polly Dedworth to
her mother)

The weather was glorious, so the mistress chose her Hyde-built Landau
for the expedition. It stood outside her house in the most fashionable
quarter of the metropolis. It gleamed. It rode upon the latest of springs
and was upholstered like a monarch's drawing room. More important, it
was completely open so that *she* could be seen by an admiring world as
she passed by, drawn by a pair of horses of staggering cost, with a liveried
driver on the box, and two liveried footmen on the step at the back.

Since it was unthinkable for such a lady to ride alone, she was in company
with two pretty little serving girls recently arrived from Berkshire, with
smooth cheeks, round limbs, and big eyes. These girls sat in the finest clothes
they had ever worn in all their young lives, even if they were only lesser
reflections of the outfit worn by their awesomely sophisticated mistress.

She wore a tiny white bonnet adorned with peacock feathers, and a
long-sleeved, yellow silk jupon that came just under the bust, over a white
muslin gown with silver embroidery that flowed to her ankles. Having
decided that jewellery was unfashionable this season, she wore none so that
others might see her and know themselves to be caught out in last year's
style. They would know that because she was one of the reigning beauties

of England: the subject of portraits by Reynolds and Gainsborough, and celebrated in a thousand prints and caricatures. She was the envy of women and the idol of men – she was Lady Sarah Coignwood.

She was Lady Sarah Coignwood, widow of the late Sir Henry Coignwood, the celebrated manufacturer of fine china, who had made such a colossal fortune and left his companies so well managed that even Lady Sarah could not spend the money faster than it came in.

"Drive on!" said Lady Sarah. The driver flicked his whip and the Landau rolled forward as the two servant girls rocked in their seats, gaping at Lady Sarah. One of them merely gaped, but the other – Polly Dedworth – gaped and thought about what she had heard of her mistress. She had an aunt – a housekeeper in a great mansion – whose influence had won Polly a place in Lady Sarah's household. But her aunt had given warning:

"She's got a temper, Lady Sarah, and some say the money weren't rightly hers. But be a good girl and you shall do well."

Polly looked at Lady Sarah, who smiled in return, and the smile was so lovely that Polly could believe no ill of her. But she did wonder exactly how old Lady Sarah might be? She was known to have had two grown up sons, one killed in the Navy, and one disappeared. Could she be over forty? It was impossible to believe. Then Polly lost her train of thought as the Landau moved through such a traffic of vehicles as she had never imagined. The streets echoed with the rumble of wheels and the clopping of hooves. Lady Sarah was constantly acknowledged by fashionable persons. She waved at some while ignoring others who were, therefore, downcast and shamed. Thus, Polly wondered if this was entirely kind?

Soon the Landau rolled into Bingham Square, one of the epicentres of London's shopping life. It was a great rectangle of noble buildings in white Portland stone, enclosing a garden of choice shrubs and flowers, within neat iron railings.

Polly stared as Lady Sarah's Landau approached a line of carriages outside the Bingham Square Bazaar, which rose upon five floors and a basement, and every floor crammed with the most exclusive wares in the city. Since the Bazaar was as full as the management could permit, there was a queue of London's finest, waiting to be admitted.

Lady Sarah waved to the drivers and occupants of the carriages, and these persons waved back with eager smiles as their drivers made way, and Lady Sarah's Landau advanced to nearly the front of the queue. But there, even *her* progress was delayed by two carriages each with a most grand and aristocratic lady within. Thus, the gold-laced drivers did not make way: not even for Sarah Coignwood. Polly saw that *one* grand lady smiled and waved at Lady Sarah while the other did not, staring straight ahead with a face of pure vinegar: another little warning.

But all was forgotten in the paradise within the Bazaar, and the respect with which Lady Sarah was received.

"God save your ladyship!" from a round, fat pastry cook.

"I trust you are in good health, ma'am?" from a lacemaker and her staff.

"Such a joy to see you today, Lady Sarah!" from the diamond jeweller.

Polly soon forgot everything except the glory of the goods on display and the items purchased, and everything on credit with never a hint of payment.

It was pure joy. It lasted for some hours and then it was time to go. Polly, her companion and Lady Sarah were in the Landau returning to Lady Sarah's house in Dulwich Square. Except that the Landau did not go to Dulwich Square. It went through streets that grew progressively shabbier. It went past Old Street towards a graveyard, next to a huge and gloomy building which looked down upon the dead.

The Landau stopped in front of the building which had a large sign over the entrance.

St Luke's Hospital and Asylum

Polly looked at the sign and wondered, and she looked at Lady Sarah who merely smiled. Then the footmen were letting down the Landau's steps and throwing open the door, assisting Lady Sarah to dismount. As she did so, the front doors of the building flew open and four men and a woman ran out. They split faces in greasy smiles; they wrung hands with limitless unction and they bowed low. Meanwhile, one of the footmen whispered to Polly.

"Never mind what you see inside," said he. "She does this to everyone."

"Just keep quiet," said the other footmen, "and you'll be alright."

Then the greasy ones were speaking.

"Oh, Lady Sarah!" they said. "Oh, the honour! Oh the condescension!"

The leader was a large man in his forties: poorly shaved, a stubbly chin and not entirely clean. He wore a grey wig like a clergyman, and a long black coat and clerical band. A woman stood beside him: fat, overdressed and coarse.

"Dr Wilson," said Lady Sarah, "and Matron Brant, I hope that I find you well?"

"Oh indeed, Lady Sarah!" said Wilson.

"Oh yes, Lady Sarah!" said Matron Brant.

"And yourself, ma'am?" said Wilson.

"I am well," she said, "and have you received my letter?"

"Oh yes, Lady Sarah!" said Wilson.

"And everything is ready for your inspection, My Lady," said Wilson.

"Oh yes, oh yes," said Matron Brant. "Anything for you, My Lady!"

"Good," said Lady Sarah. Then she turned to Polly and her companion. "Come!" she said. Just that single word.

Afterwards, Polly's memories were disordered and ugly. Though she did remember Matron Brant, saying:

"Scrupulous, My Lady. Scrupulous! We've had everyone scrubbing and cleaning and no expense spared of hot water and soap. And so there ain't no smell now." That's what Matron Brant had said, but the stench of urine skewered Polly's nose as she entered the building because, on the first floor, there was a hideous line of so-called 'wards' which were in fact cells, where mad women were chained to their beds. Some of these women were near-naked; all were in rags, and all of them were out of their minds with insanity.

"These here, we divide into *wet patients* and *dry patients*," said Dr Wilson.

"As you can see, My Lady," said Matron Brant, "the wet patients, such as cannot maintain continence, are provided with straw mattresses that can be burned, which is the best possible way with such persons."

After that, there were long corridors with windows overlooking the graveyard, and women who came in and out of wards and wandered: some barefoot; all with hopeless vacancy of expression; some talking to themselves; some being restrained by the staff; a constant noise of doors opening and shutting, and cries and moans from dark corners. Later, there were wards for mad men: equally hideous, equally shocking, and equally terrifying. The worst was the Correction Room in the basement, which had an enormous water tank with a run of steps leading up to one end of it.

"The water stays cold down here," said Dr Wilson, "and I find that even the most difficult of patients, if immersed and briefly held under, will soon cease their bad behaviour."

There was more. Much more. But finally, Polly and her companion were in the Landau, leaving the stench and ugliness behind, heading for Dulwich Square, and being told why they had been taken to St Luke's.

"Now, my dears," said Lady Sarah with a smile, "as you know, all servants see and hear everything." Her smile faded. "Do you understand?" The two girls did not speak, but Lady Sarah continued. "So, my dears, you must understand that should either of you ever speak of anything that you see in my house, then you will not merely be dismissed without a reference, but you will find yourself confined as a patient of St Luke's, such that if you are not – at first – insane, then very soon you will be." She paused to see the effect of her words, which of course was tears.

"Good," she said, because that very evening she was expecting a new lover. He was John Pitt, second Earl of Chatham, who had been First Lord of the Admiralty from 1784 to 1789, and was now Master General of the Ordnance: an organisation second in power only to the Treasury and which was entirely responsible for the great guns of the Army and Navy. Therefore, while the Earl of Chatham was not entirely to Lady Sarah's taste – she preferred young men of strong virility – she knew that the Earl of Chatham was aching to get her into bed, and that his influence within the Sea Service was colossal.

He was just the man to ensure that a certain Sea Service officer, now condemned to half-pay unemployment, should be given the command that he deserved so very much indeed. Therefore, it would be disadvantageous in the extreme if the Earl of Chatham's wife were to learn of the exercises planned for tonight. But Lady Sarah knew that she could rely on the discretion of her servants.

CHAPTER 3

I'm afraid that Mary and Josiah weren't especially gripped by the subject of aerial navigation, but my fascination was so great that I let my inclinations run away with me and they were bored something dreadful. On the other hand, Lady Patience, Sir David's wife, bore the discussion heroically having heard it all before. She wasn't nearly as old as Sir David, being a fine, pretty woman. She was his second wife after a family tragedy, which was explained when Mary got in a word to ask a question.

"And are you visiting your grandfather?" says she to Arthur, who was sat respectfully quiet in the company of his elders, so this was kindness on Mary's part, to bring the lad into the conversation.

"No, ma'am," says he, in reply. "I live here, with Grandpa and Lady Patience." He looked at Sir David silently.

"I should explain, ma'am," says Sir David, "that my son, Arthur, and his wife, and my first wife, Anne, were lost in a boating accident at Brighton. But by fortune's grace, my grandson, Arthur, and his two younger brothers were saved."

"My deepest sympathies, sir," says Mary.

"Indeed," says I and Josiah together.

"And the brothers?" says Mary. "I trust that they are well?"

"Edward and Christopher," says Sir David. "They are thriving, ma'am. They are away at school, and coming on well." He smiled. "As is *young* Arthur," says he, nodding to his grandson, "who is quite the scholar, being fluent in languages and a promising engineer." Then Sir David turned the conversation back to aerial matters, wishing to spare us from his sorrows. Soon we were in the deep of it yet again: me and him, and Arthur now joining in. So Mary and Josiah were falling asleep before we were done, and they did sleep all the way home in our carriage apart from a frigid word from my sister as we first climbed aboard.

"Jacky!" says she, "if ever I hear another word about flying machines ..."

I'll leave you youngsters to imagine the rest, and I deserved it too.

"Yes, ma'am," says I, and "No, ma'am," and so on. Repeatedly.

"I shall judge you by future behaviour," says she, "because we must of course return Sir David's hospitality. We shall have him to Hyde House for dinner: him and his charming wife and that lovely boy."

"Yes, ma'am," says I. The next day I was back at Bayley Hall to carry Mary's invitation to Lady Patience, since all such matters passed from one Lady to another. Once that was done, Sir David looked at Lady Patience, and she looked at him and nodded as if there was some understanding between them.

"So!" says Sir David, taking my arm and leading me to his study. Young Arthur was sent for, and joined us with smiles all over his face. I smiled back and thought we were in for another congenial discussion. But we were not because, although I did start to talk about steam engines, I could see that Sir David had something else to say, which indeed he did.

"Now see here, Sir Jacob. This young gentleman," says he, pointing at his grandson, "wants ..."

"To go to sea!" says Arthur. "I do! I do!"

"Huh!" says Sir David, "he wants to go to sea, and I'm asking you to take him as a young volunteer: a midshipman."

"Oh please, Grandpa!" says Arthur. "Oh please, Sir Jacob!" I smiled at that, for the light in Arthur's eyes. He was damn near jumping up and down. But I had to shake my head.

"I'm sorry, Sir David," says I. "It can't be done. I haven't a ship. I'm beached and stranded." Sir David ignored that.

"If you take him," says Sir David, "*if!* Then you must bring him home safe and sound, because if you don't, then God might forgive you but I never shall!"

"But I told you. I haven't got a ship and I'm not likely to get one!"

He shook his head. "That's not what I've heard."

"What?" says I. "No, Sir David. You must be wrong. They don't like me down at the Admiralty. They'd rather sup with Bonaparte than give me a ship."

"Hmmm," says he, looking at Arthur, then at me, "but if you did have a ship, would you take him?"

31

"I suppose I would," says I. "He seems a likely lad."

"Huzza! Huzza!" says Arthur, dancing all around the room.

"You see?" says Sir David, "there's no containing him. He's mad for it!" I laughed because young Arthur had got the sea fever and no mistake. But then Sir David came about on another tack completely. Or so it seemed.

"Sir Jacob," says he, "if I might presume upon the hospitality of your sister, I would be infinitely obliged if, when Lady Patience and I come to dinner, instead of bringing my grandson, Arthur, might we instead bring a friend? I stress that he is a most respectable person, already known to your sister's husband. He is Mr Harold Norfolk, who sits as a member of Parliament for Bishopsbourne West, which is close by."

That seemed odd, but nothing like so odd as discovering a depth to my brother-in-law which I'd never known. But first, for the education of you youngsters, let me make clear my opinion of politics, and of politicians as a class. Which is, that politicians are like a clap of the French Pox. They are a curse which wise men should avoid.

But when I got back to Hyde House and passed on Sir David's request, there was Josiah spouting politics! And him the very embodiment of a sound English gentleman, with his countryman's ruddy face, his honest features and his excellence in business – that is when led by his wife. Indeed, I had always assumed it was my sister that led him in all things. But now she sat silent while Josiah spoke in their nice parlour with the view over the very outbuildings where his carriages were made. It was astounding. How could a decent man of business also be a politician?

"Mr Norfolk is welcome here," says Josiah. "I know him because he is not only the member of Parliament for Bishopsbourne West, but is the local agent for the Whig party, in which interest he has approached me, that I might stand for Bishopsbourne East."

"What?" says I. "*You?* And a *Whig*? I thought it was Tories that were all for business."

Which I should never have said. Because it showed interest, you see? Or so Josiah thought, and by Jove but he paid me back for boring him and Mary with aerial navigation! He did indeed and delivered lengthy response, of which response I give but a shorthand so that it might not inflict upon your innocent selves, the same agonies that it inflicted upon your Uncle Jacob.

"The Whig party defends religious dissenters, of which I am one," says he, "as a Wesleyan!"

"Oh?" says I.

"And it supports the new industrialists ..."

"Oh?"

"And electoral reform ..."

"Oh?"

"... education for the masses ..."

"Oh?"

"... philanthropy... abolition of slavery ... the Rights of Man ... universal suffrage ..."

"Oh? Oh? Oh? Oh?"

"Whereas the Tories stand for ... blah ... blah ... blah."

So I had good reason to suspect that I would receive another heavy dose of the same when Sir David and Lady Patience came to dinner with Mr Harold Norfolk.

But no, because Norfolk turned out to be a charmer. He was younger than I'd expected, perhaps thirty? He was dressed in Mr 'Beau' Brummel's new-fashion, black and white evening clothes, the first time I'd ever seen such an outfit. He was slim and neat with an odour of perfume about him, together with fine curly hair and a laughing manner. Lady Patience and my sister lapped him up and begged for more. Since he had no lady in tow, I would guess that he was one of those who trod lightly, and he certainly was most amusing company.

It was a good, plain roast beef dinner: my sister and brother-in-law not being of the Frenchified food persuasion, but their dining room was exceedingly well appointed, what with the carriage business turning so handsome a profit. Josiah was even kind enough to serve a decent claret for his guests and myself, although he and Mary took only water.

As for the conversation, Mr Norfolk was generous in seeking my opinion of seafaring matters as they bore upon manning the Fleet and containing the French, and he and the ladies listened to what I said. So I liked Norfolk, despite his profession, and I was flattered by his attentiveness, and when he did turn to politics, he wasn't boring at all because he made fun of it.

"Shall you join us in the Westminster Bear Pit?" says he to Josiah. "You will be easy among us because – as a countryman bred – you will already be accustomed to the grunts and snorts of animals." The ladies laughed; we gentlemen smiled and Josiah nodded.

"You may count on me," says he.

"Splendid!" says Norfolk, "and it matters not if you are no great speaker. Because look at our Tory Prime Minister, Mr Addington! His voice has the strength of a mouse and the grace of an elephant." The ladies laughed again and later, when they withdrew, Norfolk was even more entertaining.

"Addington?" says he. "Pitt absolutely piddles on him when it comes to addressing the House, and Charley Fox kicks his arse so hard that his teeth fly out!" He was very witty, and delivered a string of tales about others of the idiots that frolic and wallow in the House of Commons. He made us laugh. But then Sir David spoke up.

"Mr Norfolk?" says he. "I think you have something to say to Sir Jacob, concerning his future at sea."

"Do I have a future?" says I, looking at Norfolk. I looked carefully because, amusing as he was, he was a very clever man who seemed to know everyone in power.

"Do you have a future?" says Norfolk. He took a breath and thought. "Do you recall the business of the Blue Star?" says he, and it was my turn to take a breath. The Blue Star was a colossal diamond of colossal worth that I had brought back from Africa and which the Admiralty wished to give to the King, but which was stolen by a gang of highwaymen on its way to Windsor Castle. In that respect, all you who read these words must truly believe that I had absolutely nothing to do with this shocking, outrageous, dreadful and wicked crime. I had absolutely nothing to do with it whatsoever. Nothing at all. Trust your Uncle Jacob.

[Fletcher defended the above statement so long as he lived, although rumours forever swirled around him and contributed much to his notoriety in Queen Victoria's reign. S.P.]

"Yes," says I, "I remember something of that robbery." Norfolk laughed. "Well, Sir Jacob, it used to be the Admiralty's reason for denying you any further employment."

"Used to be?" thinks I, in the quiet of my mind. "*Used to be?* Oh dear, oh dear."

"But somebody has been importuning on your behalf," says Norfolk.

"Who?" says I.

"Nobody knows, but it is somebody powerful because Lord Chatham ..."

"Chatham?" says I. "Who's he?"

34

"He is John Pitt, Second Earl of Chatham," says Norfolk, "elder brother of Billy Pitt so recently Prime Minister. The very same Chatham who was once First Lord of the Admiralty and is now Master General of the Ordnance."

"Oh," says I, "him!"

"Him indeed," says Norfolk. "Then take note, Sir Jacob, that Chatham is busy seeking a ship and a commission for you, in order that you might go to sea at the earliest convenience."

"Is he?" says I. "Why?"

"Nobody has the least idea *why*, Sir Jacob," says Norfolk, but the *fact* is that he is doing so. It is the gossip of the Admiralty and of Westminster."

"Westminster?" says I. "Do they know about me there? In Parliament?"

"They know about the Blue Star!" says Norfolk, and they say that Chatham has already considered and rejected, on your behalf, a number of appointments that most Sea Service officers would regard as choice and desirable. So if Chatham wishes to oblige you, and wishes to advance your career, then we wonder what precisely is going forward in this respect."

"Oh dear, oh dear." I think I actually said it aloud that time, because Norfolk smiled. But I could feel deep down in my bowels that something nasty was bearing down upon me.

Would the bastards never leave me alone?

Was I never to have peace?

They were going to drag me back to sea again.

"Therefore," says Norfolk, "as a friend of Sir David" – he looked at Sir David who nodded – "and as a friend of Mr Hyde, besides, then I am happy to count myself as *your* friend, Sir Jacob. And I advise that when the offer comes down from their Lordships of the Admiralty – as certainly it will – then you should think most careful before accepting it."

CHAPTER 4

14 Dulwich Square,
West London.
(Evening, Friday June 24th 1803)

"If there were a rating for erotic sensuality then S. C. would rank unreachable above all others."
    (Private Journal of the 2nd Earl of Chatham, entry for June 27th 1803)

When naked, Sarah Coignwood was everything that she promised to be when clothed, and Chatham could only stare in wonder as she threw aside her dressing gown, except that she didn't just throw it aside: she slid off the silk in a rustle and a swish and twirled herself to give him best possible sight of the best possible view of herself and, by God, she was lovely.

She was smooth and creamy in the candlelight with the most shapely of limbs and the most delectable bum that Chatham had ever seen in his life. What's more, she performed the disrobing as a work of art, which Chatham could appreciate as a connoisseur who'd seen the like in some of the best Houses in Paris, and the girls there hadn't done it better.

"And so!" she said, raising hands, supposedly to make sure that her hair was bound up, with ribbons and out of the way, but also to raise her breasts still higher and offer herself up as even more delectable than she already was. Chatham certainly thought so, and stiffened in anticipation as he lay in the bath. The bath was another wonder. It was enormous. It was sculpted of cedar wood; the size of a ship's launch; lined with linen for smoothness; and filled with hot scented water. Chatham wondered how the hell it had been got up to the first floor? But the bath was no more wonderful than its surroundings: walls and floors of arabesque tiling, silver candelabra, luxurious hangings over the bath, and exotic food and choice wines on tables placed conveniently for the bather. In fact, it did briefly cross Chatham's mind to wonder if all this might be in bad taste? A trifle *outré* ... even vulgar? He knew very well that *La Belle Coignwood* was not received in every lady's salon and that she undoubtedly had a certain reputation. He smiled at that, because otherwise he wouldn't be here, would he? Then all such thoughts went down any plughole that the bath might have had, as she got into the water beside him and began sliding over his body, biting his ears and kissing his lips.

"Now, sir," she said, "shall you take your pleasure of me? Or shall I take mine of you?"

"Now that *is* trite," thought Chatham. "It's lines from a melodrama!" But so what? Because – by God – she was easing herself upon him and wriggling her hips so that he entered within her, and delivered such a broadside as could not have been bettered by a line-of-battle ship. At least that's how it felt to Chatham, though Lady Sarah knew better. But she kept that to herself. On the other hand, and with her encouragement and assistance, he managed yet another broadside within less than half an hour, which was damn good going for a man of forty-seven.

After that, they lay in each other's arms, enjoying the warmth, and the steamy air, and a glass or two of wine. Thus, Chatham was entirely intoxicated with pleasure, no matter whether it was vulgar or not. Then Lady Sarah frowned, reached for a silver bell and rang it.

"Good Lord!" said Chatham, closing his knees together as the door opened, and two neat, little serving girls came in, all dressed in faux-Grecian robes that showed their legs and arms, and fine legs and arms they were too. They carried faux-Greek amphorae on their shoulders and poured hot water to warm the bath.

"I thought it was getting cold," said Lady Sarah, as the girls curtseyed with downcast eyes, and then left.

"Don't you mind?" said Chatham. "Don't you mind who sees what? Because I damn well do!" But she just laughed.

"My dear Lord Chatham," she said, nibbling his ear and whispering so that pure electricity ran up and down his body. "You may rely absolutely on the discretion of my servants, because I most certainly do."

"Do you, by damn?" said he, and couldn't help but laugh.

37

"Tell me," she said, once he was easy and comfortable again. "Tell me why Ireland is so dangerous. You have hinted before, and I should like to know, because *you* know what I want."

"Ireland?" he said. "Now?" but he was half dozing.

"Oh, go on," she said running her fingernails across his chest such that he sighed happily. "Go on!" she said, and pinched him.

"Oh!" he said, and they both laughed.

"Well, half of them hate the other half, and the other half hates them in return."

"Meaning?" she said.

"The Anglo-Irish are on top. They are Church of Ireland Protestants, and they have all the wealth and titles. But half of them live in Ireland and think they're Irish, and half of them live in England and think they're English."

"And they hate one another?"

"More or less. They certainly don't get on."

"And the others?"

"The great mass of them are Catholics. They are peasants who speak Irish, not English, and live on the land. They hate the Anglo-Irish of either kind and, of course, they hate the English. Then there are the dissenter Protestants. They're mainly in the north. They're industrious folk, not peasants, but being dissenters, they can't hold office or join the Army. They hate the Anglo-Irish and they hate the Catholics, and the Catholics hate them, and they fight one another."

"Fight?"

"Armed mobs. Organised mobs. They go round at night burning houses. The Protestant 'Peep-o'-day Boys' against the Catholic 'Defenders'."

"Can't we stop that? With the Army?"

"And start another war like '98?"

"Tell me about '98."

"Really? Now?"

"Yes. Tell me about the United Irishmen."

"Oh for God's sake, not now …"

"Now!"

He sighed.

"The Society of United Irishmen? It was formed by some of the *Irish* Anglo-Irish. It was supposed to unite everyone against the English. They got the French to back them, and a French fleet was sent. There was a hideous uprising in 1798, which we had to crush with the Army. It was the worst fighting in the British Isles since the Civil War. There were fifty thousand dead at the end of it."

"So many?"

"Yes! Fifty thousand dead and many more wounded. It was appalling."

"And is Ireland still dangerous?"

"Good God, woman! Haven't you been listening? Ireland is a powder-keg. One spark and it'll be off again!"

"Is that why no officer of the Sea Service wants to go to Ireland?"

"Yes. Nor any officer of the Army, because there's no credit to be gained and much to lose. It's not like fighting the French. It's ugly war and it's civil war. It's atrocious on all sides." Sarah Coignwood smiled and kissed Chatham with such enthusiasm that he stirred into action.

"Oh?" she said, "have you cleared for action yet again, sir?" He laughed.

"By God, yes!"

"In that case, and if you want more, you must pay close attention because this is what I want you to do with regard to Ireland ..."

CHAPTER 5

I knew nothing about Ireland in those days. That's what led me astray. But I did know about His Majesty's ship, *Tromenderon,* which is also what led me astray. It was *Tromenderon* that sent me back to sea again, contrarywise to the warning from Mr Norfolk and to my own inclinations. So I do wonder why I was so stupid and I regret it even unto this very day.

[False! False! False! These are the pretentions of a poseur. Note that as Fletcher spoke of the ship *Tromenderon* his face became alight with joy. It was as if he were in love with some beauteous lady. S.P.]

In my own defence, I offer that my last commission afloat had been as Captain of *Tromenderon,* a prodigy of design and widely regarded as the finest ship in the Fleet, being huge in size and nominally of second-rate, since she bore ninety guns, plus carronades. But since all her long guns were 32-pounders, as opposed to the usual 24 or 12-pounders on the upper decks, then *Tromenderon* was capable of greater fire-power than a conventional first-rate of a hundred guns. As well as that, she had the underwater lines of a speedy frigate. Of course, the hidden secret in all this was that she was copied from a French original that had been taken as a prize and closely studied.

This is the sad truth because there's no arguing with the fact that the Frogs built splendid ships, based on mathematical principles. So what a shame it was that they didn't *keep* mathematics, rather than going round invading other people's countries and chopping off heads with their blasted guillotine. That and eating garlic, which is an atrocity for which no decent Englishman can ever forgive them.

Shortly after Norfolk's warning, I did indeed receive the offer that he'd foretold. It came by Admiralty Courier. This offer I represent here, adding only the fact that it came on finest paper in a big round hand and embossed with the Admiralty's fouled anchor.

To His Majesty's Trusted and Well-Beloved Servant:
Jacob Fletcher, Knight of the Bath,
Hyde House,
Near Canterbury,
In the County of Kent.

Sir,
I am commanded by Their Lordships of the Admiralty to inform
you that you are to be commissioned in the rank of Commodore,
aboard of His Majesty's Ship, Tromenderon, in company with such
other of His Majesty's ships under your command as may serve
His Majesty's pleasure, and that you are requested and required
to present yourself before the Admiral Commander-in-Chief
Portsmouth, at His Majesty's Dockyard of Portsmouth and at your
very earliest convenience.

All Commissions, Documents, Papers and Instructions apper-
taining unto your duties await your urgent arrival in the hands of
the proper officials at Portsmouth.

Given this day Monday July 18th 1803.
For their Lordships of the Admiralty.

T.J. Silkin Esq.

Clerk of the Acts and Amanuensis to the Earl St Vincent, First
Lord of the Admiralty.

Mary was with me as I opened the letter in her parlour. I must have shown emotion, because the word that leapt off the paper was *Tromenderon*. That and the fact that I would hoist a broad pennant as commodore in charge of a squadron, receiving all the pay and privileges that went with that rank! I read it over a few times to be sure it was real and then gave it to her. She read it and shook her head.

"Huh!" says she. "So you'll be leaving us again?"

"Shall I?" says I.

"Huh!" says she again, and then everything went fast. There was packing and folding of clothes, bringing down my sword and pistols from the attic, and also going to Bayley Hall to inform Sir David and young Arthur that Sir David was right after all. I had indeed got a ship, and such a ship! I thought there would then be a delay while Arthur got together his sea traps, but no.

"Look, sir!" says Arthur, leading myself, Sir David and Lady Patience into a small day-room where everything was laid out: his midshipman bicornes and uniforms, his foul-weather gear, sea trunk, sextant, dirk and all the pots and potions that young gentlemen took to sea – even Dr Pilchard's powders for the seasickness. He was halfway to the moon with delight, even if Sir David was dreadful downcast at losing him, and Lady Patience in tears. But he was a smart lad and he stood straight, raised hand to brow and dropped all the skylarking. Instead, he looked at me serious, knowing that there could be no familiarity between us now.

"I am ready for duty, sir!" says he, which considering the small size of him brought absolute sobs from Lady Patience, and Sir David blowing his nose into a handkerchief. After that, we upped anchor for Portsmouth the very next day, and by the kindness of my sister and brother-in-law, and the nature of their business, we went in a travelling-chaise fit for a king. That and four matched horses, and a hired driver to the fore and two guards astern, and all our luggage in the boot.

In those days before the railways, a good average speed on land was ten miles per hour including stops to change horses. So it was a long day's journey to cover the 120 miles from Hyde House to the Portsmouth dockyard, with eleven changes. It was late afternoon when we came to the Portsmouth Royal Dockyard where God's Own Almighty Navy – the British Royal Navy – lived in the splendour of its home port. There never was a sea town in all the world so heavily fortified behind massive walls, so well guarded by heavy guns and red coats, so lavishly provided with cranes, sheer-hulks, dry-docks, warehouses, gun-wharves, mast-ponds, and clerks and officials, together with block-making machinery of vast ingenuity. That was Portsmouth, my jolly boys!

[See how Fletcher's true regard for the Navy appears, despite all the insincerity of his repeated and ludicrous protestations. S.P.]

Clippety-clop! Rumble-Rumble! We went in through the main gates, with their white pillars topped with huge golden balls, and the marines saluted at mention of my name. Arthur leaned out of the let-down sashes to gaze and gaze at the great ships in the harbour, and the busy traffic of wagons and of boats pulling out to the ships, and between the ships. All that and the smell of the sea, the gulls calling, and the seamen in tarred hats and earrings.

"Look, sir!" says he, all excited, "see how they walk! They really *do* walk with a roll!" It made me think of the first time I was ever at sea, excepting that I was pressed as a lower-deck hand which was not pleasant to recall, but you can't change the past, and must make best of the present.

And so to the office of the Commander-in-Chief Portsmouth, with more marines on guard, and old guns sunk upright in the kerb-side as bollards to discipline the traffic, a Union Flag flying above. There we found that the great man – Admiral Sir George Montagu at that time – was gone out on business. But he was expected back, so we waited in a side room off the vestibule, with the chaise outside and Mr Bayley still gazing at the ships through a window.

Fortunately, Montagu was soon with us. He came in with a retinue of officers, some in Army red and some in Navy blue. The door to our side room was open, so Bayley and I stood and were pointed out. Thus, I saw Montagu and the rest react to the mention of my name. Most of them muttered and stared, but Montagu came up to me and amazed me by smiling and offering his hand. That's not what I was used to from the Admiralty's elite. It came as a surprise, and I think it might have had something to do with his own career. He was in his fifties: a tall man with heavy brows, swarthy face and full lips. He'd served in major fleet actions but despite having risen so high, the sea gossip was that there was a hidden stain on his reputation. So perhaps it takes one rogue to know another?

"Sir Jacob!" says he. "You are expected!" He smiled again. "Fletcher the steam-navigator!" says he. "The bringer of diamonds and the submarine voyager!" Well, that was fairly said. So I liked him on sight, and all the more fool *me* for being blinded by a friendly smile! I'd have done better with one of the Admirals who damned me as a pirate and never forgave me for sinking a ship with a submarine mine, thus encouraging our enemies to do the same to us.

"Honoured to meet you, Sir George," says I.

"Come with me, Sir Jacob," says he, turning to his followers. "Gentlemen? You also!"

"Aye aye, sir!" says they and, "Yes, sir!" depending on the colour of their coats.

43

"And who is this young gentleman?" says Montagu, spotting my companion.

"Mr Bayley, sir!" says Arthur, touching his hat.

"He will follow me into my next ship," says I, "as a young gentleman volunteer."

"Excellent!" says Montagu. "You shall not go far wrong, Mr Bayley, if you take Sir Jacob as your example." By God and all his little angels! I had to gulp before I could believe that because, for all the promise of the letter from St Vincent's amanuensis, I still feared that the Admiralty might drop me in the drink with an anchor to help me float. "Meanwhile Mr Bayley," says Montagu, "why don't you take a turn around the dockyard and be back here in an hour or so? Since Sir Jacob and I have much to discuss."

Upstairs in his main office there was a big table with chairs, windows for light, a jumble of charts, papers and muster books, and a staff of lower creatures – mere lieutenants – to fetch and carry, and serve the drink. So down we sat, Montagu, myself and the rest and straight to business.

First he introduced the others present, who were colonels of line regiments, plus a couple of post captains and several officers of the Transport Board, which was that part of the Navy that hired merchant ships to carry troops, guns and stores for overseas service. I stress here that the Transport Board had a powerful reputation of efficiency in this vital work of commissariat and supply. So if they were looked down upon by so-called 'fighting seamen' – which they were – then all the more fool them, because while we could always beat the Frogs at sea, it was only by landing armies *ashore* that we could stamp 'em flat and teach 'em sense.

Then Montagu turned to me:

"Sir Jacob," says he, "you are to have *Tromenderon* now at anchor in Spithead, and your Fleet Captain will be Edward Ilford, just recently promoted from First Lieutenant." By George that was new: a Fleet Captain? You see a commodore was a temporary admiral, and his flagship was therefore ruled over by a full post captain, to spare his mightiness, the commodore, of such lowly duties. So that was another step in your Uncle Jacob's career. Meanwhile, Montagu looked at one of the lieutenants. "Commission!" says he, and the Lieutenant gave him a document which he passed to me. "There, sir," says Montagu, "that paper makes you master of *Tromenderon* and all who sail under her protection." The red and blue coats nodded. "Which protection shall include the two 38-gun frigates, *Philhemon* and *Orastices*!" Then he paused, frowned, and looked closely at me. "Now, Sir Jacob, what do you know of Ireland? And of the rebellious rising of 1798?"

"Nothing," says I, "since I was in the Far East for most of '98."

"Then know this," says he, "know that within the British Isles, the rebellion of 1798 was the most hideous letting of blood within a hundred and fifty years, and the like must never happen again!"

"Never again!" says the colonels and captains.

"Never!"

"God forbid!"

"And also know," says Montagu, "that Bonaparte is well aware of the instability of Ireland, since the French sent troops in '98 to aid the Irish rebels, and only by the providence of foul weather was their fleet prevented from landing, since we of the Navy" – he paused and drew breath – "*we failed absolutely to intercept them in advance!*" He actually thumped the table when he said that, and I don't blame him. "And therefore, Sir Jacob, you are to be entrusted with the main defence of Ireland, basing your ship, and those others under your command, upon the dockyards of Cork, and convoying to Cork a squadron of transports embarking five thousand regulars and two hundred of engineers and artillerymen, together with all heavy equipment and guns."

At this point, I suggest that you youngsters get an atlas to see how Ireland stands opposite England. Especially see how the southern part of Ireland leans westward into the Atlantic, putting Cork – second city of Ireland – as a prime location for any fleet dedicated to protect Ireland. That is, to protect Ireland from fleets coming in from the Atlantic, or coming south around England to get at Ireland. Which is all very well, but now look at the western coast of Ireland, and see the long procession of inlets, harbours and bays that wriggle in and out, and all of them with rocks. See that and remember that the prevailing winds are westerly, coming unhindered across thousands of miles of cold grey sea, where they've been gathering strength and malice.

Consequently, my jolly boys, there are some giant waves that come ashore on the west of Ireland even on good days, and when the weather turns nasty, then the whole, raw, God-save-us length of western Ireland becomes a lee shore that is death for ships under sail. Please remember that: you who've been bred up in a world of screw propellers and iron steamers, which go where they please and sneer at the wind and even if they do go ashore, they're so strong they don't break up.

Being a seaman and used to charts, all of the above occurred to me even as Sir George Montagu offered me the duty of protecting Ireland, even with the finest ship in the Fleet and a commodore's rank. In addition, I thought of Mr Norfolk's kind warning ... and so ... I could have said and should have said : *'no thank you'* or *'suddenly I feel unwell'* or any of a dozen wise and sensible things. But I didn't and I still don't know why.

[Yet again, Fletcher denies his own nature. The truth is that he was intoxicated with the prospect of command afloat, and could no more resist it than cease breathing. S.P.]

After that, and taking my silence for glad acceptance, Montagu pressed on.

"You should know, Sir Jacob," says he, "that we believe the Irish are active again, and may have been in communication with the French. Therefore, the expedition which you shall command has been in preparation many months. Our aim is to send as many troops as possible to Ireland and to strengthen the land fortifications, while *Tromenderon* herself – as flagship – was got ready and manned by that fine seaman, Sir Percival Elphinstone, until his unfortunate illness." He looked at one of the lieutenants. "Something surgical, was it not?"

"Stone in the bladder, sir," says the Lieutenant. "He was cut for it and is mercifully recovering."

"Oooooof!" says everyone, wincing.

"Pray God he continues well," says Montagu.

"Aye!" says everyone, in sincere agreement.

"Meanwhile, we were obliged – at short notice – to replace Sir Percival," says Montagu, "and your own name, Sir Jacob, was recommended at the highest level both within and beyond the Admiralty." He saw my puzzlement at that, and he laughed. I suppose he knew my reputation just as I knew his. "So you have a patron somewhere," says he. "Someone who has taken advantage of Elphinstone's indisposition."

After that it was all detail: how many transports; how they would be adapted to take soldiers, horses and guns; who would go aboard which ships; and how many warships would be in company with *Tromenderon*. It was all very well planned. I very much liked the look of the Transport Board officers, and my two frigate captains looked capable men. It was only as the meeting ended that further doubts appeared. Montagu kept me back for a glass of wine, on pretence of getting to know me. But he sent the lieutenants away so it was just the two of us. He leaned forward and raised a glass.

"Here's to you, Sir Jacob!" says he, "and Heaven help you!"

"Oh?" says I. "In what regard?"

"In regard of the fact," says he, "that you haven't the ships to do the work you're supposed to do and, concerning which fact, I never heard the end of complaining from poor Elphinstone, who constantly threatened to resign his commission!"

"Oh," says I.

"See here, Sir Jacob," says he. "We must indispensably keep our main force – the Channel Fleet – in readiness to defeat an invasion of England by Bonaparte, because that would be the end of us, since just as our Navy is better than *his,* then his Army is better than *ours!*" I nodded, because it was true: the Frogs were good soldiers and their Army vastly bigger than ours. "So," says Montagu, "we cannot spare enough frigates and line-of-battle ships to form a proper defence of Ireland, and you must just do your best with what you've got. Do you understand?" Once again I thought of Harold Norfolk M.P. By Jove he was right, and I wondered who my unknown patron might be? Could it be the Earl of Chatham as Norfolk had suggested? I thought not because he didn't know me. What had I to do with the Master of the Ordnance? I'd never even met him! None the less, somebody had contrived to hand me a poison chalice.

All I could do now was hope that it was only Irish rebels I had to deal with, and that Bonaparte's mind was elsewhere: *anywhere* elsewhere than Ireland.

CHAPTER 6

Le Ministère de La Marine,
Hôtel de La Marine,
Place de la Concorde,
Paris.
Early Morning: 20 Fructidor XIII by the Revolutionary Calendar.
(July 21st 1803)

"He was an inspiration! He spoke for all France in his ambition for an Irish revolution!"

(Translated from the diary of General Auguste Coulonges for Sunday July 23rd 1803. Note that in later years, Coulonges struck out the Revolutionary dates and replaced them with Gregorian dates.)

The company of horse clattered across the Place de la Concorde, led by their captain and lieutenants, a small group of staff officers and the man whose bodyguard they were. All the people cheered the splendid black horses and the heavy cavalrymen of the Old Guard, in their bearskin caps, their swords, boots and firelocks. They were the pick of the Army and their pride was immense. The people cheered them, but not so loud as they cheered the man who rode in front of them all.

The company rode towards the enormous Hôtel de la Marine: a perfection of 18th century architecture in fine, biscuit-colour stone. Outside the great building, the company of horse was received by marines of the Consular Guard: blue coats, gold-draped shakos, Charleville muskets, and perfection of drill. Stamp! Stamp! Stamp! Bugles called and banners waved. The staff officers and their leader dismounted; they entered the building and they were received again, this time by the Minster of the

48

Navy plus acolytes, who bowed and led the way. They passed through the richly decorated splendour of the interior, and up a broad staircase, to a room lit by rows of windows, where another company of uniformed men was waiting. These were officers of the Republican Sea Service, the Land Service, and the Bureaucracy. A small group of civilians stood gaping at the wonders around them.

Also, there were tables bearing charts, prints, diagrams and lists: all formed up in ranks like Grenadiers of the Guard.

The Minister of Marine led his honoured guest into the room, together with the tall and fabulously uniformed staff officers, who wore every colour of the military rainbow. They were handsome men, still young, who had been promoted fast by the brilliance of the New Order.

But nobody looked at them. Everyone looked at a sallow-faced little man, with black hair plastered down, and the plain coat of a mere colonel. He looked at everyone with fierce eyes, and everyone looked at him because he was Napoleon Bonaparte, First Consul of the Republic, who greeted General Auguste Coulonges – senior officer of this meeting – with these words:

"If it *is* to be done, then *when* can it be done?"

"Much preparation is already complete, my First Consul," said Coulonges, "so it can be done very soon."

"Be precise!" said Bonaparte.

"Within weeks, my First Consul." Bonaparte nodded, said nothing, then stalked up and down the line of tables in a clunking of boot heels, taking in everything at a glance. For him, any new information, however complex, was *once seen never forgotten*. He could read a book in an hour and recall everything. He studied the papers, then turned to address the roomful of men who were waiting in deep anxiety.

"I will permit this venture of Ireland," he said, and everyone smiled, especially the civilians. "But!" he said, and everyone shrivelled. "You must be lucky this time! I will not have France dishonoured by another failure." He stared at them all, and not one man present dared to meet his eyes except the civilians. He instantly went towards them. "You speak French?"

"Yes, my First Consul!" said their leader. Bonaparte turned to an officer who had followed him. Bonaparte raised eyebrows in enquiry.

"Henry Fitzsimons," said the officer, consulting a list, "Grand Master of the Dublin Lodge of the Society of United Irishmen. He is here with four others of his kind."

"Good!" said Bonaparte to Fitzsimons. Bonaparte smiled and spoke to Fitzsimons and the room relaxed again. "It is good that you speak French, because I wish to say how much I admire your revolution against the British. The British who – these hundreds of years – have oppressed the people of Ireland!" He turned to the rest. "Long live the Irish Revolution!" he said.

"Long live the Irish Revolution!" they cried.

"Good!" said Bonaparte, and took Fitzsimons by the arm, leading him towards the tables laden with papers. "And now, I shall have the details directly from you. I wish to know what organisation you have in Ireland, where your strength is concentrated, how many men you can put into the field, what arms and ammunition you require, and how soon you can be ready." He turned to the French officers. "After that, I shall wish to know how many men *we* can spare, and how many ships, and of what kind. Then, and more than anything else, I wish to know what special and particular precautions you propose, to avoid the failures of 1798. I will hear that *personally* from each one of you because each one of you will be *personally* responsible."

"Yes, my First Consul!" said the French officers, and a long discussion followed.

CHAPTER 7

I went aboard *Tromenderon* as soon as I was done with Montagu. I took a whole pile of instructions with me, giving the ships and officers under my command, together with standing orders for convoy duty, provisioning ship, and much else. I took them and Mr Midshipman Bayley, who was so full of excitement he nearly jumped out of the boat. He had to be shoved forward to get *into* the boat, when he tried to stand back for me out of politeness, not knowing that the senior officer is always last into a boat and first out.

For me, there was a considerable warmth on getting into the boat, because it was *Tromenderon's* launch come ashore for me, and the ship's First Lieutenant in command. Also, there was a crowd of dockyard folk waiting by the boat. They actually raised a cheer.

"Jacky Flash! Jacky Flash!" says they, and a great, fat sow of a washerwoman lumbered forward and had the bloody gall to grab hold of me and kiss me! That was an education for Mr Bayley and brought more cheers from all the rest, and left my ear sopping wet and ringing from the smack of it. These people have no respect. Not the women anyway. But it made me laugh.

Meanwhile, the lieutenant in command of the boat was Mr Alan Eaton, who'd served under me the last time I was in *Tromenderon*, and he'd done well to be First in such a ship for he was quite young. He grinned like all the rest and touched his hat.

"May I welcome you on behalf of all the ship's people, sir?" says he. "The sea gossip ran before you, sir. It ran like lightning and word went out to the ship, so soon as you entered Portsmouth."

"Well and good," says I, holding off smiling because you never know quite what you'll find on joining ship, and it doesn't do to be familiar straight off. You youngsters should learn that and act upon it, though in this case I needn't have bothered.

So out we went and I got cheers from some of the boats and ships we passed, because whatever the Admiralty thought, the seamen liked me, though God knows why.

[This modesty is entirely contrived, and is part of Fletcher's stubborn pretence of dislike of the sea life. The truth is – as well he knew – that whatever senior officers thought, Fletcher was universally loved by the lower-deck people of whichever ship he commanded, and this reputation spread throughout the Fleet. S.P.]

Then there was *Tromenderon* and, by Heaven, she was beautiful. Such lines, such power, such lofty masts and such excellent paintwork too! I could tell on sight that poor old Elphinstone had done a good job aboard of her before the surgeons got hold of him, so I'm pleased to add that he did survive their attentions and served for years after. So well done him, for looking after my lovely.

Then we were alongside, and Lieutenant Eaton was bawling out the ship's name:

"*Tromenderon!*" says he. It was the formal warning that a ship's commander is coming aboard, given by naming his command. Of course, Eaton shouldn't strictly have done that until I'd read myself in. But he did, and there was a stairway rigged to the entry port, with neat white steps, and brass posts with white ropes between. Up I went, and there was the entire ship's company and the Boatswain's crew sounding their pipes, and the marines in scarlet presenting arms, and I was come home. Oh God it was joyful.

"Three cheers for Jacky Flash," says someone, cheeky rogue that he was.

"Hip-Hip-Hip …"

"HUZZAH!"

"Hip-Hip-Hip …"

"HUZZAH!"

"Hip-Hip-Hip …"

"HUZZAH!"

Then the ship's band gave *God Save Great George Our King* and all hands joined in. Next, the ship's Captain – Fleet Captain, Edward Ilford – who I'd not met before came forward, hat off, to welcome me and introduce my officers. There was a deal of hand-shaking, and recognising of familiar faces and meeting new ones. Mr Bayley was introduced, and was near intoxicated with all that he was seeing.

Next, Ilford called for silence so that I could read my commission to the ship, and become her master under the King. Which I did, and then Ilford made a speech which was received with yelling and laughter from the ship's people, and one great bruiser of a man was pushed forward, barefoot and bare-chested and possessed of ugly fists. He was an African black from the West Indies and was best man in the ship.

"All hands know the manner of your coming aboard ship, Sir Jacob!" says Ilford to wild cheers all round. "And therefore, Sir Jacob, here's Mungo Johnson to greet you as you would wish!" Cheers and more cheers, and a miraculous parting of the main-deck crowd and the appearance – rigged in an instant – of a boxing ring, complete with chairs for the contestants in the corners, and buckets and sponges waiting. Seamen are good at such contrivance, and it made me smile, despite what I have said, because I did indeed have my own way of coming aboard. This way I commend unto you youngsters, should any of you be near my size and strength, for it is a gentle kindness to the men, which avoids all the cruelties of flogging and – which is worse to seamen – it avoids the depriving them of their grog. Because once they have seen me pulverise the strongest man in the ship, then – why – I never have the slightest problem of discipline.

So off with my hat and coat. Off with my shirt and shoes, and stockings too for the better grip of bare feet, and then the ship's bell sounding and myself and Mungo Johnson facing each other with fists at the ready, and, by George, he was a good 'un! Never a wisp nor whisker of him holding back, and it was hammer and tongs from start to finish. For once I didn't have to hold back either, what with him being so big and strong. But the result was the usual one and – as I've said before – there's little credit appertaining unto myself, because even when facing such as Johnson, for *me* it is as it would be for *you* to engage in fisticuffs with a child.

Finally, I helped him up, and raised his arm calling on the men to give respect to a good shipmate, a true Briton, and a credit to the Service.

"And double grog for Mr Johnson and his messmates!" says I, and the cheers this time rattled the topmasts. But we weren't done yet.

"Sir Jacob!" says Ilford, "I have my stopwatch here. All hands are ready for the final part of your coming aboard, and the order that it always pleases you to give."

"Well and good, Mr Ilford," says I, still dripping with sweat and gasping. "You may clear for action, and do so at your best time." So the marine drummers gave *Heart of Oak*, all the grins and nonsense disappeared, and a great rumble of noise rose over the ship: of pounding feet; the heaving away of partitions; the taking down to the orlop of everything moveable; the clatter and scrape of furniture moved. After that there was the casting off of sea-going tackles and the squeal and groan of gun-carriage trucks as the ship's battery was run out for action. All that and much, much more, especially down on the lower gun decks and in the magazines. But once again, credit to Elphinstone because he'd kept *Tromenderon* sharp, and the whole business – so far as I could see and hear – was done without one single order other than the beating of the drums.

In the end, when the men stood panting at their guns, and all was ready as if to engage the enemy, I stood – still half-naked – on the quarterdeck beside the ship's wheels, with Ilford looking at his watch, and Mr Bayley beside me, astounded beyond belief.

"Four minutes and thirty-five seconds, sir!" says Ilford, which was a damned good time. But there was a traditional response.

"Dear me," says I, shaking my head, "it'll have to be quicker next time!"

"Aye aye, sir!" says he, as tradition further demanded.

After that, the drums beat *Retreat* to stand down the ship from general quarters. I got myself down to my cabin below, and called for fresh water, soap and towels. Mr Bayley was sent to the midshipmen's berth on the orlop to become one of the ship's company.

I then had about a fortnight to get to know the ship once again before we set sail for Ireland, and I stress that, once the full weight of my responsibilities had fallen upon me, then just like Elphinstone, I went every day ashore, to pester Montagu with all my might. I did that until he got fed up with me.

"For Christ's sake, Fletcher," says he finally, yelling at the top of his voice for all to hear. "You can always resign your sodding commission if that's how you feel. Resign it and go to the sodding Devil!" But he got me four more ships, bless him: a sloop, a brig, and a brace of luggers. It was a rag-tag-bobtail squadron but it was numbers that counted if I was to keep watch around Cork. Also, Montagu said that there would be more vessels awaiting me in Cork, but he added, "probably," which was a worry.

As for *Tromenderon* herself, I was ever grateful to Elphinstone because of what he left behind. Thus, it was usual for a ship's captain to go aboard with a retinue of followers and servants, and always a chosen secretary or clerk, and a cook and various others. He'd normally bring those live bodies, and a great deal of lumber besides: furniture, bedding, cutlery, plate etc, etc. Of course, other than Arthur Bayley, I had neither followers nor furniture, having never wanted to go to sea again, so I was fortunate in Elphinstone leaving everything to whoever came after him. Captain Ilford explained why.

"He suffered horribly from his stone," says he, and I nodded because bladder stones were notorious for ghastly pain, when bits of them pass out in a man's water. "When finally he went ashore," says Eaton, "he'd lost interest in worldly things, and he once said to me, he said: *all my traps can go to the Devil for that's where I'm bound myself.*"

So, I had all my furnishings as a gift, but I had to work to know my crew, and you must take note that *Tromenderon* embarked some eight hundred of them, including eight lieutenants, a captain of marines and two subalterns, two dozen midshipmen, plus the Purser, Boatswain, Gunner, Carpenter, Chaplain, Surgeon, Sailmaker, Caulker etc, etc, etc. Now all these seafaring persons you would expect to find aboard ship. But the needs of eight hundred men were like those of a whole village, so *Tromenderon* also had a barber, a tailor, a launderer, a cobbler, and even a watchmaker would you believe.

Then there was the Reverend Blackhurst, our chaplain. He was over fifty, and had been a notable actor until he felt *The Call*. He was a fire-and-brimstone preacher, and the men loved him for being a big, heavy man who bumped the insolent out of his way since he was the biggest aboard after myself and Mungo Johnson, though in him there was more fat than muscle. Also he could never be shocked, since he cussed better than any hand before the mast.

Early in that commission, I gave a series of dinners in the great cabin, and one was for a dozen of the youngest midshipmen – including Mr Bayley – together with the Chaplain and Schoolmaster, who were responsible for their moral welfare. The mids got a carefully measured quantity of drink; the dinner was a fine ragout of salt pork, served by Elphinstone's excellent cook. I told some stories of sea life, and then so did Blackhurst, who had taken his full quantum of wine and was looking for more. He was red-faced sweating, and glass after glass went down. But he was never even close to being drunk. He spoke of good food, which he loved, and of bad food, which he hated.

"Cheese, gentlemen?" says he.

"I've been in ships where the cheese was so old and hard that the men made buttons of it, and the Gunner used it as trucks for the gun carriages, since it was tougher than oak."

"Oh," says all the mids, believing this ancient tale, and Blackhurst nodded and left off drinking to shovel in a mouthful of ragout. Then he looked at us with eyes twinkling in the candlelight.

"But *this!*" says Blackhurst, pointing fork at plate. "Now this is different, gentlemen. This is prime relish! And it's all because of the pork!" He took another mouthful, chewed with careful concentration, then nodded. "This will be from the batch of spring '97, or I'm a Chinaman." He turned to me with a tiny wink. "Am I right, Sir Jacob?"

"If you say so, Mr Blackhurst," says I, "though I'd have to ask the cook to be sure."

"No need!" says Blackhurst, "for I can tell by taste alone." He looked at the mids. "Thus, you should all take heed, because a story attaches hereunto this pork."

"Oh?" says all the mids, and their eyes went round as Blackhurst leaned forward and lowered his voice as if divulging a confidence.

"You see, gentlemen," says he, "all the Navy's meat: the salt pork, salt beef, and salt fish too, is prepared in the Victualling Yards at Portsmouth." He turned to me. "Am I right, Sir Jacob?"

"You are, Mr Blackhurst," says I, "and a monstrous great enterprise it is too, with great buildings and high walls and massive gates."

"Indeed," says Blackhurst, "and I thank you, Sir Jacob, for pointing out the high walls and the grim gates."

"Grim?" says one of the mids.

"*Grim*, young sir!" says Blackhurst, lowering his voice still further. "Now! It is supposed that only the choicest of livestock goes in through those gates, for the making up of dinners for King George-God-bless-him's Navy."

"God save the King!" says I, because that's what you said aboard ship when the monarch's name was mentioned. You said it even for George III, who in those days was running round mad: bare-bummed in his shirt with his tackles dangling.

"God save the King!" says all the mids.

"Indeed, indeed," says Blackhurst, and pressed on with his tale. "So it is *supposedly* only the best of cattle and pigs that enters in through the grim gates." He shook his head.

"But?" says another.

"But," says Blackhurst, "I have heard – and from reliable sources – that if you go past the grim gates on a quiet day, then you hear dogs barking and donkeys braying on the other side!" The mids gasped at that, and Blackhurst continued. "And I could say more, gentlemen" – he took another gulp – "but methinks I should not."

"Oh go on, sir!" says one of the mids.

"Yes, yes!" says another.

"Well since you ask, gentlemen," says he, "then listen well."

"Yes!" says they.

"In the spring of '97," says Blackhurst, "the Master Butcher of the Victualling Yard made a great and charitable offer. This offer came from there being an excess of meat in the yards, and a need to use it up before it rotted. All the paupers of the local parishes – those who were a burden upon the public purse – were invited to enter in through the gates to carry away that meat which the Yard could not use." He stopped for yet another gulp, and shook his head. "Which statement of an *excess* of meat was surprising, since it was generally believed that the yard was precious *short* of it that spring … that yard which takes in the living beasts to be slaughtered … and to be butchered for the meat which they bear … and all that blood-soaked business done in a trice … by razor-sharp knives in the hands of pitiless men who are expert in the arts of killing."

"But?" says one of the mids. Blackhurst shrugged.

"But that is what the Master Butcher said. He said that there was an excess."

"Yes? Yes?" says the mids.

"So," says Blackhurst, "on the appointed day, all the paupers came. They came in their thousands: men, women, children. All happy and merry with bags to carry away the meat. And they entered in through the grim gates. And the gates swung shut." Blackhurst looked round the table and fixed the mids in his eye. "And never a word was heard of those paupers ever again." The mids gasped and looked at one another. "But ever since then," says Blackhurst, "the entire world is united in declaring that the pork of spring '97 was the plumpest and sweetest ever known."

There was a long, long silence during which the creaking of the ship was heard, the yelling of some petty officer, and distant footfalls on a companionway. But then I saw the solemn faces and couldn't help myself. I burst out laughing. Blackhurst laughed too. He laughed in great booms, and then all the mids laughed. But one laughed before the rest: Mr Midshipman Bayley. He was highly intelligent, perhaps more than I'd guessed.

All I had to do now was bring him home safe to his grandpa and Lady Patience.

I just hoped that I could do it.

CHAPTER 8

The Port of La Charante,
12 miles south of La Rochelle,
The Atlantic coast of France.
5 Fructidor an XIII by the Revolutionary Calendar.
(August 23rd 1803)

"The Irishmen do not agree among themselves so I have to explain and explain."
(From the diary of General Auguste Coulonges for Tuesday August 23rd 1803.)

The five Irishmen couldn't resist the music. It was joyful and splendid, and they smiled and tapped their feet. It was military music at its finest, with high, blaring bugles and a thunder of drums. The Irishmen looked down from their hill and watched the infantry columns stepping out in their blue coats and tall shakos, with muskets clutched to the chest, and knapsacks tight-strapped. The soldiers went forward in step towards the quays and the boats, as the band played and the Drum Major jerked his staff up and down. They marched to a spine-shivering, quick march of French military music, with its drums and trumpets. They marched and they roared out the song:

"Aupres de ma blonde,
Qu'il fait bon, fait bon, fait bon!
Aupres de ma blonde,
Qu'il fait bon dormir!"

Fitzsimons nudged the man next to him, Liam Byrne.

"See?" he said. "They really are with us. We can trust them!" Byrne was still enwrapped in the music so he was smiling. But he shook his head.

"Huh!" said Byrne. "I'll be fucked if I'll trust anyone, and fucked if I should worry about anything else than the English Navy – God fuck 'em – catching us going over to Ireland!"

"Holy Mary!" said Fitzsimons. "Can you not give up with your swearing? Can you not just watch and be happy?" Byrne said nothing, but they watched the show. The five Irishmen looked down from the hill, standing in the garden of the cottage they'd been given as accommodation. Their servants and their cook stood behind them, and they all looked down the rocky slope that led to the harbour, a hundred yards below.

"Look!" said Fitzsimons. "See that officer there? He's waving at us! Wave back!"

A plumed and splendid officer was mounted at the head of his regiment, and he not only waved at the Irishmen, but yelled a command and the regiment turned eyes-right in salute. "See that?" said Fitzsimons. "Now did you not see that?" Byrne just shrugged.

"Where's Coulonges?" said Byrne. "Where's God-damn Coulonges, our bloody keeper? Where is he? Is he not supposed to be here?"

"Oh be damned with you," said Fitzsimons. "If Jesus gave you a gold piece, you'd suck it to see if it's brass! Just shut up and believe that they're on our side, out of the need to defeat the English!"

But Byrne sneered, so Fitzsimons gave up and went back to watching the show. It was a fine show. The harbour was crammed with ships. Their masts were a forest and their rigging a spider web; while ashore, La Charante was full of the French military. There were soldiers, artillery pieces, horses, wagons, sutlers and clerks. It was a full-scale expedition of fifteen thousand men going aboard ship, together with all supporting stores and gear. As far as Fitzsimons was concerned, the French were delivering their promise, and he was impressed with their skills of organisation, and the number of transport ships – all specially adapted for trooping – that were mustered under the protection of four frigates of the French Navy, and other ships promised. But even Fitzsimons was worried until Coulonges appeared. He came, running and shouting in full uniform, holding his hat and sword as he ran.

"Fitzsimons!" he cried. "Fitzsimons!" Coulonges was half Irish from his mother, and he not only spoke English, but Irish too. He was a general by merit, and a revolutionary by belief. Thus, he was Fitzsimons's friend by correspondence, and the principal advocate to the French Government, of the Society of United Irishmen. He ran up to Fitzsimons, and shook his hand still gasping from his run.

"*Tá brón orm mar sin tá mé déanach, bhí,*" he said in Irish. 'So sorry I'm late.' Fitzsimons blinked because he was *English,* Anglo-Irish, and spoke no Irish. Therefore, Byrne answered for him, because Byrne was pure-bred, *Irish*-Irish.

"*Lá maith duit Ginearálta,*" said Byrne. 'Good day to you, General', and he sneered at Fitzsimons. Coulonges saw that, and realised his mistake, because you had to be so careful with these half-comrade, half-rivals. Five Irishmen were present, but Fitzsimons was not the only one with no Irish, some even had no French, so Coulonges chose English as the lesser evil.

"What do you think?" he said, waving at the preparations below. "Is it everything that you hoped?"

"Yes!" said Fitzsimons.

"It looks very fine,' said Byrne, "but why are we starting from here, and not your main naval base at Brest? That's a hundred miles nearer Ireland and it's where your best ships are!" Coulonges sighed, having already explained this. But he was patient. He had to be! The project vitally depended on the cooperation of the Irish revolutionaries, because even if all fifteen thousand French troops were safely landed, they wouldn't be enough to defeat the English army of Ireland without tens of thousands of Irishmen rising up in support of them.

"You're right about Brest," said Coulonges. "But the English Navy knows it! They know that it's on the tip of Brittany facing out into the Atlantic. And, because of that, they keep a very close watch on Brest. So if we started from there, we'd surely be intercepted."

"Can't you fight your way out?" said Byrne.

"No!" said Coulonges. "If we could do that, we'd have invaded England long ago."

"Why can't you do it?" said Byrne, and Coulonges clenched his teeth, because this too had already been explained. He looked at Byrne and at Fitzsimons, knowing the antagonism between them, and hoping that it wouldn't pull these 'United' Irishmen apart. So he gave a polite answer to an impolite question.

"We can't fight our way out because the English Navy is too strong," he said. "Their guns fire so fast that nothing can match them. It is the one, single thing – the *only thing* –that the English do well. In every other respect they are inferior to the French. They are inferior in art, culture, cuisine – indeed they *have* no cuisine – and absolutely inferior in everything military." Coulonges gave a Frenchman's shrug. "But in sea fighting," he said, "the English are dangerous. They are very dangerous."

"And so?" said Byrne.

"And so," said Coulonges, "there will be diversionary sailings from Brest, and from other French ports, to lure the English away from here. When we sail, we shall go south into the Atlantic, far out and away from England and Ireland, and only then will we go north and then finally east, to land our forces. That way we shall avoid the English Navy."

"And will that work?" said Byrne.

"Of course!" said Coulonges.

"Of course!" said Fitzsimons, looking at Byrne. "We must make it work. We must make everything work. We must do it for Herself." He stumbled on two Irish words but persevered. "We must do it for *Cailín Draíochta!*" he said, and even Byrne nodded. He nodded in profoundest agreement.

CHAPTER 9

With so much done by Elphinstone, and with ships provisioned and manned, I was able to set sail under my broad pennant on Tuesday August 30th, and this was my squadron:

Tromenderon Flagship 90 guns, 10 carronades, 3,200 tons, 789 men
Philhemon Frigate 38 guns, 6 carronades, 680 tons, 285 men
Orastices Frigate 38 guns, 6 carronades, 650 tons, 290 men
Quickly Sloop 14 guns, 4 carronades, 420 tons, 250 men
Bull-Pup Brig 12 guns, 2 carronades, 380 tons, 260 men
Daisy Lugger 10 guns, 2 carronades, 300 tons, 210 men
Hastings Beach Lugger 10 guns, 2 carronades, 250 tons, 230 men

I should point out, for those who don't know, that 'guns' meant the standard ship's gun on the wooden carriage that even landmen recognise, usually a ship's main armament. But a carronade was a short gun for close ranges and firing a heavy shot. It was mounted on a cleverly designed carriage turning on a pivot, so it could be aimed easily from side to side. Thus, a carronade needed only a small crew but was so powerful – within its range – that it went by the sea name of *smasher*.

That was my command: those ships plus twenty-eight merchantmen, ranging from 350 tons down to under 200, from *Angelina Bonny* to *Yarmouth Bay*. But note well that while the King's ships looked down on the merchant ships, it was the merchantmen that mattered because the cargo they carried was the most precious that went aboard ship in wartime: the living flesh of soldiers and artillerymen to a final total of nearer six thousand than five. All those and sixty horses too, and just imagine how those poor beasts were hoist aboard, with blocks squealing and lines swaying, then penned down below. It always amazed me that any horse ever survived a voyage under sail.

Meanwhile, once we were cleared of harbour and out on the open sea, convoy drill put the twenty-eight merchantmen in two box-shaped divisions, each division being in two ranks, with sea-room between for manoeuvre. The first rank of the first division was over a mile long, with the second rank a quarter-mile behind that. Then came a gap of a half-mile and the second division likewise in two ranks. Of course, all of this was a compromise because you wanted the merchantmen close together so the warships could defend them, but you didn't want them so close that they ran foul of each other when the weather turned bad.

So draw yourself a plan of it, my jolly boys, and a great big arrow to show where the wind blows, and then ask yourself how you would defend those two divisions? How would you do it with the men-o'-war that I had, all lumbering along at the speed of the slowest, and the full neatness of formation never quite achieved? Because it never was, what with some shipmasters keeping better station than others, and others seeming determined *not* to keep station and obey orders. Oh yes! They could be perverse little sods could merchant captains, just you believe me.

In the event, I followed Admiralty Standing Instructions with *Tromenderon* upwind and astern of the convoy so that I could bear down upon any threat that was serious. *Quickly* was in the van, since she was the nimblest among us, with orders to scout ahead and signal any danger. Then the two frigates, *Philhemon* and *Orastices* were – respectively – to windward and leeward of the first division, with the luggers to windward and leeward of the second division, and the brig *Bull-Pup* between the divisions.

Given that, my jolly boys, you may further exercise your imaginations to conceive of the worry that fell upon your Uncle Jacob, in being responsible for all those men aboard all those transports. Because what if a French frigate got in among them? What if broadsides went crashing through their timbers? What sort of damage would a round-shot cause in a ship full of human bodies? Given that disaster, never mind what the bloody Admiralty thought, because what would *England* think of the commodore who let that happen? Remember that, when you envy the lavish accommodation of a commodore, with his great cabin, sleeping cabin and servants, and his enormous salary and privileges, because it was him that got broke if things went wrong.

In the event, as is often the case at sea, the peril that fell upon us had nothing to do with the enemy, because by chivvying with signals, and threats yelled at merchant masters, I kept the convoy in what passed for decent formation, with the men-o'-war between them and any danger. Then, when the enemy turned up – which he did – we saw him off!

'He' was a couple of Frenchmen that found us on our third day at sea, when we'd made a slow passage of not even three hundred miles, and were out beyond Land's End. Though I would point out that – as is ever my practice at sea – I'd had gun-drill every day, and every other damn drill I could think of, because you youngsters take note that you must never let the hands rest easy: not them nor the quarterdeck officers neither, for they just grow fat and slow. But I never let that happen to them, bless their hearts. Oh, by Jove, I didn't, just you ask anyone who ever sailed with me.

The weather was fair; we had a southerly wind; the sky was clear and a good twenty miles to be seen, from the mastheads to the far horizon, and no land in sight. Then up comes the signal from *Quickly* with a gun fired to draw attention. A ball of white smoke, soon blown away from her speeding hull, all heeled over under press of sail. Then seconds later ... thud ... flat and dull from the distance. All the quarterdeck officers and mids put their glasses on *Quickly's* signal hoist, and there was a gasp of glee from the pinky-cheeked young gentlemen who'd never yet been in action.

"It's number one, sir!" says the Signals Lieutenant, even though we could all see it for ourselves. It was indeed. It was flag number one of the code book, which meant *Enemy in Sight!* No wonder the mids gasped.

[Here, Fletcher refers to the fact that under Lord Howe's 1790 signals code, the flag for numeral number one - when flown alone - meant 'Enemy in Sight'. Howe's code was supplanted by Sir Home Popham's more sophisticated code of 1803. But many commanders continued to use the numerals exactly as Howe had recommended. S.P.]

"Shall you beat to quarters, sir?" says Captain Ilford.

"Not yet, Mr Ilford," says I. "Whatever *Quickly* has seen, it is still under the horizon. But if the convoy reads her signal, I don't want them coming over with the vapours, and wandering about. So signal *Keep Better Station*."

"Aye aye, sir!" says he, and up went the signal.

"Bah!" says I, when half of them didn't respond. "Make to the convoy: *Acknowledge Signal*."

"Aye aye, sir!" That did it. Now they all had the *acknowledge* hoist. At least they'd been warned. Then it was a game of many hours long, and a game of prize because, when finally the two Frenchmen came in sight, they were no possible threat, not even to our frigates let alone *Tromenderon*. Instead, they damn well shouted *privateer*. They were brig sloops: flush-decked, two-masted and with huge stay-sails. They were built for speed, heavily armed, and had French flags streaming from their topmasts. The game for them was to outmanoeuvre us, so as to dart in and snatch a prize before we could stop them. It was a game of prize, because privateers were legalised pirates, licensed by all maritime nations at war, with so-called 'Letters of Marque'.

Mind you, it was almost in my mind to let the blighters come aboard one of our transports, and serve 'em right, because there was damn-all prize value in a ship full of red coats: just angry men ready to fight! But in any case, we saw them off. My captains worked well and showed initiative. *Quickly*, in particular, did wonders in darting about, coming round on fresh tacks just as the Frenchmen did, and giving her broadside at long range whenever opportunity presented. Who knows if she scored any hits, and who cares, because it kept them at distance, and was damned exciting. *Tromenderon's* people were in the shrouds and lining the rail and cheered every time *Quickly* fired. Or at least they did until other matters intervened.

Then, when the Frenchmen split up and tried to work on either side of us, *Philhemon* and *Orastices* did their part, and finally the two privateers gave up, and sheered off. I'm pleased that my captains did well, though I never knew it until afterwards, because the unexpected peril took all my attention.

The peril was fire. Now, you landmen may wonder how fire can threaten a ship on an ocean of water? Well it can, my jolly boys, indeed it can. It's the worst of all perils when you're full of everything that burns: you're full of tar, resin, paint, sailcloth, cable, even furniture, and of course the ship itself is made of wood. Worse still, aboard *Tromenderon* there were forty tons of gunpowder in the magazines. If a fire got hold of that, then at least we'd feel no pain, because we'd all be annihilated in an eye-blink: all of us together and our ship, all gone in one thundering, catastrophic detonation.

So the one thing nobody wanted to hear aboard ship was the fire alarm, which was the ship's bell sounded repeatedly, as fast as a hand could swing the clapper. My orders were that any man who found a fire must *instantly* sound the alarm, and summon myself and my officers, and that's exactly what happened as we were enjoying the entertainment of *Philhemon*, firing at one of the privateers.

Clang-clang-clang-clang-clang! I ran. I ran to the ship's belfry as hard as I could go, with Ilford, the Boatswain, the Carpenter, Chaplain and others. Mr Bayley was sounding the bell: Mr Midshipman Bayley. He gaped at me, and kept ringing.

"Belay that!" says I, "where is it? The fire?"

"Midshipmen's berth, sir," says he. "It's bad, sir!"

Oh Jesus! Oh hell! I sniffed and could smell the smoke. There was smoke bloody well coming out of one of the gratings, and the middy's berth was three decks down! "Fire drill!" says I in a shout. "Hands to fire drill!" Because there was a drill for that too, and we'd practised it. We'd practised in harbour.

"Aye aye!" says all present, and there was a great running of men to their duties: Gunner and his mates to the magazines and by God but they ran! Them especially! They ran fastest of all of us! Then the Boatswain ran to his stores, the Sailmaker to his workshop, etc etc, and the ship's firemen mustered to their engine, which wasn't the steam-powered beast of later years: not the iron monster that never tired. It was a wooden water-trough on wheels, with man-powered pumps. It was eight foot, by four foot, by three foot deep, and was kept ready-filled on the upper gun deck near the elm pumps. It had to be near the elm pumps – two of them, made from hollowed-out tree trunks – because they raised seawater from beneath the ship. They could refill the engine's trough as fast as the firemen emptied it, or at least that's what they tried to do.

The engine itself was worked by cranks with crossbars for five men each side to heave up and down, and so long as the men's strength lasted – and the pumpers were chosen from the strongest among us – it threw a fierce jet, via lengths of canvas hose and a brass nozzle. Then there were wreckers, with axes to break open anything in the way of firefighting, and conversely there were smotherers, to slam shut the gun ports and cover hatches to keep air from the flames. Others heaved buckets overside on lines to fetch up seawater in case the pumps failed, or the pumpers fell exhausted. It was like clearing for action. It was organised chaos, and the skill of it – with so many men doing so many things – was for each to keep out of the other's way, and not trip up in the excitement.

With fire being so dreadful a threat, I went below to see for myself, giving command of the ship to Ilford. That meant running down two sets of companionways – staircases to you youngsters – from the belfry on the foc'sle, down to the main deck , and then down to the upper gun deck. There the pumpers and hose men were stood by the fire engine, under the Hose-Captain with a crew of other firemen, to run out the canvas hose lengths, couple up the brass connecters, and pass word back to the pumpers as need be: *water on!* Or *water off!*

These men and the Hose-Captain were specialists recruited by Elphinstone, from men who'd fought fires ashore, and I'm ever grateful to him for that. It was a practice I followed ever after. So the Hose-Captain wasn't stood idle. He'd already gone down two more companionways, from the upper gun deck to the lower gun deck and the orlop, where the headroom was so low that I had to crouch, and where smoke was curling. God help us because I could feel the heat, see the flames, and hear the crackle of a fire that had engulfed the middy's berth – a lath and canvas, painted-up box – against the larboard bulkhead. Thus it was in as bad a place as a fire could be because it was only ten yards fore and aft of the ship's two magazines. It was slap between the pair of them!

"Water on!" yelled the Hose-Captain, up ahead of me, and his chain of men passed the command.

"Water on!"

"Water on!"

"Water on!"

Up above, the pumpers worked their cranks, the canvas snake came alive, and the Hose-Captain aimed at the core of the flames. The water shot out with a whoosh and a rush, and even more smoke filled the close, low deckhead space of the orlop, so all I could see was the red glow of fire, and all I could hear was men coughing and the hiss of steam. It went on, and well done the Hose-Captain and his men as it looked as if the red glow was fading. But then came the boom of a powder explosion, followed by crackles and pops and things flying. The fire flared up, and suddenly the canvas hose was a mad thing. It was jumping and leaping and squirting water everywhere but into the fire. I could barely see it, but I could feel it, and the damned brass end of it hit me in the chest and the blast of it soaked me to the skin. There was nobody holding on to it, and the damned fire was roaring.

"Water off!" cries someone, and the hose fell limp; someone was crawling up the deck beside me, feeling his way up the hose.

"Like this, sir!" says he. "You got to follow the sod! With your hands! You got to kneel for the air, sir! You can't stand!"

"Aye aye!" says I, and did as he said, because he was one of Elphinstone's hose-crew and knew fires better than me. So down I went, and I could breathe better. I grabbed for the hose. Then we followed it, coughing and choking, and the fire was really getting up again; it was hot on my face, and I just hoped that the Gunner and his people were ready with buckets in the magazines. We passed two men in the smoke: one unconscious, one groaning, who were the Hose-Captain and his mate. We crawled over them.

"I've got the nozzle!" says I.

"Water on!" cries the Hose man, and the word went up the chain.

"Water on!"

"Water on!"

"Water on!"

Then the hose came alive and I damn well lost it again! It jumped and kicked and the nozzle flew out of my hands. I'd never have believed the strength of it: it was like a python of the Indies, and it was only with the help of the hose man, and the pair of us hanging on, that I got control of it and could steer the jet into the fire.

"That's it, Cap'n! That's the way!" says the Hose man. "Give it to the sod! Give it to the bastard!" So we did, sticking at it, and slowly we won. We put the fire out. We soaked the embers; we soaked the ashes. We were blind by the end of it, with eyes stung red, and smoke, stink and water everywhere. Then others of the hose-crew relieved us, crawling through the smoke.

"I got it, Cap'n!" says one of the hands, reaching for the hose. "We'll stand by now, sir. You saved the ship, sir. You can stand down now, sir."

"There's men wounded here," says I. "Pass the word for the Surgeon and his mates."

"Aye aye!" says he. "Surgeon and his mates!" and the others passed it on.

"Surgeon and his mates!"

"Surgeon and his mates!"

"Surgeon and his mates!"

We got cheered as we made our way up to the quarterdeck. The privateers were forgotten. *Tromenderon's* hundreds of men were cheering. We had indeed saved the ship, though credit went entirely to the pumpers and the hose men, who knew what to do and did it. There were more cheers as the Hose-Captain came up on deck, grinning and happy. He'd been stunned by the force of the explosion that we'd heard, and his hair was singed, one ear bleeding, but he was sound. The other hose man was worse hurt. He too had been stunned, but hit his head as he went over. So he was in the hands of the Surgeon for a week. But he too survived.

All of which was just as well, and I don't just mean saving the ship. I mean what I might have had to do, had either of those two fine men been killed: them or anyone else, because I had to find out how the fire had started and whether anybody was responsible. But that was after the Carpenter and his mates had examined the site of the fire to check the ship's timbers hadn't been weakened.

"Timbers is scorched but not wounded, sir!" says the Carpenter, soon after his examination. "They won't need no dockyard work, and my mates can trim 'em clean."

"Aye!" says his mates, and since this was on the quarterdeck with all hands looking on, there was another cheer: a cheer by officers and men united. The ship was their home, after all.

"Shall I set to and rebuild the mids' berth?" says the Carpenter.

"No," says I. "I'll want to look over it, with the Hose-Captain, to see if we can work out what started the fire." Which indeed I did, taking Captain Ilford with me as well to poke through the ashes. After that, and since the fire had started in the mids' berth, then the mids probably had something to do with it. So I had all of them, one at a time, sent down to the great cabin, where I sat with Ilford, the Chaplain, and the Schoolmaster to put the young gentlemen to the question.

They were divided up into Oldsters – those over sixteen years – and Youngsters. I had the Oldsters in first and it was a tedious process made near impossible by what Mr Blackhurst the Chaplain declared to be:

"*Omerta*, gentlemen! The code of silence of Sicilian peasants, who will never betray another Sicilian to the authorities." Ilford the First Lieutenant nodded.

"It's like school," he said. "You never tell on another boy."

But we squeezed some bits out of them and put that together with our investigation of the ashes. Finally, Blackhurst, who'd taken notes, gave a summary.

"The Oldsters we can exonerate," says he, "but when we sighted the privateers, some Youngster dreamed of a boarding action, and went below to test his pistols by snapping the locks, and some sparks fell into an oily rag he used for cleaning the pistols.

"And the little sod never noticed, and then dropped the rag on a pile of old newspapers," says Ilford, "when he heard our squadron firing, and ran up on deck to see the fun!"

"Worse still," says Blackhurst, "he left his pistol case open, with a large powder flask in it, which was set off when the fire took hold!"

"And it wasn't just one case of pistols," says I. "We found the remains of four of them, all burned out and the flasks exploded."

"Indeed," says Ilford. "It's a wonder the Hose-Captain wasn't killed when they went off."

"Right," says I, "bring 'em all back: the Youngsters!"

I had them lined up in a row, all pink-faced and nervous, ranging from ten years old to fifteen, and Mr Bayley far from the youngest. But not a word would they say of who was guilty, though they looked sideways at one Carlisle, who wouldn't meet my eye. I could have punished him alone. But I didn't because, as I've said, it wasn't only Carlisle's pistol case that had been lying about, so who knows what the little blighters had been up to?

"You can all kiss the Gunner's Daughter," says I, "each of you! A dozen of the Boatswain's cane, and let it be an education." They got it that same day, just before their dinner. They got it across the buttocks, every one including Mr Bayley, who – to his credit – never yelped. But Mr Carlisle did, later on, when the other mids took it out on him, down on the hold out of sight. He yelped something fierce, but all hands managed not to hear, because it was mess-justice and none of our business.

There was one final thing worth recording in the matter of the fire, and which I had come across earlier when I went through the remains of the middies' berth with Ilford and the Hose-Captain. We found half-burned clutter of all sorts, and among it there was a folio sketchbook bound in leather. It was scorched but not really harmed; Ilford picked it up and opened it.

"Good Lord!" says he, "these are decent-fine. And vastly clever." He held out the book to me. "See here, sir." I took the book and flipped through it.

71

"Well, I'm damned," says I, and looked at the fly leaf where a name and address were written in a bold round hand:

Arthur Bayley,
Bayley Hall, Canterbury Road,
Kent.

"The boy's a bloody artist," says Ilford, and I had to agree. There was page after page of Indian ink drawings and some of them beautifully water-coloured. There were images of the people at their duties, the anchor being brought in, and a lovely full page rendering of the Chaplain bellowing a sermon on Sunday, the hands all smiling and merry. Also, there were some intricate studies of the ship below decks. But mainly there were the most complicated flying machines, some being huge and fanciful works of imagination, but others with a practical look about them, such as the craft I'd seen Arthur Bayley aboard all those weeks ago. Also, there was a whole series of drawings of weird, bat-winged craft labelled Da Vinci 1488 which label puzzled me greatly, until I showed Ilford.

"What's this?" says I.

"Stap me!" says Ilford, "young Bayley's been to Italy! These are copies of da Vinci's designs of 1488. I've seen them myself."

"Who's da Vinci?" says I.

"Leonardo da Vinci, the genius," says Ilford, "he was designing flying machines in the late 15th century."

"Surely not," says I, "so long ago as that? 15th Century?"

"Oh yes," says Ilford.

"Did they work, these machines?" says I.

"Nobody knows," says he, "but look here at Bayley's drawings. He's gone beyond da Vinci. He's written down calculations as to how the machines might be made to fly."

So that was Mr Bayley, and it was very far from the end of his fascination with aerial navigation. Didn't I just know it.

Meanwhile I had much else to think about once we reached Ireland.

CHAPTER 10

Mr Brody's House,
Knapp's Lane,
North of the River Lee,
Cork,
Ireland.
(Morning, Thursday September 1st 1803)

"I was intoxicated. My faith was reborn after a lifetime of disillusion."
(Translated from Spanish in a letter of Friday September 2nd 1803, written in Cork by Javier, Francisco, Pablo de Torrentes, to his cousin Dom Alfonso in Cadiz Spain.)

Torrentes had found the truth. He'd found it in Cailín Draíochta. She was a miracle that had come late, but come in time. He was filled with holy ecstasy as two men led him from the room. Torrentes was old – eighty-three years old – and was moved to the deep of his soul. The emotions within him were so profound that without help he would have been unable to stand, let alone walk.

Torrentes had been a Jesuit. He'd been fiercely devout. He'd been a fine priest, a giant of a scholar, and his life's work had been inquiry into physical manifestations of spirituality: that is *claimed* physical manifestations. He'd been famous for it and his reports had been read by all five Popes, from Benedict XIV to Pius VII, because Torrentes had been active for sixty years.

But his faith had been broken by too many of his own proofs that miracles were false. Worse still, there had been too much reneging by the Popes against the Jesuits: too many charges of politics and too much envy of their financial success. Thus, Popes had damned the Jesuits, then blessed them, then damned them again, then blessed them. Because of this – incredibly for a Spanish Jesuit – Torrentes was lapsed from all reverence for Popes. He was lapsed and bitter and had abandoned his order, finding a new calling in the struggle of the Irish people: the devout and Godly Irish people. He had found a new calling in their struggle against the Protestant, Godless English.

For that at least Torrentes thanked Pius VI, who – as punishment for dissension – had sent Torrentes into rural Ireland to investigate one of the most prosaic reports that came out of peasant communities. It was a task for a novice to investigate. It was the tale of a plaster Madonna which shed tears of blood: the commonest of all supposed miracles. Torrentes had easily destroyed that falsehood, but then he fell in love with the Irish.

Now, the two men led Torrentes into the front parlour, where Mr and Mrs Brody were waiting with a teapot, and bread and butter. The Brodys came forward, putting their arms around the old man, and helping him to the best chair.

"Did you speak to her, Father?" said Mr Brody.

"And are we to call you *Father?*" said Mrs Brody. "Are you yourself again, Father? Your proper self? Because so many of us look to you. So many in the Movement." They all waited as Torrentes said nothing to them, but clasped his hands in prayer and gave thanks to God in his mother tongue, and then Latin. He smiled and looked up.

"A moment of peace?" he said. "A moment of quiet? Please?"

"Of course, Father," said Mr Brody. "We'll be just outside if you call."

"Thank you," said Torrentes, and Mr Brody ushered everyone out and left Torrentes alone. There in the quiet, with his cup of tea and his buttered bread, Torrentes was at peace for the first time in years. He was at peace because – personally and at last – he'd experienced a phenomenon that was truly unearthly, and the existence of even *one* such phenomenon was invitation to the truth of others, including the teachings of Holy Mother Church.

Outside, everyone smiled including the two men who'd led Torrentes from the presence of the girl, Cailín Draíochta. One was the parish priest, who'd discovered her as the wonder of her village, and brought her to the attention of the Movement. The other was in his thirties and was balding, well-dressed and neat. He was Cathal O'Darragh, a lawyer educated at

Trinity College Dublin, where he'd gone by the name of Davies and claimed to be Church of Ireland. He'd done so in order to advance his career and thereby serve the Republican cause that he pretended to despise.

O'Darragh was complex of mind and, like the island of Ireland itself, he was full of conflicting loyalties.

CHAPTER 11

Cork Harbour is a fine place to anchor a fleet. Or rather Cork's harbours are fine places because there are two of them. Thus, you come in from the Atlantic, south-west of St George's Channel, and pass between Roches Point and Weaver's Point into a bay four miles by two-and-a half, with a ragged peninsula on the west where the British Army and Navy of Ireland lived.

This is the lower harbour, and to the north there's a channel into an upper harbour, which channel is the outpouring of the River Lee that leads to Lough Mahon – about three miles by one – with the city of Cork on the western side, surrounded north and south by two inland branches of the River Lee.

Lough Mahon is a fine place for merchantmen, but on September 3rd 1803, when my squadron dropped anchor, it was in the lower harbour and close to the peninsula. It was near to that and the three islands close by it, which were vital to the defence of Ireland: Haulbowline Island, Spike Island and Rocky Island. All were fortified, with heavy guns to smash anything French that tried to get into Cork.

In particular, Spike Island was undergoing a truly colossal process of engineering, whereby twenty-five feet was shaved off the island's height, and levelled to make room for one of the biggest military forts in the world: Fort Westmoreland. In those days the Admiralty was constantly moving its Cork headquarters from one place to another. But when I was in Cork, the Port Admiral, Sir William Dromby, had his offices in the middle of an enormous barracks block under construction in the fort. So, once *Tromenderon* and the other men-o'-war had saluted the batteries and come to anchor, I went ashore in my barge, taking Captain Ilford with me, to present myself to Dromby as protocol demanded. I stress of course that coming to anchor of the entire squadron took many hours, with ships struggling into the lower harbour, and avoiding the sandbanks – of which there were plenty – and pilot boats guiding, and boats from the warships yelling, to get the transports into something like the lines that had been agreed in advance. But it was done at last, and with thousands of red coats lining the rails, grinning and pointing at one another's ships.

Fortunately, I could leave all that to my captains as I was pulled ashore by my barge crew, and it was a chance to see what else was in the lower harbour that was a King's ship. I saw three frigates, and six lesser ships, which wasn't much. I counted them. I had to. They'd be the ships with which I must protect Ireland. There was also a busy traffic of civilian boats, since it's amazing how the news goes round a seaport when a fleet gets in. They went past, pulling for my anchored squadron, and laden with all the things that seamen want when they come in from the sea: fresh bread, vegetables, drink, trinkets and baubles. That and boat-loads of whores.

"Captain darling? Yoo-hoo, Captain!" That was from one boat that went close by, which had spotted my epaulettes and cocked hat. It was full of trollops in bright colours, calling aloud. "Will you be wanting us, Captain?" says one. "Special cheap for you, darling!" They all laughed, and all my boat's crew grinned.

Once ashore on Spike Island, we were saluted by various Army officers and marched to the Port Admiral with an escort of regulars and small talk all the way. The island was alive with civil works and soldiers drilling. It was a builder's yard and Horse Guards Parade all in one, and there were whole regiments marching about with bugles blowing, drums beating and sergeants yelling.

"See there, Sir Jacob!" says an Army captain, pointing to a great rise of scaffolding, and picks and shovels going. "A perfect bastion! Latest design! Glacis, scarp, counter-scarp and parapet for 32-pounders, with emplacements for mortars behind."

"Really?" says I.

"The final cost will be beyond belief or understanding, sir," says he.

"Enormous!" says someone else.

"Vast!" says another.

"Oh?" says I.

"A perfect star fort," says the officer, brimming with enthusiasm – he was an artilleryman. "Two main bastions of enormous size, and four subsidiary ... etc etc." He was full of it: bomb-proof magazines, barracks for thousands, and massive cisterns to catch the rain for drinking water. He had all the details, and talked non-stop. Thus, to the Port Admiral's office, and the huge ensign hanging outside, marines on guard, and the Admiral actually waiting for me outside! There he was, God bless him, with clerks and lieutenants all smiling like good 'uns. So even then I began to wonder if this was just exceedingly good manners, or was it something else?

"Good day to you, Commodore Fletcher!" says the Admiral. "I'm Dromby and glad to see you!"

"Good day to you, Admiral," says I. "May I introduce Mr Ilford, my Fleet Captain?" Everyone shook hands before moving inside, where wine and cakes were ready, and glasses raised to the King beneath a huge picture of His Royal Self. It was a fine painting: life-sized, in coronation robes, done before he went barmy.

So, my jolly boys, that was when your Uncle Jacob got the first definite sniff of a certain smell. It was a smell that I encountered frequently in Cork and elsewhere. It wafted up from the King's own men: the officers of His Land, Sea and Political services, and it was the smell of passing the buck. You see, my lovely lads, Dromby was too helpful and too obliging. He just couldn't be more obliging.

"In whatever decisions you make, Sir Jacob," says he, "I shall be your support!" "Oh yes!" says his acolytes.

"I will provide everything that you need in your campaign," says he. "Ships, men, guns, stores!"

"For your campaign!" says the acolytes. "Your campaign, sir!" says they, all heavy on the *your*. Even Pontius bloody Pilate couldn't have washed his hands cleaner. The others in the room were the same, so it wasn't just Dromby and Co. Ilford spotted it too, and mentioned it on the pull back to the ship.

"I don't know if I should say this, sir," says he, lowering his voice.

"Say what?' says I, though I'd guessed.

"I got the feeling, sir ..."

"Go on," says I.

"There was a certain stepping back, sir. Stepping back from responsibility."

Of course, he was right, and I learned more later when I thought I'd found a friend, because – as is always the case when a fleet anchors – the great and good of the town invite the officers to dinner. In this case the leader of the great and good was no less than the Governor General of Ireland, who happened to be in Cork with his wife. He was Charles Philip Powel, the Earl of Portwicke, together with Lady Elizabeth Powel.

The dinner was a good 'un and a big 'un. It was given in the new barracks block in Fort Maidstone, where the noble Earl had a suite of rooms when he wasn't staying in Cork itself. I was invited with a selection of my officers so I brought along the captains of my men-o'-war, which is something you youngsters should always do, for the good it does in encouraging loyalty to yourself, and the bad it does if neglected, and for two very good reasons. First, because it is an important step up socially for a young captain to get his knees under an earl's table, and second because the first dinner of a fleet's arrival is well known as the occasion when a young officer scans the table to see which pretty wives have lost interest in boring husbands.

So I took my captains, and with room for one more, I took Mr Blackhurst, the Chaplain. Thus, the dinner was excellent, with ourselves in full dress. The table was dressed with silver and fine china with rows of candles, and liveried servants in attendance. All the prominent men of Cork were there, with sashes and orders, the elder ones of them with white-powdered hair, and all the ladies in fine gowns. Which gowns, I should add, were of a style of gorgeousness not seen before or since, and were forever a favourite of mine, because they barely existed. They were drapes of close-fitting muslin, a few of them in colours but mostly white. This left the arms bare, but for long gloves, the neck bare all the way down to the titties, and the titties pushed up from below. That and various turbans, and feathers curled round the head. By George, they were lovely!

As guest of honour, I was sat next to Lady Elizabeth, with Mr Ilford beside Earl Portwicke, and what a bold animal Lady Liz turned out to be. Mind you it was hardly surprising. Portwicke was a decent sort, very mannerly and noble but he was old, as Lady Liz made clear.

"The dear man is so understanding," says she, a tickling whisper in my ear, and her hand squeezing my thigh under the table. "He is no impediment whatsoever, so long as one is discreet," says she, which wasn't the usual behaviour of ladies at dinner, so perhaps it was something in the Irish air? But whatever the case, and even sorrowing for my lost love in Africa, there are things that a man needs. Aside from this, Lady Liz was luscious, and everything popped up so splendid from her muslin gown;

she had big blue eyes and fresh skin. I'd have had her on the table, given the chance. But that would have spoiled the dinner. So we did nothing but talk – on that evening anyway.

After so many courses of food that I lost count, we toasted the King, and the ladies withdrew, leaving us gentlemen to the port and cigars. Then it was politics, politics, politics because Portwicke took my arm, and drew me aside with a group of Army officers behind him. They were generals, colonels and the like, and they nodded their heads off at everything Portwicke said, as he read me the rule book about Ireland.

Portwicke was thin, and had once been tall but was now stooped, showing his age for a man that couldn't be more than sixty. He'd lost some teeth too, but he was sharp as a razor, and I thought he was an honest man trying to help me.

"You must understand the quintessential importance of Ireland to Britannia," says he.

"Yes-yes!" says the colonels and generals.

"In what way?" says I.

"Ireland is divided into factions which hate each other, but hate the English more. Do you understand?"

"I suppose so," says I.

"Do not suppose!" says he. "Believe!"

"Believe!" says the colonels and generals.

"Oh," says I, and Portwicke was off. He poured out so many words that I don't remember them all but only an overall impression.

"I support the emancipation of the Catholics," says he, "but many others do not ...

The last time Ireland rose, the atrocities were hideous on all sides ... Ireland is a knife ready to be plunged into England's back ... If the French land in force, it'll be appalling ... With the men you brought, we now have thirty thousand regulars plus many more of militia and cavalry ... but no man wishes to order another such bloodbath as last time ... Fortunately we have agents among the rebels ... reports that something *devilish new* is coming ..." Then he was interrupted because Chaplain Blackhurst let out a huge roar that drowned everything else.

"Toby!" says he. "You little love!" Everyone looked. Blackhurst had taken a bucket or two of drink, and was struggling to get out of his chair. Two of my captains took pity and heaved him up and he lumbered towards someone who'd just entered the room. "Come to my arms!" says Blackhurst. The newcomer was a tiny man, elaborately dressed, wigged and brocaded, and he strutted along with one hand at his waist. He was in his fifties and bearing a full cargo of rouge and powder about the face.

"Donny!" says the newcomer. "Donny Blackhurst or I'm a bloody Chinaman!"

"Toby!" says Blackhurst, and embraced the other, swinging him off his feet. "Toby, you mincing little bugger!' says he.

"Donny, you big fat sod!" came the reply, and everyone laughed. The pair of them were so comical. Even Portwicke laughed.

"That's Mr Toby Cartwright," says he to me, "principal of the Theatre Royal." Portwicke shrugged. "He's whispered for a knighthood," says he, "following his Henry V on Drury Lane."

"Oh," says I.

"He has the habit of late arrival," says Portwicke, "to make an entrance." Meanwhile, Blackhurst put Cartwright down, and they conversed in loud voices for all to hear.

"So tell me everything!" says Blackhurst.

"My love," says Cartwright, "you are here by act of Divine Providence!"

"How so?"

"Because Charley Blair has strained his back, rogering Dolly Morris!"

"That old tart?" says Blackhurst. "Does she still need a quick one before going on?"

"Every time," says Cartwright, "she likes it standing." Blackhurst nodded. "Yes," says he, "and the gentleman must heave her up, and lift her on."

"And Charley ain't man enough for the work," says Cartwright, "not fully."

"I know," says Blackhurst, shaking his head. "It took me all my strength last time I had her." He looked down at Cartwright in puzzlement. "So how do *you* manage?" says he.

"I get up on a box, dear boy," says Cartwright, "and I think of art." He stood back. "And speaking of art," says he, "how's your Falstaff?"

"Ah!" says Blackhurst and he struck a pose and bellowed even louder than before: *A plague of all cowards, I say, and a vengeance too! Marry and amen. Give me a cup of sack boy. Ere I lead this life long ... "* There was much more, but I'll spare you, since it was bloody Shakespeare which is too cruel to inflict upon the young, and all schoolmasters should be hanged who do so. But Cartwright was delighted.

81

"Sublime!" says he. "Then Donny, my love, will you be our saviour and play the role until Charley is recovered?"

"Why, Toby," says Blackhurst, "*'tis my vocation, and 'tis no sin for a man to labour in his vocation!*" Which was more Shakespeare, and everyone cheered. Later, I gave Blackhurst leave to perform, so long as he delivered his sermons on Sundays. Of course, all hands in the Fleet wanted to see him perform. Even the soldiers wanted to see him, and Toby Cartwright got full houses for weeks. Even I went for the first night. I went to the Theatre Royal on George's Street: a fine big building with a good auditorium and boxes. I went because I was invited by Lady Liz, who was to have come with friends, but came alone.

"Where are the others?" says I as I met her in the foyer, crowded with all the bright and beautiful of Cork, and every gentleman grinning when they saw who I was with.

"Oh them?" says she. "They could not come." She smiled. She had on another of those half-transparent muslins, this time in blue and gold, but with the gleam of her shining through something precious tasty. There were the same round arms too, and the outstanding upperworks. So I heard little of Blackhurst playing Falstaff, because it's dark in a private box once the curtain goes up, and especially dark behind the curtains at the back. I soon discovered that Lady Liz wore nothing under the muslin. Indeed, she was so keen for me to make that discovery that she guided my hand in the doing of it. Then she sidled up against me all soft and perfumed, and bit my ear, the little madame, leading me behind the curtains, where I damn near spoiled everything by thinking of Charley Blair and Dolly Morris, which made me laugh. But being so strong as I am, and always thinking of the lady before myself, I took a grip of the starboard and larboard cheeks, and hoist away with ease. I got her aboard, and thereby passed the only performance of Shakespeare that I ever enjoyed in all my life. I think she enjoyed it too, because we went back behind the curtains twice more before the play was done.

But life is very much ups and downs, my jolly boys, and a number of worries came upon me in the days that followed. Thus, I realised that I'd been given the worst posting that it was possible for a Sea Service officer to receive, because nobody else wanted it! Dromby, the Fleet Admiral, didn't want the job of keeping off another French invasion because the Admiralty wouldn't allow enough ships to do it. Meanwhile, Portwicke didn't want to be responsible for turning the British Army on the Irish people if they rose up again. Consequently, they and all the rest were looking for someone to take the blame while they stayed safe behind the fortifications around Cork and Dublin, hoping that the Irish would behave.

So that's how it was for your Uncle Jacob in Cork in 1803, and don't bother looking for any of this in the history books because things like this never appear. But that's how it was, and I could only wonder why the buck had been so completely passed to me? I even wondered if someone was working against me at a high level.

Which wasn't all of it, because the very day after my outing to the theatre, and with all the troops now embarked from the transports, I was in the middle of drawing up plans for patrols of the Irish coasts with such ships as I had. I was seated at the table of *Tromenderon's* great cabin, with Ilford and a dozen of my other officers, when the cabin door was opened by the marine sentry on duty outside.

"Beggin' your pardon, Sir Jacob, sir?" says he. "It's Mr Venables, sir, the Carpenter, sir, an' he begs a word most urgent, sir." I groaned, because we were already trying to do too much with what we'd got, and everyone knew it, and Venables wouldn't have interrupted the meeting without something important – probably bad – to report.

"It was the fire in the mids' berth, sir," says he, standing in front of the table, with his hat in his hand, and everyone looking at him. "As you know, sir, it still stinks of smoke, even now."

"And?" says I.

"And we thought no great harm was done." He shrugged his shoulders.

"Get on with it!" says I.

"Well, sir, the core of some of the heavy timbers must have been rotten within, and the fire has been smouldering, and working its way down them. We've drilled and tested, my mates and I and ..."

"And so?" says I. The Carpenter stood straight and touched his brow.

"The ship ain't seaworthy, sir," says he. "She must be docked, and the rotten timbers cut out – them which is still a-burning deep within – and good ones let in, and it's months of work, sir, and I'm sorry but that's God's truth."

That was very bad news, my jolly boys. It was very bad news indeed that my magnificent flagship was out of action. I'd have to transfer my broad pennant to another ship and pray that if the French did come, then they wouldn't come with line-of-battle ships. That's even if we managed to catch them and they didn't slip past us as they had in '98!

In the event, I shouldn't have worried about either of those things. I should have worried about something else entirely: I should have worried about something *devilish new*.

CHAPTER 12

Mr Brody's House.
Knapp's Lane,
North of the River Lee,
Cork,
Ireland.
(Evening, Friday September 9th 1803)

"If I must be judged, then let it be by what I sought to prevent, not by what I sought to gain."
(Extract from the pamphlet *My True History, My Precedents and My Rebuttal* by Cathal O'Darragh LL.B., published by John Murray of London.)

The parlour room was hot and crowded. Too many men were there for comfort, and these men could never be comfortable together under any circumstances because their beliefs and even their accents grated upon one another, while the Irish language itself was mother tongue to some and detestable to others.

The only man that everybody respected was Father Torrentes, the Jesuit. He was also the only man sitting, because he was too old to stand for very long. He had a chair and a small table, and two men stood behind him. One was a parish priest; the other was Cathal O'Darragh.

"So," said Torrentes, "we have heard her words. We have heard her words in the room next to this, and note that she has the English as well as the Irish, being the daughter of a schoolteacher."

"Yes," said some.

"*Chuala muid í*," said others: '*we heard her*' since Irish has no words for 'yes' or 'no'.

"Good!' said Torrentes. "We have all heard, and we have all seen a true miracle of inspiration, and if any man will still not be united with the rest … then let him speak now!" He looked round and there was silence as each man sighed and struggled with ancestral hatreds. But there was silence.

"Good!" said Torrentes. "And now we come to secrets so deep that any man who betrays them is surely damned to Hell. Does any man disagree with that?" There was silence. "But," he said, "I shall not ask you to swear silence in the name of God, because we all worship *different* gods." He smiled to make a joke of a thing that was deadly serious, and seriously divisive. But he was a Jesuit, and the Jesuits are clever, so the little joke worked, men smiled and some of the antagonism left the room. "So, I now ask for word from the Green-Leaf Men of County Mayo, to confirm the place where the French shall land." One of the men nodded and spoke.

"It'll be up north in Ennismullet Bay, Father. As agreed with the French."

"Good!" said Torrentes. "Now I call on the Cork Lodge of the Society of United Irishmen, to declare *when* the French will land."

Another man spoke.

"Father, we have just learned that the French squadron left La Charante on August 24th so they should be approaching Ennismullet Bay. They should be there within a few weeks from now, though you can never be sure with a sea journey."

"Good!" said Torrentes. "So I look to all of you to be ready for the great battle when the time comes."

"We'll be ready!" they said, *"Beimid réidh!"*

"And more than that," said Torrentes, "we must now destroy any fear among us that we cannot trust each other!" He rose to his feet in the passion of the moment. "Listen to me, you men of the same land." They blinked and shuffled under the intensity of his stare. "We must show each other that we really will fight. So I call on you now, to send out your armed men to take advantage of the enemy where he is weak, and more important still, to *prove* to each other that you will stand together when the time comes." He paused and drew breath. "Do you hear me?" he said.

"We hear you," they said, *"Cloisimid tú."*

"Finally," said Torrentes, falling back into his chair, "I call on the Sons of all Ireland of Trinity College to tell each man, in his turn, where Cailín Draíochta will be, so that she may bless your men for what they have done so far, and for what they must do in the future." He looked at O'Darragh, who spoke.

"Cailín Draíochta is precious," he said, "so I shall tell each man just the *place* where he shall muster his people. That and no more!" He looked at Torrentes. "Only the good Father knows when she will come, and that will be told later." He looked back at them all. "Do you understand?" They nodded.

"Yes!" they said.

"*Tuigim!*" they said: I understand.

"And," said O'Darragh, "I shall not speak the name of the place aloud but I shall give each of you a paper, with the place written on it. Do you understand?"

"Yes!"

"*Tuigim!*"

O'Darragh handed out his papers.

"Remember!" he said, "without Cailín Draíochta, our whole cause may fail, because who else shall bring us together?"

Later, when the meeting ended, and each man went on his way, O'Darragh walked through the streets of Cork to his lodgings on North Main Street. He raised his hat to the fashionable people who acknowledged him. He was well known. He was greeted by name. He was respected. As a lawyer and a wealthy man, his lodgings were in a fine new building of Portland stone, with a pillar-and-pediment entry and a fanlight over the door. Inside there was excellent furniture, clean linen, porcelain, polish and servants.

Thus, O'Darragh was living the life of the Protestant Ascendency while remaining a Catholic Nationalist at heart. There could be no doubt as to his true loyalty. There could be no doubt whatsoever.

CHAPTER 13

Philhemon was small after *Tromenderon,* even though she was a fine ship and well manned under a bright young fellow named Eustace Watling. Which indeed he should have been, since she was fast sailing, capable of a point closer to the wind than any other ship in my squadron and bearing thirty-eight, long 18-pounders, six 32-pounder carronades, and two 9-pounder bow-chasers.

I chose her because poor *Tromenderon* was sick, and because of information from Governor General Portwicke. For this, I was summoned ashore early on September 10th. I met him in his office in Fort Westmoreland with his generals and colonels, and a big map of Ireland on the wall.

"Here!" says he, pointing at the map. "Ennismullet Bay, that's where they'll land: the French! They're coming in strength, with thousands of men. It's a whole fleet: warships and transports." I frowned. How could he know that when it was only guesswork that the French would come at all? Portwicke and the rest were landmen, so what did they know of fleets and the sea? It was me that was supposed to be keeping an eye on the ocean.

He saw my expression but got shifty-eyed rather than angry, which worried me.

"How do you know that?" says I. "How can you know?"

"We have our sources," says he.

"What sources?" says I.

"Sir Jacob," says he, "it is enough that you know that the French will land at Ennismullet Bay. Note well that their fleet left La Charante in France on August 24th, and might very soon be upon us, and it is therefore indispensably vital that you take out your squadron to intercept them!"

"Yes! Yes!" says the colonels and generals.

"But I ask again," says I, "how can you know? Because if they really are at sea, and they land somewhere else other than Ennismullet, then God help us all!" After that there was more argument, but not another word of how Portwicke knew what he knew, but I guessed that it was from informers. By then, even I knew that with so many mixed loyalties among the Irish, there were some that the rest could not trust, and because of that – among the Irish – an informer was detested beyond anything that the English can imagine.

So there was myself at two bells of the first dogwatch on September 11th going aboard *Philhemon* in Cork Harbour, with my traps and baggage and my broad pennant to fly above her. I took those things and I took Mr Bayley, since I'd promised to look after him.

I was aboard *Philhemon* to lead out every warship I could get hold of, to cruise the southern and western approaches to Ennismullet Bay. I went aboard with just two followers: Mr Bayley and Mr Chaplain Blackhurst, who had surprised me by asking to come with me.

"It is my vocation, Sir Jacob," says he, having asked to see me in the great cabin. "It is my calling to preach the gospel to the ungodly, and none are more ungodly than seamen. Also, I am told that there is no chaplain aboard *Philhemon*, which is a severe lapse and contrary to Admiralty instructions."

"Indeed it is," says I, "but what about your acting? I thought you liked being Fal-whatever-his-name-is?"

"Falstaff, Sir Jacob," says he, "and indeed I do enjoy the role." He paused, stood straight and looked up at the deckhead. "But we are speaking of a calling from *on high*." I looked at him hard to see if there was some sarcasm behind his words. But no. He meant it. He really did. He really did want to be an angel-maker. Well, that was a surprise, but it was an undoubted fact that the people liked his sermons and he made them cheerful on Sundays.

"What about *Tromenderon's* people?" says I. "Don't they need a chaplain?"

"She is in port, sir," says he, "within easy reach of numerous churches and places of worship." Again I wondered if he really meant what he was saying, and it did occur to me that perhaps Blackhurst liked me and wanted to follow me? Very odd, my jolly boys, but such things happen.

"By all means, Mr Blackhurst," says I, "come with me if you wish."

So there was the three of us, aboard *Philhemon* where I deeply missed

Tromenderon's heavy guns. But *Philhemon* was a smart, neat ship and I was very well received: too well in fact, because Watling had the hero worship on him the moment I came over the side. The Boatswain's calls had barely stopped trilling before Watling was offering me the ship's bully-boy for fisticuffs, and getting ready to run his guns against the watch.

I never did understand such fawning behaviour, not in all my time afloat, because I got it from others, not just Watling, and was obliged to make the best of it. I suppose it was my name in the newspapers that did it, because nobody would believe that I never wanted to be in the bloody Navy in the first place.

[As ever Fletcher is perverse in his refusal to accept that many in the Service, and especially among the junior officers, admired him enormously and chose him as their exemplar of seamanly leadership. It was all part of his lifelong refusal to admit his love of the sea. S.P.]

So off with my coat, which I gave to Mr Bayley, and I knocked down their champion as fast as I could, then watched while *Philhemon's* drums rolled and her people cleared for action. It was a decent performance since Watling was a gunnery enthusiast, who practised regularly.

"Four minutes and twenty seconds, sir!" He looked at his stopwatch. "But, of course," says he, beaming all over his nice young face, "it'll have to be quicker next time!"

And all his crew cried, "Jacky Flash! Jacky Flash! Jacky Flash!"

Watling laughed. "We're all Fletcher-fashion, aboard this ship, Sir Jacob!" says he, "every man of us!"

"Aye aye!" says his officers and mids all gathered round.

"Aye aye!" says the ship's people stood panting by their guns.

Which was all very nice. Yes, Watling was keen and so were his crew, and that's good. But they were too familiar. There was too much *Jacky Flash*, because – and be warned you youngsters – you must never let the hands think you're free and easy, because then they'll take liberties. On the other hand, in *Philhemon* there was a quick way to stamp this out, because all I ever had to do in that ship was scowl, and the silly damn blighters near wet themselves for fear they'd upset me. So if that's hero worship, my jolly boys, then it's no use to a seaman: not such a seaman as myself.

[**Note this rare admission by Fletcher that he was indeed a seaman. S.P.**]

Better still there was urgent need to get the squadron to sea, which is the best place to put right indiscipline.

"Mr Watling?" says I.

"Sir?" says he.

"Do you recall your sailing orders?"

"Aye aye, sir!" says he, reeling them off from memory, just as I'd given them earlier that morning when I had my captains in *Tromenderon's* great cabin. So Watling gave it back to me: "*Philhemon* in company with *Orastices,*" says he, "together with the three Cork frigates which are seaworthy, to establish offshore blockade of Ennismullet Bay, while other ships of our squadron shall place themselves in such positions in the western and southern Atlantic as to detect the approach of the French squadron, now expected most shortly."

That was my plan, and all I had to do now was make it work. So we pulled up our anchors, and got ourselves out of Cork, with my frigates in line-astern of *Philhemon*, and the smaller ships far ahead as a vanguard in a spread out line-abeam. Once we got out into deep blue water, this line would stretch over the horizon, with each ship in signalling distance of those on either hand, and the centremost of them within signalling distance of the flagship. In this formation I hoped to scour the west and south coast of Ireland, so the French should not escape us. But much depended on chance and – of course – on the weather.

On the second day out from Cork, having made little progress under contrary winds, we were barely past Bantry Bay, which lay to the leeward of the squadron. The vanguard was in sight from our tops, and the frigates came on under all plain sail, astern of *Philhemon* in a sight worthy of an oil painting.

I was forward of the ship's wheel, looking at the squadron with my Dolland three-draw glass, with Watling and the quarterdeck people beside me, and the ship running smooth on a freshening breeze. A huge swell was rolling in from the west, and Watling was constantly yelling at his topmen to make all neat and tidy above, which I imagine was to impress me. But it did no harm, and I do grant him that his ship sailed easy on a heavy sea because not all ships rise well to the waves, and it's not just a matter of ship-building. It's also down to the captain's mastery of his vessel: in the sail that he carries in the present weather, and the trim that he chooses of his ship's burden and guns. So well done Watling in that respect. But then he wanted to talk because he was a chatterer, though at least he had the good manners to ask his First Lieutenant, rather than interrupt my thoughts.

"Do you think we shall catch them?" says he, and all the officers, mids and people pricked up their ears.

"Depends on how far they cruise out west," says the First Lieutenant, "to avoid the Channel Fleet, and whether they really did set sail on the 24th." At this, everyone looked at me, for my opinion.

"Gentlemen," says I, speaking without looking at them, because that's what you do to supress idle gossip. "Gentlemen, I have it from the Governor General that the French sailed on that date, and assuming a deep passage into the western Atlantic, before turning east for Ireland, they have at least fifteen hundred miles to sail, and sail at convoy speed. With today being the 13th of September, our friends the French might drop anchor in Ennismullet Bay any time between a month to come ... or a week gone past! We must, therefore, withhold all speculation and await Signal Number One of the code book, so soon as it comes in from the ships of our vanguard."

That was telling 'em, my jolly boys, because I wasn't happy and I didn't want the bother of their pointless questions as I had no idea if the French really were heading for Ennismullet, or if they were even at sea at all, or if Portwicke's informant traitor was telling the truth, or whether I'd have been better ignoring him and attempting the impossible of searching the entire Atlantic with the few ships I'd got, and which task needed ten times that number! So I was carrying all the worry that a fleet commander normally bears, and worse besides.

It was like that for days – miserable days – as each one followed the other, and the bells gave ship's time, and the watches changed, and ship's routine proceeded: up-hammocks, breakfast, swab decks, noon observation, dinner, gun-drill, supper, music and hornpipes, down-hammocks, lights out! Thus, we rolled slowly up and down the western coast of Ireland, and I had the vanguard change formation to curve around ahead of the frigates and to the west, such as to observe what might be coming in from the deep Atlantic. Meanwhile, I kept the frigates close enough inshore, to observe movement along the coast but far enough out to avoid the dangers of a lee shore. In addition, I chose occasionally to heave-to the entire squadron, and send boats far inshore just to check that the naughty French weren't hiding deep in some bay or other.

Thus, we plodded our patient beat and, on any other time, I would have remarked on the great beauty of the Irish west coast, as many aboard did, getting up into the shrouds, and peering over the hammock nettings from the carronades. Because Ireland is wild in a way that England is not. There are thundering great runs of dark cliffs: vastly high and stretching mile upon mile, all sombre and magnificent. There are enormous yellow beaches that catch the morning sun bright and cheerful, and there is a world of green inland, and rain and sunshine something wonderful and magical, because Ireland is a magical place. But you don't think of that when your bowels are churning with responsibility, and you're wondering if you've been sent out deliberately to take the blame, while others stayed safe ashore.

The only thing that kept my mind off worrying was Midshipman Bayley and his kites, but first I should mention one of the things that landmen don't expect on a ship of war. It's like the fact that when a ship leaves port on a long voyage, she's a floating farm that's heaving with livestock penned up on deck. There might be cows, pigs, goats, chickens and ducks, which come aboard to provide the ship with fresh meat, when otherwise it's only salted down in the cask.

The other big surprise for landmen is that one of the normal sounds of a ship at sea is that of boys at play: the ship's boys and the younger mids, which sound was as natural aboard ship as the ship's bell, since the little blighters must run off their energy, just as a young dog must. This was as true for the younger midshipmen as for the boys, because young gentlemen are also boys. It was often the case that a bright and seamanly midshipman would organise the boys' play, and Mr Midshipman Bayley was good at this. He'd divide them into teams, think up games and bring order to their disputes, which was excellent for his own training as a future officer.

I'm pleased to say that the other mids liked him, and so did the boys, because some of the games he organised were so fascinating. He had them running, jumping and playing tag of course, but also he had them making kites to fly off the fo'csle on the lee side of the ship, and competing for colour, shape and height of ascent. This sent the boys rummaging the ship, begging for thin sticks, paint and paper and glue, but that too was a part of Bayley's games, to show who was best at rummaging. The hands approved of this, and would cheer on the lads and laugh as kites fouled each other's lines and went down into the sea. So it was good for the morale of the people.

But eventually I had to stop young Arthur as one of his games went too far. He had them competing for the biggest kite, and he turned out with a real whopper. It was an odd design: he called it 'a Leonardo' after this da Vinci person, and it was great spread of spidery wings with him hanging on in the middle, and the kite secured by a line to a pin-rail for safety, which was just as well, because it caught the wind something fierce and pulled so hard that he was hauled off his feet, to screams of fright from all round, and it would have pulled him overboard. But seamen are quick to act, and two hands leapt forward, grabbed the line, hauled it down with Bayley aboard and a third seaman cut the line with his knife.

"Ahhhhhh!" cried all the boys in sorrow, as the big kite flew away, trailing its line, vanishing into the sky and never coming down. It just went up and up in the wind.

"That's enough, Mr Bayley," says I to him later, on the quarterdeck where everyone was grinning. "I'll have no more giant kites aboard this ship. Just little ones from now on, because we must navigate the ocean, not the air." It was a weak joke that got a strong laugh because we all thought well of Bayley and, thereafter, he kept his kites small, producing all manner of designs.

After that it was back to dull routine until the enemy came to my rescue, ending all the tedium and all the doubting. So God bless the French, which sentiment I thought I'd never entertain, let alone set down for you innocent youngsters to read. God bless the French indeed, because finally they did indeed turn up, and it was indeed a large fleet of them, with transports and frigates and – God bless them twice over – not a single ship of the line was among them! Oh joy! Oh happy day! Oh rejoicing! Didn't the bells of Heaven just peal in delight?

You see, my jolly boys, with politics there's little a decent man can do to preserve his arse intact, what with deceit, lies and skull-duggery. But when the enemy heaves up over the horizon – why – you can lay alongside of him, and give him round-shot, grape and cannister, and blow away his masts and dismount his guns, and then go aboard and take the sword off him in surrender. That's a simple matter and every man knows what he's doing and why he's doing it, and didn't they just know that aboard *Philhemon*? And my other frigates too? Because all hands cheered themselves silly when a puff of white came from one of the distant vanguard and the *thud* of a gun for emphasis, and every glass was on her signal hoists … and there it was: Signal Number One, flying in the wind!

We had first sight of them on September 22nd when my four frigates were stationed off Ennismullet Bay, and our vanguard spread out up and down the coast. I had the four frigates plus a dozen of brigs, sloops and luggers. What was coming right into our arms, coming in from the Atlantic, was a French squadron of transports – some fifteen to twenty of them – rolling along in ranks and files, with a pair of frigates on either side them, and a line of lesser ships out ahead, just like my own vanguard. Our first sight of them wasn't too clear because it was soon after dawn and there was mist out westward of us. But there they were, coming out of the mist, coming into sight, and never a doubt that it was them.

I sighed with relief that we'd not missed them. Watling was yelling and calling on his drummers to beat to quarters, and to his First Lieutenant to take the ship into action, and again, to give him credit, he bellowed out all the things I'd have said myself.

"Fire only as the guns bear!" says he.

"Aye aye!" says his people.

"Steady aim, and on the downward roll!"

"Aye aye!"

"Double shot *only*, when close alongside!"

"Aye aye!"

When he'd done yelling, he stamped foot and touched hat to me, bless him, and all the quarterdeck people beamed in pride of how fast their ship had cleared and run out. I nodded in approval, then made sure that they knew what to do next.

"Go for the transports, Mr Watling," says I, in a voice for all to hear.

"Aye aye," says he, though the smile went right off his face.

"And remind me of why?" says I. He paused a bit, remembering the fighting instructions I'd given in *Tromenderon's* great cabin.

"Because it's only soldiers that can threaten Ireland, sir," says he. "Ships can't do that, sir."

"Very good, Mr Watling," says I. "So what shall we do about that?"

"Your Fighting Instructions, sir," says he, "are that we shall aim to bypass the enemy's men-o'-war and engage the transports." He didn't like that and he paused again. "We're to fire into 'em, sir, and sink 'em if we can."

I nodded. I'd learned, you see. Having myself guarded transports packed with troops, I'd learned what was important in warfare and what was not, because it's truth beyond denial that a battle fleet cannot bring about invasion and conquest. Only soldiers can do that. So it'd be useless to win a victory over the French warships – however complete and glorious – if all the transports got safe ashore.

"Precisely, Mr Watling," says I, "and I look to you as flag-captain, to set the example to the rest of our squadron."

"Aye aye, sir!" says he. He did his best in that respect, and the battle of Ennismullet began with the ships of our vanguard attempting to pass the French vanguard, to get at the transports as ordered. Some made it, though the French – not being fools – did their best to keep their transports safe. So it was hammer and tongs, and powder smoke, and wreckage flying, and waves of cheering from *Philhemon's* crew and the crews of my other four frigates, as each of them cracked on sail and raced to join the fight. There was even a band blowing hard on one of the ships: *Sweet Lass of Richmond Hill*, the *Irish Washerwoman* and much more.

It was a race, and just for the swagger of it I had Watling hoist the signal to *Engage the Enemy More Closely!* They say that this was Nelson's favourite, but he wasn't the first in that respect. Then, being a fast ship, and already ahead of our other frigates, *Philhemon* pulled steadily away and we closed on the ships trying to get into Ennismullet. These French ships had blue-white-red banners hoist, drums beating, bugles blowing, and men jumping up and down on the decks as Frenchmen do. Soon we could see two of their frigates come round – very neatly too – and bear down upon *Philhemon* determined to engage us in defence of the transports. With their speed and ours combined, we were closing at near twenty knots to the hour. They heeled and we heeled, and the white water fizzed under our bowsprits. But yet again, well done to Watling in the handling of his ship because it was clear that we were going to get between the pair of them, to prey upon the lines of transports behind them.

Meanwhile two of the British frigates astern of *Philhemon* were well caught by the French ships, and the four of them were soon heavily engaged, broadsides pounding, holes blown through sails and the ships seeking advantage by manoeuvre. But that still left two of ours free to get in among the French transports to work mischief, and then … yes … yes … I counted and saw that our frigates were out-firing the French by two broadsides to one. A Frenchman took a hit to his foremast even as I watched, and it went over, trailing canvas, rigging and wreckage, so I had little doubt of the outcome if it turned into a fleet action, after all.

So wasn't it all most jolly and bright? Wasn't it just, my lads, until we saw something nasty: something that was coming out of the mist that had hidden it so far. But now I could see it, and I sighed as I realised that it had placed itself behind and upwind of its squadron, exactly as I had done with *Tromenderon*. It was a line-of-battle ship.

CHAPTER 14

Aboard the French Republican ship
Treize Vendémiaire,
Off Ennismullet Bay,
Ireland.
(Dawn, September 22nd 1803)

"Our ship displayed all the precautions demanded by Napoleon to avoid the failures of 1798."
    (From the diary of General Auguste Coulonges for Saturday September 25th 1803.)

Claude Verchet was a fervent intellectual revolutionary, because just a few years ago he had been a mere captain's secretary in the Bourbon Navy. But now, at under thirty years of age, he was a rear-admiral in command of a fleet, and he owed everything to the French Enlightenment, which prized logic and promoted merit. Verchet now wore a magnificent uniform, and had a magnificent ship under his feet. She was *Treize Vendémiaire,* a 74-gun line-of-battle ship, heroically named for the Revolutionary Calendar date when Napoleon's artillery supressed a Bourbon rising by pouring grapeshot into the Paris mob: a glorious day indeed with hundreds of counter-revolutionaries slaughtered!

    "Vive la Republique!" he cried, and every man on the quarterdeck responded.

    "Vive la Republique!" they cried. Cheering rumbled and echoed through all the decks of the big ship, as their ship passed through the fleet of transports, under a press of sail, and with the soldiers of the transports cheering as they went past. They cheered in their thousands. It was a very great day for Verchet, and his spirits soared.

He leapt forward and embraced the ship's Captain and First Lieutenant. Then he embraced General Coulonges: also splendidly uniformed, also a full and proper revolutionary. Then Verchet forced himself to embrace the trail of Irishmen who followed Coulonges: Byrne, Fitzsimons and the others, who were either priest-ridden Catholics immune to the Enlightenment, or joyless Protestants immune to the Enlightenment, and each one secretly hating all the others. But Verchet embraced them because it was necessary, since only they – or rather the organisation they represented – could turn out the hordes of Irish cannon-fodder without which the French could not take Ireland from the English. The only puzzle that Verchet could not solve, was how these Irish managed to cooperate with one another at all?

But enough puzzlement. The dawn mist was clearing, the whole squadron was becoming visible, and Verchet judged that a speech was necessary.

"Citizens!" he cried, and his men cheered, "and comrades," he added, looking at the Irish. "There is the enemy!" He pointed and everyone looked down the length of the big ship, past masts and sails and shrouds. Everyone looked through the mass of transports, and past the frigates that were turning to get into action. They looked past the distant screen of smaller warships, already throwing out clouds of smoke with guns booming. They looked and saw the English under fire from the French, including a line of frigates with one ahead of the rest.

"Citizens and comrades," cried Verchet, "the English have one trick and one trick only. They give quick broadsides. But consider the broadside which our ship can deliver! Consider it and – for the moment – ignore our upper-deck battery! Likewise ignore the guns of our forecastle and quarterdeck! Ignore these guns because" – he paused in emphasis – "we have thirty-six guns on the lower deck, and these guns were specially brought aboard to deal with the quick-firing English. They are the heaviest guns anywhere at sea and the English have nothing like them. They are guns throwing 42-pound shot!"

CHAPTER 15

That was a very bad moment, and how I wished that I had *Tromenderon*. But I didn't so I did what I could, and made a hard decision.

"Captain Watling?" says I.

"Sir?" says he, with the same glum face as everyone on the quarterdeck.

"Make a signal to the Fleet," says I.

"Sir?"

"Make '*Follow fighting instructions Emphatic*' then, '*I will engage the enemy flagship*'."

Yet again, all credit to Watling and his ship because the silly blockheads cheered. I don't know what they thought we could do against a ship of the line, with its massive thick timbers and many times our weight of broadside, but they still cheered. They were a keen ship, as I've said before, and that was good because what mattered was keeping that French line-of-battle ship from interfering with what my squadron had to do, which was prevent the French from landing troops. If one frigate got smashed into splinters, then what did that matter? Not much, my jolly boys, unless you happen to be aboard that frigate. Mind you, most people in those days were bloody fools enough to believe that any one British ship could beat any one of the French no matter what its size. So, God help the British ship that had to do it.

Then the signal was hoist, with a gun to draw attention, and every glass in *Philhemon* studied our squadron to look for the *acknowledge*, which was hoist over some but not all, what with them being busy with their French opposites, and trying to get at the transports. But I had to put up with that.

"Straight at her, if you please, Mr Watling," says I, pointing at the big ship, "and see if you can get under her stern and fire in through the Captain's windows!" That got another cheer, even though it was the obvious ploy when engaging so heavy an opponent. Thus, a ship's guns were mostly on the beam and the clever trick – if you could manage it – was to avoid the main battery and fire down the enemy's length, which was double-better if you could do so from the stern, which was the weakest point of any ship, since much of it was only the glass of the stern-cabin windows, and any shot that did get in would run the length of the enemy's decks doing dreadful harm all the way.

After that I had just one more order to give, before I stood back and left Watling to the work.

"Hoist battle colours," says I, "colours to fore, main and mizzen peaks. Let 'em know we're coming and who we are!"

"Aye aye!" says Watling. Up went the huge Union Flags and up went another enormous cheer, because you have to do these things to keep the men happy for all that it's stuff and nonsense. Even the other frigates cheered us and copied us. What nonsense it all was. What nonsense.

[The nonsense was in Fletcher since the contradiction within him was never more gross. When he spoke of hoisting battle colours, the emotions within him were so great that he could barely articulate, thus his speech came in gulps and he must needs grip the arms of his chair to steady himself. S.P.]

So, it was all up to Watling, and having got *Philhemon* well past the French frigates, which were now engaging ours, and with a widespread struggle going on downwind of us, he shortened sail to fighting canvas. That was normal in those days, to reduce the need for sail-trimming and put the greatest possible number of hands to serving the guns. That meant tops'ls and t'gallants aloft and mainsails furled.

I looked at the French two-decker and saw her do the same, and with some smartness besides. Also, she came round a point, getting ready to swing her broadside to bear on *Philhemon* as we approached. We could even hear, dimly, the roll of drums aboard her, and we could clearly see her ports open, and the muzzles of her guns run out. Each of us tried to outmanoeuvre the other, like a pair of pugilists circling before blows are struck. It was a careful and considered approach, and it was slow, so there was time for discussion.

"He'll come about and give a broadside," says I, "any second now."

"Aye aye, sir," says Watling, "and as he does, I'll cut across his stern, and rake him. I'm waiting to see which way he'll turn."

"Well and good, Mr Watling," says I. You should note that I stood by his judgement in this matter, because he knew his ship better than I did and it must, therefore, be his judgement as to when he might choose his moment. He had his glass raised and was doubtless watching the enemy's topmen for any sign of trimming before she came about. I was doing exactly the same, and saw the topmen move, and saw the two-decker heel over.

"Stand by to go about!" cries Watling, in a hail-the-masthead shout. "Put up the helm! Bring her to windward! Cross his stern!"

"Aye aye!" says the helmsmen. Round she came and the deck heeled.

"Fire only as the guns bear!" says Watling, and you youngsters should take note that this wasn't a piece of bluster that you said for the saying of it, because in those days the aiming of a ship's guns wasn't a captain's business, since it was so hard to change a gun's point of aim, given the clumsy nature of the carriages. So, the best any captain could do, was get his ship into a favourable position opposite the enemy and leave the rest to the gun-crews.

With a north-wester blowing, Watling was depending entirely on his ship's ability to sail close to the wind and I soon saw that my duty was to stand back and keep my mouth shut, because several times I'd have given orders contrary to him, and I'd have been wrong because I didn't know *Philhemon* as well as he did. In the event, he did damn well and nearly made it unscathed, only nearly because the two-decker could see what he was doing, and gave us a broadside even though we were closing on her bow, and nothing like alongside. Then, never mind the morning mist, because out poured a great rolling cloud of powder smoke and sulphur-stink, and the two-decker absolutely disappeared from sight as all our ears were pounded by the tremendous, sickening noise of a ship's full battery fired into our faces.

Firing from so awkward a position, the two-decker mainly missed us and his shot flew wide, though some crashed into the sea and threw waterspouts hundreds of feet up which came down and drenched our ship. None the less, some of their shot struck home. It was only a few – two or three at most – but they must have been enormous shot because one of them struck a quarterdeck carronade with an appalling clang, and utterly smashed it, hurling cast-iron shards in all directions. They ripped my coat sleeve and the shirt beneath; they took buttons off my coat; they punched holes in my hat, and never even touched me: not so much as a scratch, though I staggered as if hit by a hammer. It was such a shock as you could not imagine and I felt myself all over to see if I still had my eyes and limbs.

But that was nothing because I was alive, while nice young Watling, and his First Lieutenant, and his Sailing Master, and various others were no longer human beings. They were bits of rag, and puddles of blood, and butcher's meat. I found some pieces of them spattered on to me. I threw them off with a hideous shudder and you'd not thank me for describing them so I won't. But that's how it happens in war. Some are slain and others are spared, and without the least drop of reason, or sense or mercy. So, if you youngsters dream of the King's Service, then ponder on that.

I looked round. I wasn't a spectator any longer. I was in command. I tried to clear my head of dizziness and fear. I tried to take a grip and I wondered what to do next.

CHAPTER 16

Aboard the French Republican ship
Treize Vendémiaire,
Off Ennismullet Bay,
Ireland.
(Morning, September 22nd 1803)

Admiral Verchet and his officers frowned as the English frigate steered towards them.

"What are they doing?" said Verchet, while his Captain snapped shut his telescope and shook his head.

"It's got to be some sort of trap, Citizen Admiral," he said, careful to use the correct form of address to this highly political officer. He nervously drew out his glass again, and searched the ocean. "There must be some heavy ships close by, otherwise it's madness. It makes no sense." There was agreement among the sea officers on the quarterdeck, and all of them – like their Captain – were searching for English two-deckers, three-deckers, or anything at all that they hadn't already seen. But there was nothing. The dawn mist was gone, and there was nowhere for a big ship to hide.

"Look!" said Verchet with his own glass on the frigate, "he's signalling. See his flags! And look, his other frigates aren't even coming up in support. They're fighting our own frigates. Look!" Everyone nodded. They saw the red stabs of flame, the clouds of smoke, and they heard the rumble of gunfire, and especially the rapid *thud-thud-thud-thud* of English broadsides.

"What's going on, Admiral?" said General Coulonges, with his Irishmen alongside him. Verchet waved a hand as if to brush off an irritation.

"A frigate doesn't challenge a ship of the line," he said. "That's not the purpose of a frigate. It's not built for that. It's nonsense."

"But *that* one is coming right at us," said Coulonges, and his Irishmen agreed. The fact could not be denied so Verchet shrugged.

"Why don't we just ignore it?' said Coulonges. "Surely our main purpose is to get the troops ashore? To protect the transports?"

"We can't ignore him," said Verchet. "We can't just sail past. That would give him the chance to fire at us as he chooses." Verchet shook his head. "No! We have to engage." He smiled. "We shall engage, and accept the gift of an easy victory over our main enemy!" All the sea officers smiled. They liked that. They were fed up with being told that the English were invincible at sea. But Coulonges frowned.

"The English Navy isn't our main enemy," he said. "Not here and now. Their Navy is a distraction. We have to get our troops ashore. That before everything."

"Yes!" said the Irishmen. But Verchet disagreed. There was a seaman inside him somewhere under the dross of politics, and he wanted – just for once – to beat the English Navy. But he still used politics to get his way.

"Citizen General?" said Verchet, "I think you are showing the wrong attitude, and if you continue, I may have to report it to my superiors." Coulonges blinked. A man had to be so careful these days. There was still a guillotine in the Place de la Concorde, and Coulonges didn't know what influence Verchet had in Paris. Therefore, he looked away and Verchet won the argument, though he won at great cost because Coulonges now despised him as one who got his way by threatening a stab in the back. That was the coward's way: not a soldier's way. But Coulonges kept quiet and Verchet smiled.

"Good!" he said, and turned to the ship's captain. "Citizen Captain?" he said.

"Citizen Admiral?" said the Captain.

"That damned Englishman there," said Verchet, "if he wants to be battered and sunk, then kindly oblige him! You will run out your guns, and bring them to bear as soon as you may."

The drummers beat to quarters, and the gun-crews of *Treize Vendémiaire* cheered as they worked, and they did their best for Verchet, knowing that he was political but also efficient. Thus, he'd worked hard to get their ship the monstrous 42-pounders with the massive shot that was so hard to heave into the guns, but which must surely bring victory over the English.

Of course, some of the old sweats grumbled. They said that 42-pounders were obsolete and a thing of the past. They said that experience had shown they fired too slowly as compared to 32- or 24-pounders, and that's why the Rosbif Navy didn't use them. But that experience came from the days of the Royalist Bourbon Navy, and what did that matter in these Enlightened times?

Treize Vendémiaire cleared and ran out, closing with the English frigate. She closed under reduced fighting canvas so everything slowed down. Everyone waited, and the lower-deck hands chattered and pointed, while up on the quarterdeck, Verchet and his officers judged their moment, and eventually:

"Now, Citizen Admiral?" said the Captain.

"At your command, Citizen Captain!' said Verchet. Orders were given and *Treize Vendémiaire* began her turn to bring her whole broadside to bear on the English frigate. The gunners cheered. But the English frigate was watching carefully.

"Damnation!" said Verchet.

"Why?" said Coulonges.

"Why?" repeated the Irishmen. Verchet sighed. It was so obvious.

"He's anticipating," he said. "Look! He's put up his helm to try to come around us before our broadside can bear. He's not a fool, and he's got a weatherly ship that sails close to the wind."

Meanwhile, on the lower deck, the gunners heaved and sweated, with their officers yelling, and they threw their weight on handspikes to heave the 42-pounders around from their normal pointing, to swivel around and point towards the bow. But the guns were mounted on standard ship's carriages with squat truck-wheels that were happy if asked to move the gun fore and aft, but which didn't like being scraped sideways, and they groaned and squealed and resisted. The guns had barely turned when the English frigate came under their aim, and trigger-lines were pulled, and the guns roared and bounded back, and the world disappeared in smoke and flame.

But the gunners went through their routine as gunners did, even half deaf and half blind.

Sponge out!

Ram cartridge!

Load shot!

Load wad!
Ram home!
Run out!
Prime lock!
Then they waited for sight of the enemy as the smoke cleared.

CHAPTER 17

Watling was dead, but his ship was intact: the ship that he'd trained and inspired. So, whether or not I was dazed did not matter, because we'd lost only half a dozen men and a carronade. Luckily, our rigging and sails were untouched, and our main-deck battery was hammering away at the big Frenchman as we slid past, their gunners replying. We were only a musket shot from them, and I could see their upper guns spouting and bounding in action, while the heavy guns of the lower deck were inching round in the attempt to bear upon us. But they were slow, slow, slow, and thank God for that, because one full broadside from them would have been ruin for all aboard of us, because they were outsize pieces bigger than anything even *Tromenderon* mounted. But the bigger the gun, the slower the rate of firing and aiming.

Meanwhile Watling's gunners were outshooting the French upper-deck guns by more than two to one; you could see the wreckage and splinters fly off his sides, holes punched in his timbers, and spars falling, which is a fine sight to see when he's doing much the same damage to you! We suffered great harm from that, because even his upper-deck guns were heavier than our 18-pounders, even if they were firing slower. We lost more men and more guns as we went past, and saw it happen: I saw our bulwarks stove in, dust and splinters fly, guns thrown over and men killed. But then I was yelling at the helmsmen to follow Watling's orders and bring *Philhemon* round under the Frenchman's stern.

"Aye aye!" they cried, or rather their lips moved, but you can't hear speech when the guns are firing, and I didn't even hear a spar smash high above me, nor see it coming down. Thank you, Mr Bayley, in charge of one of the surviving quarterdeck carronades, who did see it and pushed me clear. Then he and others were hacking at the wreckage with axes and heaving it over the side, and Bayley acting like a man.

Slowly, slowly we got round and there was the big ship's stern looking at us with some long name in heathen French, all picked out in gold: it was Vengence or Vendemery or the like, with a Roman number in front of it, and a pair of Froggy flags at either end, all carved in the woodwork and painted.

[*XIII Vendémiaire* – *Treize Vendémiaire* – as Fletcher well knew, because the battle was subsequently reported in the press. But he would never use French spelling of his own free will, and by then I knew better than to attempt correction. S.P.]

Whatever the name and whatever the flags, *Philhemon's* guns blew it all to scraps and shards as we went under the enemy's stern and fired down the length of him, smashing and wrecking. We heard the noise of our shot crashing into iron and steel and oak. It was the classic stroke of sea warfare with not a gun to answer us as we went past. But that was the end of the battle for both ships, because both were heavily battered.

Aboard *Philhemon,* we'd suffered from the exchange with the Frenchman's upper-deck guns, while he'd been sorely wounded by our raking fire. So, both of us had to haul of action for immediate repairs, in fear of being caught by the other while unable to manoeuvre and fight properly.

I was fully in command by then, with one of *Philhemon's* lieutenants in assistance. I ordered the helmsmen to take us clear of the enemy, though the ship was barely under way, having been hurt aloft more than I'd realised while the action was hot. The masts were standing, but the only sails still fully drawing were the fore tops'ls and t'gallants; while there was canvas hanging, ship's boats smashed, and guns blown out of their carriages. But seamen are drilled for such as this. They're bred up for it. I put the Gunner in charge of the dismounted guns, the Surgeon's mates in charge of the wounded, and with the Boatswain killed, I rated one of his mates as acting Boatswain, and put him in charge of rigging and sails. Finally, I put the mids in charge of clearing the decks of wreckage, which included those of the dead who were still in one piece, who must be set aside for proper burial later. But that's the sea life, my jolly boys, and you'd be amazed at how fast it turns you into a man.

Of necessity we parted company with Vendemery or whatever her name was, because both of us were avoiding the other, concerned only with repairs. *Philhemon's* warrant officers came to me on the quarterdeck to report, because – and once again that's the sea life for you – even with their popular and much-respected Captain Watling so recently struck down, there was no time for grieving and someone had to be master of the ship. That's hard reality. They came to me with hats in hand, though I should point out that this wasn't a tidy business such as might go forward on Captain's Sunday inspection, because there was furious activity going on all round, with shouting and men doubling to their duties, or heaving on lines, or trying not to get in each other's way; saws and hammers going, and poor souls crying out in pain as they were carried down to the Surgeon.

"Three guns lost and a carronade," says the Gunner, "but five others are dismounted which can be made good."

"Thank you, Mr Gunner," says I.

"Beg to report fifteen dead and twenty-five wounded, sir!" says a surgeon's mate, "and Surgeon says, might I be excused at once to return to my duties, sir? which is urgent, sir?"

"Go to it," says I.

"Jury rig to main and mizzen, under way, sir!" says the new Boatswain. "Fresh sails brought up to be bent to the yards, and all hamper and wreckage cut away and falling astern of us, sir!"

"Well done, Mr Boatswain," says I. Then it was the Carpenter's turn, just up from below, and I could see by the look on his face that he had bad news.

"We're hit below, sir," says he. "Must have been one o' them heavy shot from the beginning of the action. She's bad holed in the bow, sir, and where it's hard to get at; it's all hands to the pumps, if you please, sir." He touched his brow respectfully, and I nodded.

"Take all the men you need, Mr Carpenter," says I, "and God speed to your work."

"Aye aye, sir!" says he, and off he went. There were others reporting too, but eventually I had a moment to look round, and decide what to do next, which normally would have been to renew action against our French opponent so soon as we were in fighting trim. But there was something more important to consider. I drew my glass, and looked across the sea to where a sizeable action was under way between the rest of the French squadron, and the rest of mine. It was some miles off, and closer inshore than we were, with the long line of the Irish coast behind them, and themselves obscured by powder smoke. But plenty of ships were visible and the thud and boom of their guns was continuous.

I couldn't see what was going on and needed to know. But I'm too big to be a nimble climber, some of the shrouds were still wounded, and more than that, I was needed here on the quarterdeck. But Mr Midshipman Bayley was close by.

"Mr Bayley?" says I.

"Sir?" says he, and I gave him my glass.

"Get aloft, as high as you can, and look to our squadron, and particularly look to the French. I must know if our ships have prevented the French from landing their troops. Go on! Get aloft!"

"Aye aye!" says he, and up the main shrouds he went like the sea monkey that he'd become. He went all the way up to the cross-trees, way above the main-top, and the highest look-out post in the ship. Then he drew the glass and searched the sea.

But here I pause, my jolly boys, because you might think that this was your Uncle Jacob not just quoting Nelson, but acting like him: acting for the King's Sea Service, and in Britannia's name. If so, you might wonder where was the Jacob Fletcher who never wanted to be in the Navy? Where was the man who wanted only a career in trade?

Well wonder no more, because I was there all the time, and very much acting in my own interests because, after much thinking, I had come to the sure and certain belief that I'd been sent out to Ireland to take the blame for others: Governor General Portwicke and Admiral Dromby to begin with. In that case, if my squadron prevented the French from landing troops, then happy day and Hallelujah. I might even get some credit from it. But conversely, if the Frogs did get their men ashore, then I had to get this information to Portwicke and Dromby with utmost speed, so they couldn't pretend I'd not told them, and – more important still – so that I could drag them squealing and complaining into some responsibility for the horrible mess that would follow and not take the whole blame myself.

What I absolutely could *not* do was see the French transports land their men, and either pretend I'd not noticed, or continue in a pointless battle against the French warships. So very much indeed depended on what Mr Midshipman Bayley might see from the cross-trees. I looked up and there he came, scampering down, and myself glad that it wasn't me behaving like a circus acrobat.

"Sir! Sir!" says he. "They're ashore! Some of them at least! Our ships are mainly engaging the French men-o'-war. I saw it, sir. I clearly saw it. Some of their transports are bad mauled, but a lot of them are in Ennismullet Bay with nothing between them and the shore."

O Hell fire and damnation. They'd done it.

CHAPTER 18

Aboard the French Republican ship
Treize Vendémiaire,
Ennismullet Bay,
Ireland.

(Early evening, September 22nd 1803)

The ship was anchored in Ennismullet Bay. She was safe but the balance of power aboard her had shifted. General Coulonges stamped his foot and argued right back into Admiral Verchet's face. He argued in front of the quarterdeck officers and the Irishmen: Fitzsimons, Byrne and the rest, and in front of everyone else aboard ship who could hear or who would later hear from his shipmates.

"You did *not* win the fight with that English ship!" said Coulonges, "and you can't pretend that you did, because we came away like a horse with a broken leg!" There were growls of agreement, and not just from the Irishmen but from Verchet's own officers. He'd never been tremendously popular with them, because he had no warmth of personality, and right now they all knew how badly their ship had been hit below deck. The rudder was smashed, the pumps ruined, and the mizzenmast split by three direct hits of 18-pound shot. Thus, the Carpenter's crew were still straining to bind a hawser round the mast to hold it together. *Vendémiaire* had suffered all that, and had dozens of men killed and wounded.

The whole ship knew it, and Verchet knew it too. But under the Revolutionary Enlightenment, it was madness to admit to either fault or guilt. Or at least that's what Verchet believed.

"Citizen!" he said staring Coulonges hard in the eyes. "You need to take great care of your words. You need to know that you may answer for them in ..."

"Oh, shut your mouth!" said Coulonges. "That won't work any more. You can save that bucket of crap for your friends in Paris. Just look round!"

"Yes!" said a dozen voices and Verchet couldn't help but look round. He looked round the fine natural harbour that was Ennismullet Bay. Outside the bay, the weather had got up; the sky was darkening, but a few ships – English and French – were still visible. Verchet sighed at the sight of a ship firing her last few guns for the honour of France, while a pair of English ships poured rapid broadsides into her.

"Ahhh!" said everyone, as the French ship struck her colours in surrender even as they watched.

"There!" said Coulonges, "the bastards have won their usual victory, which even includes kicking *this* ship in the balls!"

"They did not!" said Verchet.

"Oh shut up," said Coulonges, pointing out to sea. "They beat our warships as the bastards always do, and I blame *you* bastards of the Sea Service for letting them do it! What's wrong with you? You've got better ships than them, and bigger guns. Why do you let them win every time?" The Sea Service officers winced at that. They sighed and looked at their boots. But Verchet didn't give up. Being political, he couldn't give up.

"We do not *let them do it!*" he said.

"Shut up!" yelled Coulonges. "Because the bastards also wrecked half our transports, which are now running before the wind with pumps going. They've gone God-knows-where down the Irish coast, taking thousands of good French soldiers with them."

"Yes!" said everyone.

"But!" said Coulonges, "and no thanks to you, *Citizen*" – he sneered at the word – "look over there!" He pointed towards the shore. "There's the rest of our transports anchored, and their boats taking the troops ashore."

"But only under the protection of this ship's guns!" said Verchet instantly. "We're anchored with a spring on our cable, to direct our broadside against any English ship that tries to come into the bay."

"And what else should you have done?" said Coulonges. "Run away?"

"I do not run from the enemy!" cried Verchet, but Coulonges didn't bother to reply, because he was looking across the bay. Some ships already had their boats in the water and the seamen were pulling for shore, while the blue-coated soldiers, with their packs and shakos and plumes, sat on the thwarts with muskets between their knees. Other ships were swaying out their boats, and on the smooth-sloping beach, people were running down towards the boats and waving. There were men, women and children, and they were happy.

"See that?" said Coulonges to Verchet. "It's up to the Army now, and I'm going to join our men: the soldiers who know how to fight for France. I'll thank you for a boat, *Citizen*, so I can go ashore with my Irish brothers." He looked at them. "Are you with me?" he said, and the same in Irish: *"An bhfuil tú liom?"*

"Yes!" they cried.

"Táimid Leat!": we're with you!

Coulonges nodded. That was good. Even if all the transports had landed all the French troops, then a mass rising of the Irish would have been vital. But now it was indispensable.

CHAPTER 19

Philhemon was barely seaworthy. All hands did indeed take their turn at the pumps: the ship's chain pumps that threw out water by the ton, but they did so only with men heaving on the iron cranks that drove them. It was the worst and most painful labour in a ship, and you youngsters should bless the power of steam that saves the backs of men from such effort today. I went down myself to take my turn from time to time, because that's what you do if you want the hands to stick at such work. I heaved away and sweated and grunted with all the rest, and was very glad when my turn was done.

We crept along, downwind and away from Ennismullet, and found ourselves in distant company with some of the French transports that my squadron had knocked about. They were worse off than ourselves: tangled with wreckage, with men working to put things right, trying to keep offshore and not swamped by the big seas and the foul weather. No doubt they were hoping to get round the south of Ireland, and head eastward towards France and home. That's if the sea was kind to them. Even if I'd wanted to go after them, I could do nothing since my ship and crew were in no condition to chase and board.

Also, I had other things in mind, because there had been no possibility of poor, battered *Philhemon* working upwind to join my squadron. I'd been forced to leave them to defeat the French warships, and do whatever they could against the French landings. But the Service is used to such cases, so whichever of my captains was most senior would take command, and the rest would follow. That's how it works, my jolly boys. That's how it has to work.

Given that, my plan had been to sail directly to Cork and the Great and Good of British Ireland, bringing urgent news of the French landings.

116

So, I summoned *Philhemon's* surviving navigating officers to the Master's cabin for a look at his charts.

As usual aboard a warship, the Master's cabin was under the break of the quarterdeck, opposite the Captain's day cabin. It wasn't very big and it was a tight press for myself, the senior Lieutenant – fresh promoted by me to Number One - and two master's mates. I also sent for the new Boatswain, because he happened to be an Irishman bred on the west coast, which is another sign of the divisions among the Irish, if such a man as him was voluntarily in the King's Service.

It was late in the day, it was dark, and we were crammed around the chart table, with a lantern swinging over our heads. We had to duck when the ship rolled, and roll she did. She rolled and creaked and groaned, still taking water heavily, and the clank of the pumps sounded from below. So, we got out the best chart of Ireland and considered it.

"We're here, gentlemen," says I, pointing at the spot, "having left Ennismullet Bay, and come around Bellmullet Head." They nodded. "And so," says I, "if we sail southward, keeping safe offshore, and finally eastward around Castletown, Goleen and Rosscarby, we'll come to Cork." I paused and stepped out the distance with a pair of dividers. "That's about four hundred sea miles, which would normally be three or four day's sail for this ship." They nodded again. "So, Mr Boatswain," says I, "how does that compare with an overland journey to Cork?"

"God bless you, sir," says he, "'cos only God knows how long that would be on Irish roads, where there ain't no turnpikes nor posting inns, since most of Ireland is wild, west of Dublin or Cork."

"Yes," says the Lieutenant, "and in the present condition of Ireland, I doubt we'd be safe ashore. Not even if we could find the horses."

"But," says I, "this ship won't carry us four hundred sea miles. Not with the pumps just ahead of the leaks, and the weather blowing nasty. So, whether or not it's safe, we shall have to go ashore. Does anyone disagree?" They sighed and looked at one another; then one of the master's mates spoke for them all.

"Best not to press the old ship too hard, sir," says he. "She's strained hard, and she's broken below."

"So," says I, looking at the Boatswain, "where would be a safe place to go ashore?"

"Oh, that'd be here, sir!" says he, putting a finger on the map. "That'll be Ballydoran. There's a good harbour there with two batteries to defend it, and a barracks full of red-coats. We'd be safe there, sir, and it's close by."

That was it then: Ballydoran. *Philhemon* gave her best, even though the weather was fierce. So it was on Saturday September 24th that we crept into Ballydoran Bay, barely afloat as we were. Ballydoran was a good, natural harbour, where some of the dark cliffs of the coast had given way to beaches and green land, and there was a round bay, about a mile across. We came in under reefed tops'ls, and the lead going in the fore chains, just to be sure, though the charts said the harbour was clear of shallows.

The weather had eased; we had grey skies over us and a bit of rain, but there was good sunshine coming up from the east, and the ship's bell had just sounded the Morning Watch. Best of all, once we'd anchored and weren't under way, the sea didn't come aboard so fierce, and the pumps got well ahead of the leaks. That was good, but other things were not. I was on the quarterdeck with my officers looking hard at the bay, and at the two forts on rising ground on either side of the entrance ... and seeing that one of the forts was in ruin! Its guns were thrown out, and down on to the beach, and there was massive disturbance to the walls.

"The magazines have gone up," says the First Lieutenant. "Someone's blown the powder magazines."

"Yes," says I, "but who?" And there was more. Within the bay there was a stone quayside, with a few small boats anchored, a warehouse behind, and a rectangular barrack block to one side with a flagpole and a couple of field guns beside it. But barracks and warehouses were burned out, with wispy smoke still rising; there was no flag flying, and nobody about. Worse still, a good careful look through a glass showed bodies laid out in front of the buildings: bodies in red coats. They were jumbled about, and there was a communal groan at the sight of this from those around me, and from the hands who'd got themselves in the shrouds for a good view ashore. But I couldn't allow that.

"Shut your bloody traps!" says I. "Get your duties or I'll come among you!" You have to say such as that on such occasions, but I said it with a heavy heart that day because something was dreadfully wrong in Ballydoran Bay.

"Look, sir!" says the First Lieutenant. "The other forts is sound!" I looked. He was right. The Union Jack was flying, and men were looking out through the embrasures.

"Salute the fort," says I to the First Lieutenant. "Then clear for action, lower the longboat and muster the marines. I'm going ashore."

"Aye aye!" says he, so we dipped our flags and fired a blank charge, and the fort dipped and fired in return. Then there was busy activity, as the ship's people worked hard with the wounded *Philhemon* to get her guns run out and the heavy longboat lowered, and the lookouts wary every second, watching for any dangers that might appear ashore. It had to be the longboat because all our other boats had been holed in the action, but that was good since there was plenty of room in a longboat. I landed at Ballydoran's little quay with six tars at the oars under the Coxswain, plus thirty marines with their subaltern and sergeant. They had ball cartridge loaded and bayonets fixed, and I had my sword and pistols: the curve-blade Henry Tatham fighting sword, and my barkers by Nock of Ludgate Street, in Service calibre and complete with belt hooks.

I was first out of the boat, running up the stone quayside steps with the marine subaltern behind me and his men behind him.

"Hup-hup-hup!" he cries and boot nails crunched on stone, as the marines doubled around me and fanned out, watching for whatever might happen as I stared at the smouldering barracks and the red-coat corpses just twenty yards off; all of them were stripped of their weapons and cartridge pouches. Their boots were gone too. I noticed that. I saw the white, bare feet. Someone had wanted not only their muskets but their boots. I looked round. Ballydoran would have been a miserable place at any time. There was no village, no fishing people. It was a military harbour, rigged out for military purposes with grey stone and grey cobbles. There were low hills behind, and a muddy road leading off into the green and misty morning; the Boatswain was right: the road was a mud bath full of holes.

"Sir!" says the marine subaltern. "Party coming down from the fort, sir!" I looked. The fort – the one still whole – was about half a mile off, linked to the quay and the barracks by a proper road, and half a dozen men were coming down that road. They all wore red coats, and one was obviously an officer. They were extremely wary in their movements, with muskets in hand, and looking to either side even though there wasn't much cover for anyone to hide in. But perhaps they knew the dangers better than I did.

"With me!" says I to the subaltern, "at the double."

"Sir!" says he, and formed up his men around me as I set off up the road at a quick march.

"God bless you!" says the officer when we met. "Thank God you've come!" He grabbed my hand and shook it. He was an elderly man with a white-powdered wig under his hat, a style years out of date. He was untidy and dirty, his men looked exhausted and they were constantly looking round in fear. "I'm Bletchworthe," says he, "Colonel Bletchworthe of the hundred and twenty-first. Might I have the pleasure of your name, sir?"

"Fletcher," says I, "Commodore Fletcher." He nodded and looked me up and down.

"Ah!" says he, "you'll be Jacob Fletcher. *Sir* Jacob Fletcher? The *tradesman?*" He peered at me, the ungrateful old sod, because he was obviously one of the anti-Fletcher brigade. But perhaps I was unkind. He'd had a bloody awful time and was deeply shocked by it, as he instantly explained.

"Rebels, sir!" says he. "Ragged savages from the interior. They came in their thousands, howling and screaming. Barefoot savages with pikes, sir! Nothing but pikes, murdering the wounded where they lay, and dragging out others to be murdered, with the poor souls screaming all the while; and setting all afire, *and men even thrown into the flames!* Thrown in to burn alive, sir! We heard them beg for mercy, then we heard them shriek, and the villains laughing all the while."

"What about the garrison?" says I, pointing to the barracks.

"Reduced, sir!" said he. "Reduced so small as to be useless. Most of them marched to Cork in these troubled times, which the filthy swine must have known and taken advantage of! Someone betrayed us, sir! Someone betrayed his King! They fell on us at night, sir, and many of the rebels were killed, with them having no firelocks. But still they came, and came howling and screaming and giving no quarter."

"But what about the fort?" says I, looking at the ruins. "How did they get in? Wasn't the fort defended?"

"Ah! Ah!" says he. "Such iniquity, sir! We have Fort George and Fort Charlotte here in Ballydoran, sir." I nodded. "And Fort George – which is my fort, sir – has a complete circuit of walls, but by the iniquitous parsimony of the politicians, sir, Fort Charlotte was given only a crescent moon of walls facing towards the sea. More than that, sir, our numbers were so reduced – with men sent away to Cork – as to be barely capable of defence. Instead of a hundred men each fort, we barely had thirty!

Thus, they stormed Fort Charlotte from behind, but made no attempt on Fort George with its walls, and which was a fortunate grace because had they come, sir, then I doubt we'd have held out. But Fort Charlotte's garrison was murdered before our eyes, and the fort set afire to explode with appalling violence. We saw it, sir! We saw the great effusion of flame and smoke, and guns thrown tumbling into the air like shuttlecocks, and great stones raining down afterwards." He shook his head. "It was horrid, sir, horrid!"

With that he fell into floods of tears, and gulped and moaned and hauled out a handkerchief to catch the slobber. I suppose he'd kept control of his emotions as long as he was in charge, but had given in now that rescue had arrived. I felt sorry for him even if he was an anti-Fletcher. So I put an arm round him.

"Never mind, Colonel," says I. "These things happen in war."

"But it's not ... not ... not ... even war," says he, gasping. "It's bloody rebellion."

"So," says I, thinking what was best to do now, "have you any horses, Colonel Bletchworthe, because I must get to Cork with what I know."

"We have none, sir," says he. "Some few as we had were stabled behind the barracks and were stolen by the rebels. And, and," says he, clutching my arm, "you'd be mad to go, even if we did have horses!" I nodded. I agreed. It was a relief to know that I wouldn't have to try.

"Well," says I, "I'll take you aboard ship, Colonel: you and all your people, because you can't be left here. We'll be safe out in the bay with the ship's battery to defend us. But I'm afraid we'll have to spike your guns because we can't have the rebels turning them on the ship. And we'll have to blow your magazine if the rebels look like returning, so they don't get hold of all that gunpowder."

"God bless you, Sir Jacob," says he. "God bless you and thank you. You are a far better man than your reputation suggests."

I suppose he meant that kindly.

We got him and his men aboard with whatever they could not leave behind. It was several boat trips and we had to make shift, accommodating him and his men, turning out some owners of precious cabins, since Bletchworthe ranked equal to a Sea Service captain, and had two Army majors with him who must also have cabins. Then I had marines posted ashore to watch the road for danger, and we had to bury the dead. I sent

121

a working party ashore to do that, with crosses made by our Carpenter. It was grim work because some of the bodies were half burned, and others had been mutilated beyond any need to kill them. They'd been stabbed and hacked many times over. I saw them and it wasn't nice. It was my first taste of how ugly a war in Ireland could be.

Also, I sent *Philhemon's* Gunner and his mates to spike Fort George's guns, which – in case you youngsters don't know – means to hammer nails deep into the touch-holes of the guns, so that they can't be fired. Besides this, the Gunner and his crew laid slow-matches ready to blow the powder magazine of Fort George, once the ship was ready for sea. But fortune didn't favour us in that respect, because the damage below to *Philhemon* was worse than we'd feared, and day followed day without the Carpenter being able to vouch for the ship's safety at sea.

It was on 28th September, just as the tide was on the ebb in the first dogwatch – that's about four in the afternoon to you landmen – that we were surprised by something fearful, which came into Ballydoran so fast as to send our marines running and waving towards the quayside. It was a formation of cavalry. They came with a loud rumble of hooves and with horses tossing their heads.

There was a great number of them and they were a puzzle, being so mud-spattered that we had no idea whose men they were. We couldn't tell by their uniforms because cavalry of all countries wore the same fancy dress in those days: lancer caps, fur hats, off-shoulder pelisses and the like. It was because of the enormous vanity and tiny brains of the commanding officers.

But we soon saw they must be British, because they made no move against our marines, riding forward onto the quayside little more than a hundred yards off. There they reigned in, and formed up most remarkably neat. They did so right in line with our broadside where they would have been minced with grapeshot had they been French. Then the officers drew swords and saluted. So, yes, they were ours and I suppose they'd have looked good enough on parade in Dublin or London when cleaned up. They had fur-trimmed helmets, and blue jackets with silver trim. There were officers of various ranks, and trumpeters and banner-men, and as a team they looked fit for purpose.

I turned to Colonel Bletchworthe, who was standing beside me with his majors in tow.

"Who are they?" says I. "Do you recognise them?"

"May I trouble you for a loan of your glass, Sir Jacob?" says he.

"Here," says I, giving it to him. He fiddled with the instrument and took a good look.

"It's Walton," says he, handing back the glass. "Walton and the 27th Light dragoons. It's a full squadron of two troops. It's the 27th Light! Look at them: no pistols because Walton despises them. Only swords and carbines."

"You know him, then?" says I, "him and his regiment."

"Oh yes," says he, "Walton's famous in Ireland." He pointed. "That's him in the middle there."

"I see," says I. "What sort of man is he?" Bletchworthe paused and didn't quite answer my question.

"Sir Joshua Walton," says he. "He's the baronet now his father's dead, and he's a lieutenant-colonel."

"Yes, but what sort of man is he?" says I. Bletchworthe looked at his majors who avoided his gaze, then he spoke to me quietly. He'd forgiven me for being Jacob Fletcher and he was grateful for being safe aboard ship, so he said quite a lot about Walton.

"It's his family," says he. "They have properties near Durham. Coal mines, you see, which are vastly profitable. They have sugar-money too from the West Indies, and lands in Berkshire besides. Josh Walton was the last of eleven children, all girls, and he was raised as the family's darling, you see, and he could do no wrong." Bletchworthe paused and looked round again. "Nasty temper," says he in a whisper. "His father was the same, don't you know. Both of them rigid for rules: debts paid instantly, strict-honest in everything, never strays from his wife, dogs whipped and men flogged if they transgress." Bletchworthe shook his head. "His regiment's tremendous-well organised, which is good, but it's all rules with him: all hard edges ... *that* and a nasty streak."

As Bletchworthe spoke, Sir Joshua Walton dismounted and spoke to his men such that a couple more dismounted. Then he spoke to the Coxswain of the longboat asking questions, and the Coxswain replied, pointing this way and that. Finally, Walton nodded. He and his men got into the boat, and the boat pulled out towards us.

"Stand by to give honours," says I.

"Aye aye!" says the First Lieutenant, and soon the marines were presenting arms, and the Boatswain's mates sounding their pipes, as the dragoon officers came over the side. They were stained with campaign dirt but gave proper respect to a King's ship, by saluting the quarterdeck. And so I met – and took instant dislike to – Lieutenant-Colonel Sir Joshua Walton of the 27th Light Dragoons: a creature who I'd not put in charge of a pigsty for fear of offending the pigs.

He was in his twenties, handsome under the dirt, with a big chin and fine eyes. He was nearly as tall as myself though much less in bulk. He moved boldly and well, with self-assurance bursting out of him. But, by George, I took against him. I did so for the look on his face. He looked at me as if I was a turd that he'd stepped on, and that was odd, my jolly boys, because nobody looked at your Uncle Jacob like that. I'm so damned big that folk are wary of me, as they're wary of any big and dangerous beast. But Sir Joshua Walton had been bred up to believe that he was superior to all others: including even me.

We did the introductions, and everyone shook hands with everyone else, while the ship's people stood by in the waist to see what was going on. Then, if I hadn't already despised Walton, he did something that would have done the trick all by itself. He stepped past me to the quarterdeck rail, and made a speech to my ship's crew: *my* crew aboard *my* ship and without a word to me first.

"Men!" says he, loudly. "I have heard what happened here. I have heard of the Godless and appalling rebellion! The rebellion of savage primitives! The rebellion of creatures that deserve no mercy and shall receive none, but only fire and the sword!" He went on for quite a while like that, and when he was done, he turned to me. "Commodore Fletcher," says he, "let us now go below to make plans. You will be so good as to show me the way." By Jove, if he'd looked down his nose any further, he'd have fallen over backwards. It was a very bad start indeed.

CHAPTER 20

The Big House,
McCullough's farm,
Ballintorm,
County Galway,
Ireland.
(Night, September 30th 1803)

"It was not her words alone which exalted the soul, but her very being, and her very self."
(From a letter of Tuesday October 4th 1803, from Patrick McCullough to his cousin Sean McCullough in Boston, Massachusetts.)

It was very dark. Liam O'Connor saw the torches coming down the path. He nodded. That was good. He was old and getting tired, but there was hope now because there was a great number of torches, a black shifting mass of bodies below them, and a gleam of pike-staves. O'Connor turned and went in by the parlour door. There were lots of candles – an expensive lot of them – because it was an important night, with important guests in the house, and their horses in the stables. A group of young men – well-dressed city men – sat round the table and looked at O'Connor. He nodded to them, then went to a man sitting asleep in an armchair by the fire. He was old like O'Connor and couldn't keep awake. O'Connor shook him.

"Mr Flynn, sir," he said. "Wake up. They're coming."

"Ah!" said Flynn. "I'll fetch *Himself*. I'll fetch him."

They spoke English, being widely travelled men who could equally have spoken French, because they'd fought under King Louis of France: O'Connor as a captain and Flynn as a colonel. They were men greatly esteemed by

Himself – McCullough – who was the greatest man in Ballintorm even though he didn't have the Irish speech. He'd been raised in England, God help him, which was strange for such an Irish patriot. Therefore, it would be mostly English spoken this night in respect of Himself.

Flynn got up, straightened his clothes, and went towards the stairs. But he didn't have to fetch Himself because McCullough came down into the room. He was a tall, shrivelled outdoors man in his sixties, who had to duck his head as he went through doorways. He wore a woollen cap because he was bald, and he was a famous sportsman and rider to hounds. He was a man of presence, and everyone stood in respect, in a rumble and scrape of chairs. Then everyone looked over McCullough's shoulder. But she wasn't with him. *Cailín Draíochta* wasn't with him.

"She's in prayer," said McCullough. "She's asking God's help."

"Ah!" said everyone.

"Let's go out now, and see what's coming," said McCullough. Everyone went out, putting on their greatcoats because it was cold for September and the weather was bad. They looked at the oncoming procession of torches that flared in the night. They could hear the tramp of feet and the singing. They could see the pike-heads glittering. There were hundreds of them: many hundreds. McCullough spoke to Flynn.

"Can we get them all into the barn?"

"Yes, your honour," said Flynn.

"And do they understand that I'm as much an Irishman as any of them? I may have lived in England, but I'm Irish in my bones, and I've paid for the stores the French will need when they land: the cattle and grain and bread. Do they know that?"

"Yes, your honour," said Flynn. "The priests have told them."

"And do they trust the priests?"

Flynn thought about that. He looked at the rabble of pikemen that was approaching. They were close enough to be seen in the torchlight. They called themselves *Buachaillí an bhanna glas*: The Boys of the Green Band. The average of them was undersized, underfed, illiterate, barefoot and stinking. They held homemade pikes in black-nailed fingers and their backs were stooped because they'd never stood straight in all their lives. There was no discipline among them: not proper discipline. Only a few had served in the British Army, when the choice had been to serve or starve. They'd been sergeants or corporals, so they clouted and kicked when

126

the Boys were mustered on parade. They clouted and kicked them into ranks and files, while their women and children looked on and laughed. The one thing the Boys would do was charge. Oh yes. They'd do that with a shriek and a scream, every man of them together, in a thundering rush that nothing could stop or control, because once they charged, they were beyond any other command. They were savage and mad and brutal.

"Mr Flynn?" said McCullough. "I asked you a question."

"Of course, your honour," said Flynn, but the question was a hard one. The Boys of the Green Band were all Catholics – good Catholics – except that what the priest taught was only topsoil over the deeps beneath, because the Boys believed in witches, leprechauns, the evil eye, and a thousand superstitions. But just for once that was all to the good. "They'll trust the priests this night, your honour," said Flynn, "because they've come for a magic show. They've come to see the magic fairy. They can't wait. Then once they're in front of her, they'll believe anything she tells them." Flynn sighed. "Who wouldn't? If she told me to put my hand in the fire, then I'd do it."

"But she wouldn't," said McCullough. "She'd never say such a thing." He turned to the young city men. "Gentlemen," he said, "will one of you go into her presence, and will you tell her that I shall send word when all is ready?" He looked at the Boys of the Green Band. "Meanwhile we'll get them into the barn."

There was a great deal of shoving and bustle as the horde of ragged pikemen crammed into the cobbled yard in front of the barn. They packed in, one man against another, and the animal smell of them stank foul in McCullough's nose. There was a great shouting by Flynn, and O'Connor and others, not a word of which McCullough understood because now it had to be Irish. McCullough looked at the pikemen and was surprised at how small they all were, how weather-beaten and wrinkled, and how lacking in anything other than scraps of clothing and their pikes. But they were good natured, cheering him when Flynn called on them in Irish and thrust him forward, and said words that sounded like praise. The Boys yelled and cheered and waved their pikes, and McCullough was greatly relieved to know that he was accepted among them.

He was relieved because there were so many different parts to the plan. McCullough and other educated men had approached the French, and McCullough and others had paid for the droves of cattle, and wagons of bread that would feed the French when they came. That was vital, but so was a great number of Irish peasants who must take the field and fight. It was all part of the great plan, and the plan had to hold together. Different men with different beliefs had to hold together. Therefore, McCullough was hugely relieved when the pikemen smiled upon him.

Finally, they were all in the barn, and McCullough went back to the big house to say that everything was ready. He sent one of the young men to beg that she might come down, which she did. She came downstairs, into the room and she smiled. At this, McCullough fell to his knees as did every other man in the room. They couldn't help themselves. Such was her power to inspire reverence.

CHAPTER 21

Down we went into *Philhemon's* great cabin: Walton of the 27th, his two officers, then myself and my first and second lieutenants with Colonel Bletchworthe and his majors, and Mr Chaplain Blackhurst too, because I trusted Blackhurst's judgement and, in any dealings with Sir Joshua Walton, I wanted plenty of witnesses on my side.

So, we sat down, my men on one side of the table, Walton's on the other. Then the obligatory wine was served, and the Cook sent in some of his best fancy biscuit to go with it. He sent that, and some cheese and pickles, and nuts and raisins. He did it for the honour of the ship, with visiting officers come aboard. He did it for courtesy. But Walton and his two captains were delighted and tucked into the food as if hungry.

"We must first talk of supplies, Commodore Fletcher," says he to me.

"In what respect?" says I.

"In respect," says he, "of my regiment and others being sent out urgently and with little preparation to search this pagan realm, and to live off the land; but ourselves near starving since the land was already scoured of food and cattle." He paused and looked at a last piece of cheese on a plate in front of me. "Shall you eat that, Commodore?" says he.

"No," says I, and off it went on the point of his knife, and into his mouth.

"So," says he, and – without looking – he stretched a hand to one of his officers who handed him a paper, "here is a list of supplies which I shall need at once, and which must be delivered up into the saddle bags of my regiment for my departure this very day." He gave me the paper. It was a list: a long list. I looked at it and frowned, not so much at the quantities but because I was in no mind to oblige him.

"This might be difficult," says I, "since I cannot leave my ship's people short of food." He waved a hand as if brushing off a fly.

"That is a small matter," says he, "as compared with my duty to find the witch and bring her to justice."

"Witch?" says I.

"Witch?" says Mr Blackhurst. "Did I hear the word 'witch'?"

"Of course!" says Walton, frowning. "The witch!" says he. "The witch who is the linchpin of rebellion. Do you not know?" I looked at Blackhurst, and the rest. They all shook their heads. "Ah!" says Walton, "I see that you are in ignorance. Then let me inform you that the Governor General of Ireland – His Grace the Earl of Portwicke – has been informed that this present rebellion of the Irish is fomented by a witch-woman – probably some hideous old hag – brought forward by the Catholic priests to dazzle the peasantry with magic and to set them against their lawful king." He saw our surprise, and leaned back in his chair. "Did you not know?"

"No," says I. "I was told by the Governor General that the French would land at Ennismullet. I was told that but nothing more." Walton smiled and waved away the fly again.

"That is a matter for the Sea Service," says he. "It does not concern me. I am concerned only with seizing the witch, and thereby snuffing rebellion at a single stroke." He looked round the table. "Have you any more cheese?" says he.

"Wait, wait," says I. "When did Portwicke hear about this witch?"

"Oh, weeks ago," says Walton. "His Grace told us about her when he sent us out, and gave us the names of the places where she will visit."

"Well, he didn't tell me that!" says I. "He damn well didn't!"

"Oh, he wouldn't," says Walton. "It was most secret information reserved only for the colonels of regiments sent out to find her and seize her."

"And what's this about *places*?" says Blackhurst, "places she will visit?"

"His Grace is informed," says Walton, "of all those places where the rebels shall be mustered for the witch, so that she might work her magic, and thereby coerce them into rebellion. Thus, he knew *where* she shall be, but unfortunately not *when*."

"And so?" says I.

"And so," says he, "every available cavalry regiment is out trying to catch these musters in progress, and thereby seize the witch." He frowned, while on my side we all looked at one another, wondering what was going on, because we'd seen the reality of fighting and rebellion. We'd seen men killed and ships broken, and here was Walton talking fairy-tale nonsense!

"Well, Sir Joshua," says I, "I don't know about magic witches, and musters God-knows-when, but I can tell you as fact – and it is vital that I tell the Governor General – that the French are landed in force, and that every red-coat in Ireland should be marching to oppose them!" There was a growl of approval from my side, and fists thumping the table. But Walton merely smiled. It was the infinitely self-satisfied smile of a man who sees others as mere children at play. "I see," says he, "so you failed. You of the Sea Service failed to stop the French." He shrugged. "No matter, I shall take the witch tomorrow, because I have interrogated the peasantry and know where the witch shall be, and ..."

It was his smile that did it. That and his damned landman, blockhead soldier's insult to the Service. This time I did the interrupting. I did it at the top of my voice. The ship's people heard me from taffrail to bowsprit, and the pair of us ended up standing and yelling into each other's faces. It was one of the few times in my life that I entirely lost my temper and it's only a few words of what was said that I remember.

"Witches?" says I. "What a bloody damned bucket of old cods-wallop!"

"Damn you, sir!" says Walton. "Do you not know who I am?"

"I don't give a shit who you are! Sod you, you bloody lubber!"

"I come of the highest in the land! Beware, sir, beware!"

"Beware? Beware says you? Bollocks says I!"

"How dare you, sir! I am a lieutenant-colonel in His Majesty's Service!"

"Oh? Oh?" says I, seizing my opportunity. "A lieutenant-colonel, says you? Well, I'm a bloody post captain, which equals a full colonel in the Army, and I'm a commodore besides, so I bloody well outrank you and you can sit down and bloody well shut up!"

Jesus God Almighty. The perversity of human nature. All you young-sters take note that I ought to have won that shouting match by being the biggest and loudest. But that wasn't what did it. What did it was Walton frowning, and then pausing, and then thinking, and finally realising that I'd just played the Ace of Trumps. I bloody well *did* outrank him, and for such as him there was nothing he could do than obey. You could see it in his tight-arsed face. So, he sat down and shut up. Mind you, he hated me for it ever after, and never forgave me. But he sat down like a good boy, and I read him the book of rules.

"Listen here, Sir Joshua Walton," says I, "because this is how it'll be. You can take all the supplies you want from Fort George, because I'm going to blow it up anyway, and there's plenty of food in the lockers there." I looked at Colonel Bletchworthe. "Am I right, sir?"

"You are right, sir!" says he, grinning. He really had forgiven me now, because he didn't like Walton any more than I did.

"So," says I to Walton, "you will give me a horse, and your regiment will escort me to Cork as hard as they can ride. You will do that so I can warn the Governor General that the French are landed, because that is far more important than witches, elves, fairies and dragons. Do you understand me?"

"Mumble, mumble," says he with deep-down surly look on his face.

"Do you understand me?" says I, leaning across the table.

"Yes," says he in a little voice.

"Good!" says I. "Then we're done talking here. You get your regiment ready to march, or ride out, or set sail, or whatever damn word you use, and you can fill your saddle bags with salt pork and whatever else you need from the fort. Is that understood?"

"Yes," says he.

"Then we're done here," says I, which we were. So, Walton and his officers were rowed ashore to do as I'd said, and I gave command of the ship to the First Lieutenant, telling him to get her under way as fast as was safe, and bring word to Cork in case I failed.

"And am I to explode the fort, sir?" says he.

"Yes," says I, "on sight of the rebels, or when you up-anchor."

"Aye aye!" says he. After that I got my greatcoat, my sword and pistols, and finally I had a word in private with Chaplain Blackhurst, who had something to say. We went far aft on the quarterdeck, and he surprised me with what he knew of the Governor General.

"Charley Powel!" says Blackhurst, "that was him as a boy, who is now Governor General, Charles Philip Powel, the Second Earl of Portwicke. I knew him at Eton."

"You were at Eton?" says I.

"Don't look so surprised, Sir Jacob," says he. "How d'you think I got my post as chaplain in such a ship as *Tromenderon*? Family influence, sir! Walton isn't the only man with a rich family."

"Oh," says I, "and yet you were an actor."

"For the love of it," says he. "And the despair of everyone, until I had The Call."

"I see, so what about the Governor General?"

"He was a liar, a sneak, and a coward. No good at games whatsoever."

"And so?"

"Don't be surprised if he wasn't straight with you," says he. "I'm old enough now not to trust mine arse with a fart, and I wouldn't trust Charley Powel with anything."

"What about Walton?" says I. "Do you know anything of him?"

"I knew his father," says Blackhurst, "savage brute, but honest. He was one for the written law and no mistake. No charity in him."

"I see," says I.

"Be warned," says Blackhurst. "You gave Sir Josh a considerable battering, so he'll do you down in any legal way he can. But he'll try nothing dangerous. Too many pairs of eyes in a regiment, and I don't think his men like him much. The pair that came with him were grinning when you were shouting at him."

"Were they?" says I.

"Oh yes!"

Blackhurst was right in that, because when I went ashore to join the 27th, one of the captains came forward and saluted me. He had a number of his men with him, all junior officers. They were waiting as I came up the steps at the quayside. Some of my marines were there too, and they presented arms, and I saw a traffic of horsemen going up and down the road to Fort George. I supposed that they were stuffing their saddlebags, and I wondered if they'd found some nice big cheeses for Walton.

The Captain and his men saluted. He was one of those who'd been aboard with Walton and had seen me face him down. But he was friendly. He was smiling.

"Beg pardon, Sir Jacob," says he, "I beg permission for a word."

"What is it?" says I.

"It's this, sir," says he. He took a breath and rattled off a prepared speech: "Sir Joshua sends his compliments, sir, and is ready in all respects to deliver you safe to Cork. But he points out his sure and certain conviction that the Irish witch will join a muster of rebels tomorrow at Ballintorm. And since Ballintorm is almost on the road to Cork, the deviation from your journey, sir, would be very small, while the advantage – in suppression of the rebellion – would be very great. Thus, Sir Joshua urges and requests that we go first to Ballintorm, before proceeding on the road to Cork."

He finished, stamped a foot, saluted again and looked at me. They all looked at me and, friendly or not, they had eyes and ears and I realised that Walton had manoeuvred me into a trap. I couldn't now deny that I'd been warned of an opportunity to snuff the rebellion. So if I didn't agree to chase the witch, and if the witch turned out to be real, then I could be blamed for the rebellion. Blackhurst was right again. Walton had found a legal way, if not to do me down then certainly to get his own way. But I had to be sure.

"How does Sir Joshua know?" says I, "that this person – this witch – will be at Ballintorm tomorrow?" The Captain looked uncomfortable. He shuffled his feet.

"Sir Joshua interrogates the natives," says he, "the peasants whom we catch. He interrogates them with Sergeant-Major Congreve." He said no more. He just looked at me.

"And they give information, these Irish peasants?" says I.

"Yes, sir."

"And how does he persuade them to give it?"

"I cannot know, sir," says he, "since the interrogations are private." That's all he said, but his expression said "*please don't ask any more.*" I looked at him and I looked at his men, and they all had the same look about them. I had to make a quick decision, because it seemed that Walton was a lot nastier than I'd thought. So, was I going to be entirely safe? Riding with him and his men? You know me, my jolly boys: Heaven help the man that comes at me face-to-face! But I'm not proof against a shot or a knife from behind, and I had to assume that Walton hated me, and wanted revenge. I could easily turn about, get back in the longboat and pull for *Philhemon* and safety, and hope the ship could soon be got right. But what if she couldn't be made right? What if I didn't take news of the French landings to Cork? And what if the witch was real and she escaped?

It even occurred to me that, if I did get blamed for another Irish rebellion, the Admiralty would doubtless throw me out of the Service, just as I'd always wanted. So, my jolly boys, perhaps it would be best if I stayed aboard *Philhemon* and let the Irish rebellion take care of itself? Because then I might end up ashore for good. But then I wondered if they'd be content at merely throwing me out of the Service? What if they turned really nasty: the Admiralty and the bloody Government? What if I was court martialled for not doing my best? They famously did that to Admiral Byng, and he didn't end up safe ashore: he ended up dead!

[Note that on 14th March 1757, Admiral John Byng was executed by firing squad aboard his own flagship on a charge of *failing to do his best* to prevent a French fleet from taking Minorca, which failure was regarded as cowardice in the face of the enemy. S.P.]

Oh, dear me. Oh, dear me indeed. What should I do? In the end, never mind what the Admiralty thought, I wondered what *Philhemon's* crew might think. Would they think I was a coward? That's pure vanity I know, but it made up my mind.

"So, Captain," says I, "where's this horse you've got for me? I hope it's a big 'un, if we're going to Ballintorm as well as Cork." I got a smile from all of them for that and felt better for it: better and safer, because if Walton hated me, his men did not.

I was led to Sir Joshua Walton, who said hallo and welcomed me to his regiment, but it was frosty-face formal.

"It is then agreed that we go first to Ballintorm?" says he, "sir?"

"Yes, Sir Joshua," says I, noting that he'd said sir. Then he stretched out his hand without looking – that irritating, superior gesture again – and a minion handed him a paper which he waved at me.

"This, sir, is the Riot Act of 1714," says he, "which by delegation of the Governor General, I am authorised to read in the face of rebellious assembly, and to use deadly force if they do not disperse." He handed it to me. "Here, sir," says he, "see for yourself." So I did, and found that it wasn't quite what he said, but a printed summary of the Act of Parliament, with a separate paragraph that must be read aloud to rioters as a warning. But beneath the print, in the Governor General's own handwriting, were the words:

Given into the hand of Sir Joshua Walton, Baronet,
and to be used at his judgement.
Charles Earl of Portwicke,
September 10th 1803.

Well, my jolly boys, what leapt off the page at your Uncle Jacob was the phrase: *to be used at his judgement*. If Walton couldn't see that was Portwicke's way of avoiding blame if things went wrong, then serve Walton right for putting his wedding tackles on the block while Portwicke held a cleaver! Mind you, Walton hadn't had Chaplain Blackhurst's warning never to trust Charley Portwicke, so I had the advantage of him there. It's all politics in the end, my lads, and a dirty business too. Meanwhile, since I thought that all this talk of magic fairies was nonsense, I was happy to go first to Ballintorm and find nothing there, and then onward to Cork.

So, I gave Walton back his paper.

"It seems to be in order," says I, "though I'm no expert in these matters and I leave them to your judgement." That was *myself* being political, standing in front of witnesses as we were. "I just hope you've found me a big horse," says I and indeed they did. It was the biggest in the regiment. They offered me a sword too, but I didn't want one. I had my own sword and pistols.

And here I must pause to give my usual opinion on the riding of horses, which is a thing that nature never intended me for. Yes, I knew how to ride, and could get a horse to go forward or aft, larboard or starboard. I knew to hang on and not fall off. But I'm too big for horses, poor beasts, so they don't like me and who can blame them?

Then, well done the 27th for being a campaigning regiment, because they rode with kit muffled so it didn't jingle, and brasses left dull, but swords kept sharp and firelocks clean. We were off before the end of the day, once the men and horses had been fed, and we advanced on the mud track that led to Ballintorm and, beyond that, to Cork. It was my first run ashore in rural Ireland, which was green, and misty and rolling: it was the sea made solid in grass, and it was empty in a way that England is not. England has towns and villages everywhere and it's full of farmer's fields with hedges round them. But not Ireland. You can ride for miles and when you look at the natural wild of it, and the little streams and waterfalls, and when you look at the great stones raised up by ancient peoples, you can even believe in elves and goblins hiding out of sight. Why not after all? Don't sailors believe in the sea serpent? And the mermaid? And Davey Jones, the demon, who looks up from the deep if you glance over the side in the full moon?

So, I hung on, and looked at Ireland as the 27th advanced in column of threes, and Walton and his sergeant-major peered at maps. This was Sergeant-Major Congreve that Walton obviously thought so much of, because he was alongside of Walton, up front and ahead of us all, while I was in the second rank with one of the captains and a lieutenant. The Captain was the one who'd met me at the quayside. He saw me looking at Congreve, as the sergeant-major rode aside from the column to halt and take bearings with a pocket compass.

"He's a fine soldier," says the Captain, "thirty years' experience."

"Is he now?" says I.

"Oh yes. He's fought with the Russians and Hungarians, and the Turks."

"Has he now?" says I.

"Oh yes, and he learned their ways." He looked at me and shrugged, as Congreve kicked spurs into his horse and rode up beside Walton again, and pointed.

"Left at the fork, sir!" says he. I heard that, and Walton nodded.

There was a lot more of such navigational practice, and I realised that finding the way in the depths of Ireland, where signposts were precious rare, had much in common with deep sea navigation when out of sight of land. Also, there were halts to rest and feed the horses, and periods when we all had to dismount and walk. But that's cavalry on campaign. It's not all thundering charges and bugle calls. But as I've said, the 27th were good campaigning soldiers, and fully skilled in their craft.

So, they found Ballintorm, did Walton's men; they found it after many hours of careful riding. Then, guided by Sergeant-Major Congreve, they got themselves into position around it. They got around it in four separate divisions, widely spaced out, and they did this at night, without trumpets or noise or shouting, and with scouts gone out ahead so that if anybody got surprised, it wasn't going to be the 27th. It was well done. Well done indeed. And then, if I thought a sea fight was a blood-stained affair, I had much to learn about fighting in Ireland, and much to learn about the 1796 light cavalry sword, which was the main weapon of the 27th.

This sword has a well-designed hand-guard: the so-called 'half-stirrup' and the whole thing weighs just a couple of pounds, while the blade is two inches wide, thirty-three inches long, and deeply curved. It is designed purely for cutting, and it sits in the hand so neat and comfy that the *urge* to cut is irresistible. It is the finest cavalry sword ever made, but here, my jolly boys, the praise must end, because the sword was beautiful but the using of it was not. The using of it was butchery.

CHAPTER 22

The Big House,
McCullough's farm,
Ballintorm,
County Galway,
Ireland.
(Dawn, October 1st 1803)

"We were caught by surprise: so unlikely an event that I suspect betrayal by an informer."
(From a letter of Tuesday October 4th 1803, from Patrick McCullough to Sean McCullough in Boston Massachusetts.)

McCullough was downstairs and busy as soon as there was light. He was rousing O'Connor, Flynn and the young city men who'd brought Cailín Draíochta to his house. McCullough never slept much at any time, and last night not at all. He'd worried the whole night through, and begged the dawn to come. He'd worried because the responsibility of having her in the house was so great, so very great, and now that she had spoken to the Boys of the Green Band, and roused them to a screaming, yelling fury against the English, it was time to get her safe away, on to the next muster.

"Up! Up!" said McCullough. He went round the room kicking men awake, and stepping over bodies, because it wasn't only his own men and the city men who were there. Some of the Boys of the Green Band were on the flagstones, still insensible with drink. They lay snoring with mouths open and eyes shut. McCullough sighed. That was the uisce beatha - water of life: raw spirit brewed in the secret stills of the countryside, where the English Revenue could not find them. There could be no mustering of the Boys of the Green Band without uisce beatha, even if it did leave them paralysed by midnight. "Get up, every man of you!" said McCullough. He was already dressed for the road: spurred and booted with a pair of pistols in his belt over his riding coat. "Up! Up!" he said. The room came to life and men roused themselves; the old soldiers, O'Connor and Flynn, were saluting, and the whole room stunk with bad breath and the sweat of last night's emotions. "Outside!" said McCullough. "Horses and saddles! Bring her horse to the door! Get it done! I'll fetch her down! Get to it! Now!"

O'Connor and Flynn were beside McCullough. They'd had enough self-discipline to avoid being soaked in drink, and they were hauling men to their feet, trying to get the Green Band Boys awake, which was barely possible though some of them staggered up like corpses from the grave.

The city men likewise did their best, even with a bare few hours of sleep. They blinked and licked their dry lips, pulled on coats, and stumbled outside, where most of them felt a sudden need to empty their bladders. This they did against the front wall of the big house, while O'Connor and Flynn ran to the barn to rouse the main mass of the Green Band Boys. But even crossing the cobbled yard they had to step over snoring men: dew-soaked, wringing-wet, snoring men who'd left the barn to dance in the night, with torches burning. They'd danced to wild Irish music of bone flutes and bodhran drums, till they fell down drunk and exhausted.

Inside the barn, dense packed with men forced suddenly awake – or half awake or a quarter awake – O'Connor and Flynn yelled and shoved, trying to get the pikemen outside and armed, and in some sort of order in case of danger. The few of the Green Band Boys who'd been sergeants or corporals got themselves up and joined in, calling on men by name, and calling on them by duty. Finally, a great herd of them shuffled out into the light, blinking and scratching and grinning, and each man trying to find his own beloved pike among the thicket of them left leaning against the barn walls. Then there came a great cheer as women came into the yard: women from the village nearby, bringing firewood and pots, and the makings of hot food, and water and milk to drink. There were whoops of joy at that and much calling out to the women.

But then sound came from every direction: dreadful, threatening sound, the sound of horsemen coming on at a steady trot. They came from the fields and the village, from four separate directions. There was no getting away from them.

"Beárla!" cried the Green Band Boys, *"Sasanach!"*: The English!

There was no escape and soon the English were in sight: formed bodies of cavalry with swords drawn. They poured over the yard wall, and stood in a dense mass with gleaming swords. An officer rode out in front of them and yelled at them in English, which none of the Green Band Boys could understand. Then he produced a piece of paper and read it out, which nobody could even hear for the shouting and anger. Stones were snatched up and thrown at the English, and horses began to snort and stamp; an English trooper got knocked senseless and fell from his horse.

"Seasamh daigean!" cried Flynn, once a colonel under King Louis: *stand firm!* He shouted and shouted, knowing how utterly and hopelessly the Boys of the Green Band were trapped. But the Boys of the Green Band were full of the fire poured into them by Cailín Draíochta, and even without that fire, no man in a thousand years had ever accused the Irish of cowardice in the face of the enemy. Not ever! Not them! The Boys of the Green Band rushed to the thicket of pikes, grabbed and jostled and got in each other's way, and the English officer in command of the cavalry put away his paper, drew his sword and nodded to his trumpeter who sounded the charge.

CHAPTER 23

I took no part in the fighting at Ballintorm. The four separate squadrons of us closed in at dawn. Three came in from the fields surrounding a large mansion and barn, and the other came in through the village of Ballintorm. We closed in at a steady trot, without trumpets or any noise that might give warning. We rode forward in the dim light, over soggy grass that muffled the hooves.

I was behind Walton and Sergeant-Major Congreve, with the horsemen in two ranks, and the men dressing their lines as we went. Once again, I have to give them credit for their craft, because our squadron was the first to approach a vast cobbled yard in front of the mansion. The yard was enclosed by a dry-stone wall, and while the troopers could easily jump it, there wasn't room for the whole line of us within it, not side-by-side. So, Congreve turned in the saddle, waved arms in signal, and the two ranks magically turned into four, in a denser and more narrow formation.

More horsemen joined us outside the stone wall, having come in from other directions; then there was a brief pause as lines were straightened again. I don't know about the rest of those horse-soldiers but my heart was bumping in the anticipation because we'd obviously caught the rebels, not just with their britches down, but their drawers too. There was a straggling group of men in the yard, trying to raise up others who were laid out on the cobbles for God-knows-what reason, while a great horde of rag-tag, matted-hair men, were clumped in front of the barn. These mostly had their backs to us, but turned in fright as they heard us come. They then surged in a mass, towards a clutter of long staves – pikes they were – leaned against the barn. They were a miserable sight, not soldiers in uniform, but a tribe of peasantry, and there were women too. They were in the middle of the yard, clutching pots and pans, and gaping at us. Walton rode a horse-length forward, and shouted.

"In the name of King George, I command you to disperse!" says he, and was totally ignored. The ragged men just yelled, and cursed, and some picked up stones and threw them. The stones whirled up through the air, and mostly hit nothing, but some caught the horses, while a man near me took a clump to the head and fell senseless. "So!" says Walton, following the rule book to the last, "I shall now read the warning as prescribed by law." He took out his Riot Act paper and began to read from it. But the men in front of him just grabbed at their pikes as Walton persisted, reading every last word. Then he put away his paper, drew his sword, and looked to his trumpeter, who just had time to blow the charge, before a horde of pikemen were running forward, screaming and shrieking.

But they were lost men. The 27th rode into them and over them, and it was pure butchery. No living thing in that yard was spared. The curve-blade swords went up and down, and they cleft heads and lopped arms and split shoulders. There was a howling and yelling, and horses screamed and trampled, and the men of the 27th cried out in rage as some of their comrades got speared, with pikes running through the silver-trimmed blue jackets, coming out bloodied and greasy.

But mainly it was swords against helpless arms and heads, because most of the poor damn rag-men never got hold of their pikes. I think I heard a couple of gunshots but, on such occasions, you never quite know, because you're concentrating on not falling off your horse, which is death in such a fight as that.

It didn't last long: five minutes? Ten? I wasn't counting. But it was soon over and I took no part because I couldn't. In such a melee, if you're not trained up to it, then it's just not possible to have control of a horse, keep yourself in the saddle, draw a sword and use it. So I hung on as best as I could, and struck no blow.

Finally, the last squadron came up: the one that had come through the village, and we counted our dead and wounded. Seven were dead and one wounded: the man knocked out by a stone. He was up and holding his bloodied head. As for the ragged men, most were deathly still, while the rest lay groaning such as was pitiful to hear.

So, it was all over, and the only thing that I did do was fall into another argument with Sir Joshua Walton: him and his sergeant-major. I did so with horses steaming and shuffling, and the men of the 27th looking round for anything more to fight. One poor creature did get up and try to fight. He got up with one arm hanging half-severed and blood flowing; he picked up a pike with his good hand and stood screaming at the top of his voice. He was barely on his feet, but he was ready to fight the world. I suppose he was crying out in the Irish language because I didn't understand him. Nobody did. We just sat our horses in a ring around him until Sir Joshua Walton called out to his sergeant-major.

"Yours or mine, Sarn't Major?" says he.

"Yours, sir," says Congreve, saluting with his sword. "I think you're nearer, sir."

"Your courtesy is appreciated, Sarn't Major," says Walton, returning the salute. Then he sheathed his sword, drew his carbine from its holster, cocked the lock, and rode over to the poor devil standing with his pike ... and casually shot him dead. Walton smiled as he did it. He was enjoying himself.

And so, my jolly boys, that tipped me over again.

"Walton!" says I in a mast-head bellow, "you bloody-minded villain!"

"What?" says he, turning his horse to face me. "How dare you, sir: in front of my men?"

"You didn't have to do that, you vicious bastard!" says I, and there was indeed a gasp from his men.

"Damn you, sir!" says he. "I have already despaired of you as a gentleman and ..."

"Gentleman?" says I. "You don't know a gentleman from a dog's dick!"

"How dare you, sir?" says he. "The Admiralty shall hear of this!"

"Bollocks to the Admiralty," says I and pointed to the man he'd shot. "That poor sod was bad wounded, and there's others the same all round. Are you going to murder them all? Even the bloody French don't murder the wounded, and we damn well don't do it in the Sea Service! In our service we bloody well give aid to the wounded whoever's men they are! So, are you going to do less? Are you going to do murder in the King's name? *Against the King's law?*"

He went quiet at that: rule-following, legal-minded little shit that he was. He went quiet but his men did not. I got a mumble of agreement from them. They were looking at me and nodding, and I think I'd turned even Walton my way. I'd certainly turned his men. But then something else happened. There were gasps of amazement, then shouts of surprise.

"Sir! Sir!" says several voices.

"Here, sir! Look, sir!" says others.

*"I shall bear the guilt of it so long as I live, but I was helpless. I could
do nothing."*

(From a letter of Tuesday October 4th 1803, from Patrick
McCullough.)

McCullough ran out of his house. Three of the city men were behind
him and they gaped at the slaughter, and were deafened by the noise. All
were struck helpless by these horrors except McCullough, who saw that
the English cavalry weren't yet at his front door, nor the stables behind.

"Horses!" he said. "Get them while you can! Get her on a horse and
get her away! I'll guard the door!" The three were lucky. The English
were so busy at their killing that they missed the men who ran to the
stables and came back with three horses, which suddenly became two
when one kicked and screamed in terror, sending its handler flying. It
galloped off and was gone. "Here! Here!" said McCullough, shouting so
loud that an Englishmen heard him and turned in the saddle. He yelled
to his companions, wheeled his horse in a clatter of hooves, dug in spurs
and charged with sword raised.

Bang! Bang! McCullough let fly with his pistols. The cavalryman
took a ball in the chest and his horse was seared along one flank by a
near miss; the beast staggered and reared and threw its dying rider, and
cannoned into the two horses still held by the city men. Unused to
horses, the city men shrank back, let go, and both horses would have
been away except that McCullough – horseman since the age of four –
grabbed the reins of one, hauled himself into the saddle, and tried to
take command of the hysterical animal. But it couldn't be done. The
horse was mad. All McCullough could do was keep the saddle as the
horse fled in terror of its life, galloping so fast through a formation of
English cavalry coming through the village, that they never had time
to strike a blow.

Therefore, McCullough of McCullough escaped. He escaped but few
others did. O'Connor and Flynn died fighting. The young city men –
scholars who'd never been trained to fight – ran back into the house
thinking only of her, and the need to defend her in any way that they could.

But still McCullough escaped. Given the choice he would have died rather than run. He would have given his soul to protect Cailín Draíochta. Instead, he was carried off helpless, and she was left to the enemy.

"Here! Look, sir!" says one of the troopers and we all looked at the front door of the mansion. A woman was standing there with three men trying to pull her back into the house, but she spoke to them, and they let go, and they bowed to her as if she were the Queen. Then she stepped out into the yard, looked round and lifted her chin. We all fell silent. Even the rag-men wounded stopped moaning once they heard her voice, and they turned to look as best they could.

"Who is in command among you English?" says she. "Who will bear the shame of this atrocity?" The voice was very lovely, though if you ask me, all Irish women have lovely voices. But this one was different. It was special. Walton rode forward with Sergeant-Major Congreve behind him, and I kicked my mount to get alongside Walton, because I didn't trust the murderous bastard. But he stopped a few yards from the woman, and looked at her and his manner changed. He dismounted, and strike me blind if he didn't draw sword and salute her!

"Ma'am," says he, "I am Lieutenant-Colonel Sir Joshua Walton, and I am at your service." I heard that rather than saw it, because I can't get off a horse all neat and smart. With me it's more like a fall from the main-top. But, at last, I was beside Walton and looking at the lady. Without even thinking, I took off my hat as she looked at me, and the force of her hit me like a round-shot.

She was young and exceedingly beautiful. She was beautiful in a way unlike any other woman I ever met, because women can be beautiful in many ways. There's the plump and luscious kind that makes a man lick his lips 'cos he can't wait to get at her. Then there are women who are beautiful in beautiful clothes, like a work of art. Still others have the gift of causing men to know that they are as much above the common herd, as a racehorse is above a carthorse. It's usually the female aristocracy who do that, but a lovely actress does it too, because it's in her manner and bearing. I suppose there are other forms besides, but the woman in front of me was different from all of them, because the look on her went right into my brain.

She was deadly serious, with not a twitch of expression on her face, and it was a small, pale face with a pointed chin, red lips and perfect features;

her eyes – very blue and very large – were drilling right into me. Then there was the confidence of her! She was looking out on a field of her own people all dead and wounded, and she was looking at the men who'd done the killing, and who now held total power over her. Yet when she looked at me, I felt like a fishmonger who'd come to the front door, not the servant's entrance. I felt that and two other things. First, that she was profoundly more intelligent than me, which was a cold and powerful thing. But second, she stirred me hot and deep, causing me to know that I could never bear to see harm done to her: not a scratch, nor a bump, nor a harsh word.

And that, my jolly boys, is the best that your Uncle Jacob can do, to put down in words the feelings that hit me as I looked at that woman. It is my best attempt but it is not enough. So if you want to go out beyond reason: out among the Irish mist and fairies, then I'm not surprised because I do not – and I cannot – look down on the Irish peasanty who certainly thought she was magic. They called her Cailín Draíochta, which means The Magical Girl, in their language. I learned that later, but we didn't call her that then.

"Ma'am?" says Walton. "Might I ask your name, and your reasons for being in this place at this time?"

"I am Mary Murchadha," says she, "and I am here, at this mustering of loyal Irishmen, to convince them of the rightful need to throw off the chains of occupation, and to join with our French allies in driving the English and their king from the soil of Ireland."

"Oh," says Walton.

"Oh," says I, because that was treason, pure treason. She'd condemned herself and a hanging must follow. It couldn't be plainer than that.

"Ah ..." says Walton, and I said nothing.

"And what shall you do with these poor wounded souls?" says she, sweeping a hand towards those lying on the cobbled yard. "Do you consider yourselves Christians or are you heathen savages?" By George, what a woman! She sunk us in shame and guilt. I felt as if I'd pissed the bed, and even Walton was embarrassed.

"No, Ma'am," says he, "not at all, Ma'am. I shall ... I shall order my men ... I shall ..." Then he turned round. "Sarn't Major?" says he.

"Sir?" says Congreve.

"Succour the wounded!" says Walton. "Give all such aid as lies within our power!"

"Sir!" says Congreve, and off he went and had the 27th off their horses and binding up wounds. It was something amazing to see. Meanwhile:

"And … ah …" says Walton, still thrown aback, "and who are these … ah … gentlemen?" He looked at three young men in good clothes that were stood just behind Mary Murchadha and who looked deadly afraid. She looked at them, then turned her gaze back on Walton.

"They are virtuous patriots who are under my protection," says she.

"Yes, Ma'am," says Walton, though he had the beginnings of a frown on his face. After all, this was utter nonsense. Virtuous patriots? Under her protection?

"Enough!' says she, "come inside!" She turned to the three young men, and pointed to the furthest wall of the room. "You will stand there, and say nothing," says she.

"Yes, Cailín Draíochta," says they. It was the first time I heard that name spoken, and they stood where she said, then kept silent.

But did you follow all that, my jolly boys? She was taking command. She was giving orders and that was even greater nonsense, but we all did what she said. So she stood in front of us, myself and Walton, and she delivered a lecture. There wasn't a dull second in it, and we were nodding much of the time. She started with history.

"You must understand," says she, "that your ancestors came into Ireland six hundred years ago, and took it by force of arms against the will of our folk …"

Now, it would sound deathly dull if I wrote down what she said, but when I heard her say it, she was so damned lovely that I couldn't take my eyes of her, and she was so damned clever in her arguments that I couldn't disagree with her, not even when she argued that everything the English had ever done was wicked and bad. There was even something else. She had the intuition – magic if it must be – to spot that I was the weaker of the two of us where she was concerned, and she began to look more to me than to Walton. When I nodded at some point she made, I got a smile in return – which Walton certainly did not – and by God and all his little angels, the feel of that smile was wonderful. I'm susceptible to women at any time, but that smile touched my soul. It was like when you're a young lad and you get the first smile you've ever had from a girl. Thus, she went on, until she was done, and left me deeply confused about England, Ireland and King George.

"So!" says she, finally, "you have heard me, and now you must look into yourselves to learn what kind of men you are." With that, she looked at a chair by a table, and her young men rushed forward to pull it out for her, and sit her down. Then she looked at me and Walton and waited. We were quiet a moment, then Walton spoke to me. He spoke in a whisper.

"Outside!" says he. "We must talk!" So out we went and he looked me in the eye, while Sergeant-Major Congreve and a couple of corporals stood by, and 27th piled up the dead and tended the wounded. "She's mad!" says Walton. "Mad, mad, mad! She's a lunatic and a dangerous one."

"She damn well isn't!" says I.

"She is!" says Walton. "Did you not see how she gave orders? And expected to be obeyed?"

"Well yes," says I.

"She's the witch!" says Walton. "By Heaven she is. Did you not feel the power of her?"

"Of course I did!" says I. "Who wouldn't?"

"There you are then, sir, and it all depends on her. Do you not agree?"

"The rebellion?"

"The rebellion!" says he. "Everyone says it all depends on her, and it does. Do you not agree?"

"I suppose so."

"So, without her, there'd be no rebellion. Do you not agree?"

"I suppose so," says I, and he leaned closer, dropping his voice still more.

"So! If there's no rebellion without her, and as she is a traitor by her own words, and the sure and certain fodder of the gallows, then what if ..." He looked at me and fell silent.

"What if *what?*" says I.

"What if she were to disappear? Because that would snuff the rebellion at a stroke. No battles, no bloodshed, everything back to rights. Whereas if the rebellion flares up, there will be thousands killed. Tens of thousands. Do you not agree?" He paused and whispered: "So what if we were to *make* her disappear?"

I should have shot him, but didn't.

I merely tried to wring his neck.

I tried very hard.

I'd have done it too.

But Congreve hit me on the head from behind, and his men dragged me off still dizzy, looking back at Congreve and Walton yelling at me, then taking carbines from their men, and going into the house.

That roused me again.

I put up my fists.

Smack! Smack! Down went the two troopers holding me and I was running at the door, but it was locked. So, I backed up and charged. Crash! The lock burst and I was inside as two shots sounded. Mary Murchadha was standing with three young men in front of her, and two of them were clutching wounds and falling, while Walton and Congreve dropped their fired weapons and each took up another. Walton saw me and shouted.

"Shoot her!" says Walton. "I'll get him!" Instantly Congreve ran forward and pressed the muzzle of his gun between the Irish girl's breasts, while bang! Walton fired at me but the ball went over my shoulder as I drew my pistols and fired at Congreve. Bang-bang! I hit the bastard, but that wasn't enough for me. I dropped pistols, drew sword and cleft him to the chin such that the sword stuck and I had to haul it out, while Walton was levelling at the girl with yet another gun, with the last of her men trying to get in front of her.

"No!" says she, and shoved her man clear. "I defy you!" says she to Walton. So I tried, I really tried, but I'm too big to move fast, and Walton shot that beautiful, wonderful creature, for whom a hundred thousand Irishmen would have given their lives. He shot her dead, and I failed to stop him. But, by George, when I was done with him, he wasn't recognisable as human. He was mincemeat, for all the good that it did, because it didn't bring her back to life.

Memory fails after that. I'm told that more of the 27th ran in and tried to attack me, and got themselves chopped. I was in a rage, you see. I wasn't myself. Finally, I was exhausted, and the sword too heavy to hold, and that captain of the 27th was shouting at me: the one who'd been friendly before.

Then I was arrested.

CHAPTER 24

Transcript of a letter of October 30th 1803,
from
Sir John Pitt, Second Earl of Chatham, Master of the Ordnance,
to
Sir Spencer Perceval, Attorney General of Great Britain.

My dear Sir Spencer,

May this find you well, and may it find you able to give the following your urgent attention.

You will have heard of the events of a month past, wherein Commodore Sir Jacob Fletcher was involved in opposition to a landing by the French in Ireland. As regards the French, matters are in hand to deal with them and need not concern us here.

But you will also have heard allegations that Fletcher might not have behaved quite entirely within the law as regards the late Sir Joshua Walton and others, following the action of the 27th against rebellious persons in County Galway. As regards Walton, you know my opinion of him – and of his father before him – and I know that you share the same opinion yourself.

None the less, whatever Fletcher may have done – and six dead is no small matter – the final outcome of the 27th's action is most excellent. Thus, the matter should be left undisturbed since Ireland is now quiet, and I would venture to guess that you, likewise, share that same opinion.

It is, therefore, my resolute conviction, and that of the Prime Minister and others to whom I have spoken, that the interests of the State would best be served if no legal action whatsoever be taken against Fletcher. This is additionally the case, given Fletcher's intimate knowledge of certain past and secret actions of His Majesty's Government, together with the eagerness of the newspapers to give voice to Fletcher.

Therefore, my dear friend, and with deepest good wishes to yourself, Lady Spencer, and your children, I trust that I may leave this matter in your hands?

Sincerely yours,

John Pitt.

Post Scriptum:

Do you recall the lawyer Cathal O'Darragh of Cork, who attended Trinity College under the name of Davies? He was the informer who told us where the Irish mystic woman was to preach, thereby enabling us to deal with her. Being a complex creature who informed not for money but from principle, he has left papers – soon to be published – justifying his betrayal, but we must presume that he was burdened with guilt, since he has been found in his lodgings, hanged by suicide.

JP

CHAPTER 25

Aboard the French Republican ship
Treize Vendémiaire,
Ennismullet Bay,
Ireland.
(Afternoon, Sunday October 30th 1803)

"The English were both reasonable and unreasonable. But what could we do?"
(From the diary of General Auguste Coulonges.)

Coulonges stood on the quarterdeck with the English Sea Service officers:
five of them, and a company of English marines. He was there because
his fluency in English could not be denied. He envied Admiral Verchet
and the rest, who kept apart in muttering groups, attempting to be unin-
volved in this abject surrender. They were thinking of Bonaparte and the
guillotine, and so was Coulonges.

"Is that the last of them, General?" said one of the Englishmen: a
captain called Edwards. Coulonges looked across the bay, and saw boats
pulling out from the shore with French soldiers aboard, who'd stacked
their muskets on the beach and left them under guard of the English red
coats. There were thousands of stacked muskets. The beach was full of
them. There were artillery pieces too, and ammunition cases: spoils of
war to the English.

The boats pulled clank-clank towards French transports waiting to
attempt the long haul south and east, around Ireland and so to France.
Then Coulonges looked at the cluster of French warships anchored in
the bay. The English weren't letting them go! The ships had surrendered
and their crews taken aboard the transports.

"General?" said Edwards. "Did you hear me, sir?" Coulonges sighed.

"Yes," he said, "those are the last." Then he tried once again. "I protest!" he said. "I protest that you will not give liberty to our flagship, so that our senior officers might withdraw with honour, according to the usages of war." Edwards just shook his head.

"No, General," he said, "we've said all this before. This ship becomes prize, and you officers will be held until your ships and men are clear of Ireland and England; then you'll be sent back to France. Those are the terms we agreed!"

"Aye!" said the other Englishmen.

"But it's an outrage!" said Coulonges. "Thousands of Frenchmen are sailing home in damaged ships, under threat of being fired into by your men of war, should they not obey!"

"Can't be helped, General," said Edwards. "But it's something you might like to discuss with Monsieur Bonaparte, since he ordered this invasion in the first place!" The English all laughed. "Never mind, General," said Edwards, "at least you'll all have your freedom: seamen and soldiers too."

"Only because you dared not keep us prisoners of war in Ireland," said Coulonges, "for fear of another Irish rising."

"Oh no," said Edwards. "There'll be no rising now. There was some sort of witch behind it, but someone shot her. She's dead now, and the rebellion has fallen apart. Half Ireland's in mourning for her, and the rest are fighting among themselves." Coulonges nodded. He thought of the antagonism – hatred almost – between Fitzsimons, Byrne and the other Irish revolutionaries he'd brought out from France. They'd spoken of a mystic woman. But the Irish were not rational like the French, so Coulonges wondered if she'd even been real?

CHAPTER 26

Brighton,
England.
(Afternoon, Monday October 31st 1803)

"I did not see everything myself, but he was mad for that woman. Everyone knew it."

(From a letter of Tuesday November 1st 1803, from Mr Arthur Worsley 4th Under-Butler to the Prince's Pavilion, sent to his mother Mrs Matilda Worsley, of Cartwright Mansions, Bath.)

The Perch Phaeton was the world's fastest and most dangerous vehicle. With a tiny seat high up on springs over four incredibly light wheels, it was fearfully easy to overturn on bends, throwing the occupants to certain death.

A Phaeton was usually drawn by two horses, but the leader in this race was drawn by *four*, and the driver – a celebrated beauty– wore a grey driving coat with grey hat, gloves and boots as she leaned forward and cracked her whip. Even the whip was grey, and all the people cheered as she flashed past, and all the ladies ordered a grey driving outfit the very next day.

She was Lady Sarah Coignwood, and the people cheered for her and for the passenger hanging on for his life, because he was the fat, forty-one-year old Prince George – *Prinny* – eldest son of the poor mad King and effectively ruling in his name.

Five more Phaetons came thrashing along behind in this, *The Prince's Race*. They shot down Pavilion Parade, then Old Steine, then screeched right, in dust clouds round Castle Square, with drivers rising in their seats to lay on with their whips, urging the frothing, thundering horses into the final turn between the twin lodge houses at the entrance to a lavish green parkland. Every inch of the way was lined with yelling thousands.

But Lady Sarah was first! She was the clear winner. Her horses broke the tape between the lodge houses. She smiled and let the horses slow – the losers following behind. She progressed sedately towards the main entrance of the huge, white stone, weird construction of Indian-Islamic minarets and domes, and fretwork-pierced arches, that was Prinny's Royal Pavilion. It was like Prinny himself: uniquely clever, uniquely creative, and – to some – uniquely ludicrous.

But no matter. The great and the good of Brighton were assembled in gowns, jewels and sashes outside the main entrance, where the band of the Royal Sussex Regiment gave *See the Conquering Hero Comes* in shivering brass and thumping drums. Prinny was helped down from the Phaeton, and the gilded ones pressed forward in congratulation.

"Magnificent win, sir!" said the Lord Lieutenant.

"A triumph, sir!" said the Bishop.

There was much more of the same, but Prinny was a mannerly creature and turned at once to Lady Sarah, who needed no help to dismount.

"Ma'am," said he, kissing her hand. "You drive like the Devil with his arse on fire!" Everyone laughed, including the Bishop. She smiled.

"I know," said she. "I've been told that before," and again everyone laughed. Then she looked at her pocket watch. "None the less, four hours and twenty-three minutes is a good time from St James's Palace."

"Indeed Ma'am," said Prinny. "Fifty-six miles and five changes of horses."

"Well done, sir! Well done, Ma'am!" said the beaten drivers pushing forward, all dusty and tired.

"There's no racing against La Belle Coignwood," said one of them.

"She's too fast!" said another, and everyone cheered. She smiled and curtseyed in acknowledgement because she was indeed a fast driver, but that alone had not secured victory, because, well before the race, she had won the bribing contest to get the best horses for herself at each posting inn, and the worst for her opponents.

Later there was a dinner and ball in the fantastical interior of the Pavilion, lit by huge glass lamps shaped like upside-down umbrellas, yet brilliant and lovely. Everywhere there was colour in exquisite style. It was a place of wonder. It was Prinny's work. He had immaculate good taste. Later still, there was an enormous bedroom, and an enormous bed draped in woven silks of exotic patterns matching everything else: carpets, curtains and furniture, decanters, cutlery and plate.

Prince George and Lady Sarah were together. She was naked but he was not, because good taste – and a good mirror – had warned him always to be covered by a sheet when entertaining ladies. But Lady Sarah slid a hand under the sheet and tickled such that Prinny rose again, even when he was sure he had nothing left.

"Oh! Oh! Oh!" he said, then frowned as the tickling stopped. He looked at her, entranced. By God she was lovely. There was no woman like her. But Prinny had a conscience.

"I *can't* do it and *won't* do it!" he said.

"You *can* do it," she said. "You're King in all but name. You can even dismiss Parliament if you want, and appoint Prime Ministers."

"But *why* should I do it?" he said. "I've heard of him, yes, but I don't know him and he's never done me any harm."

"You'll do it because he's done *me* harm," she said.

"But *what* shall I do? What do I know about such things?"

"You know about the Duchess Ekaterina."

"Yes. I hadn't thought of that. But *why* should I do it?"

"Because you'd like some more of this," she said, and tickled again. "Oh! Oh! Oh!"

CHAPTER 27

They left me alone until April of the next year: 1804. The Admiralty didn't come near me until then. So, they ignored what I'd done to Walton and his men. I never did find out why, but they ignored it indeed, to my very great amazement and relief.

I was set free and sent home to Kent and my family, and I even got my back pay. I got Mr Midshipman Bayley too, who declared he'd follow no other captain. He came home and, since he'd grown quite a bit, he strutted something amazing among the girls. Meanwhile I was happy once again to be in trade, though I did get a warning.

It was because of Hackney carriages. There were thousands of them in London, and all cheap rubbish. My sister and I planned to buy up as many of them as we could, and replace them – at rent – with cabs of our design. Thus, I was on my way down St George Street to meet the owner of some cabs we wished to buy, when I met someone unexpected. The shops were bustling, the traffic loud, the pavement crowded and I stepped aside to let a pretty lady pass, and walked straight into a Sea Service officer in uniform.

"Dammit, sir!" says he, "have you no eyes in your head?" He was an admiral, middle aged and with a pock-marked face and red cheeks.

"My apologies, sir,' says I, and doffed my hat.

"Ah," says he, "you're Fletcher! Fletcher of the submarine boat." I was used to being recognised, while he was puzzling what to make of me. So, we eyed each other up as men do to see who's the stronger, and each of us saw a fine, bold, swaggering dog who took no nonsense and was used to command: in fact, a man just like himself.

"Huh!" says the pair of us together, and nature worked some alchemy because we became friends for life.

[The two were most amazingly similar in character. Many times have I seen them together, laughing and drinking excessively and boasting of outlandish exploits, which remarkably proved to be true. S.P.]

"I'm Pellew," says he, "Edward Pellew."

I was impressed. Pellew was one of Britannia's heroes: renowned for victories over the French, and for his action in '96 when the East Indiaman *Dutton* ran aground off Plymouth Hoe. All aboard were feared lost, until Pellew swam out through raging seas, carrying a line whereby tackles were rigged and the people saved. He was made a baronet for that.

"Sir Edward!" says I, sticking out my hand.

"Sir Jacob!" says he, taking it. "I'm off to Saint's Club for a bite and a bottle. Will you join me as my guest?"

"Gladly, sir," says I, "if it could be in an hour's time? For I've business to attend."

"Ah!" says he, "Fletcher the tradesman?" He smiled.

Later we sat together in Saint's – a club for Sea Service officers. We were given a good table and profound respect for Pellew. I liked Saint's: oak panelling, sea paintings, white tablecloths and good food. But, at first, Pellew didn't look at the menu.

"I've a warning for you, Sir Jacob," says he, and he waved away the waiter, lowering his voice. "I'm fresh from the Baltic," says he.

"So, who's the enemy this time?" says I. "Danes? Russians? French?"

"All of them," says he. "It's a cockpit of alliances."

"And so?" says I.

"This isn't about them. It's about Prinny," says he, and I smiled. Prince George was a figure of fun, caricatured by every print shop in the land.

"Have a care, sir," says he, "because Prinny's promised a lady that he'll always pull her out of the mire."

"Oh?" says I. "Has he got one of his tarts in the family way?"

"No!" says Pellew. "It's someone special: a Russian Grand Duchess! Ekaterina Michailovna. She's shut up in a Baltic castle and Prinny wants her out."

"Russian?" says I. "So why don't *they* get her out?"

"Politics," says he. "Don't ask details because I don't know!" He leaned forward. "Mine was the third squadron sent in," says he. "Two previous attempts came away riddled with shot and decks running with blood, because the only way to that castle is up a river lined with batteries."

"Can't it be done by landings?" says I, "putting troops ashore?"

"No," says he, "the shore's swarming with rival armies, and rival politics we dare not touch." He sighed. "I lost most of my men, and had two ships sunk."

"Sorry to hear that, sir, but why are you telling me this?"

"Because Prinny is still determined to get her out, and he's probably looking for someone cunning and devious to do it: someone like you!"

I just laughed. I was out of the Service now and Prinny didn't run the Service anyway. So we had a jolly good meal, he gave me his London address, and we parted good friends. Then, next day, my sister and I went home satisfied with our Hackney carriage business, and juicy profits did indeed flow from it in due course. So I was happily engaged in trade, and I thought I was safe and free. But I wasn't because I received a letter in mid April, delivered by a grim-faced lieutenant who insisted on getting a signed receipt. I watched him ride off from the window of our counting house, with my sister and various clerks looking on. He'd come all the way from London to deliver that message.

"Oh dear," says my sister.

"Oh dear," says I when I read it because this is what it said:

To Captain Sir Jacob Fletcher, K.B.,
Hyde House,
Near Canterbury,
Kent.

Sir,

You are commanded and required to attend at Admiralty House, Whitehall, London, at your earliest possible convenience, having been recalled into the Sea Service of His Majesty in matters of serious importance to the prosecution of the present war.

You will bring with you this letter, and you will approach the Officer Commanding the Division of Land Service Affairs, arriving in all respects imminently prepared for a commission afloat.

You are warned that any delay or prevarication will be at your peril.

In His Majesty's Name, This 15th of April, 1804, Admiralty House, Whitehall, London.

Did you note that there were no names or signatures? And the *Division of Land Service Affairs*? I'd never heard of that. I worried and worried.

"Don't go!" says my sister, and I nearly didn't. But I went in the end in case they came after me for the Irish business. As I've said, I had no idea why I'd been let off and I feared the firing squad or the gallows. But I needn't have bothered about Ireland. They never even mentioned that. They threatened something else that I just laughed at.

Because, my jolly boys, your Uncle Jacob went to London, took his sea chest, found a hotel, and *attended* the massive edifice off Horse Guards Parade, which is the Admiralty. I wore full dress, and was saluted by marines who puzzled over my asking for the 'Division of Land Service Affairs', and had to take advice before leading me to a room with large windows, a long table with chairs, and nobody in it. After a while there entered a first-rate among minions, in expensive clothes and a lawyer's wig. He wore round spectacles, and carried a bundle of papers. He never gave his name.

"Sir Jacob Fletcher?" says he, and sat down opposite me.

"Yes," says I, "and who might you be?" which question he ignored.

"These are for you," says he, putting down the papers. "They are for you, *Commodore*."

"Oh?" says I. "Am I promoted again?"

"You are, sir," says he, tapping the papers, which included a large map. "Your commission and all else is here, as regards your duties in the Baltic." That's when I smelt the same rat as I'd smelt in Cork. This wasn't proper: no names, no signatures, and a 'Division' that probably didn't exist. But I kept calm.

"The Baltic?" says I. "Are their Lordships, by any chance, offering me the same duty that was given to three others, including Sir Edward Pellew?"

"Ah!" says he, much embarrassed. "Pellew? Who told you about him?"

"*He* did," says I.

"Oh," says he, looking distinctly nervous. At this stage I hauled off a point or two, so as not to scare him, because that's all too easy for me with little worms like him. So I smiled and sat back in my chair: moving away, you see, which is reassuring. All this I did because I wanted him calm and listening, not shaking with fright.

"So!" says I, seeing him brighten up a little. "I have spoken to Sir Edward Pellew, and considered the perilous situation of the Grand Duchess Ekaterina Michailovna. I, therefore, have this to say."

"Yes?" says he with expectation dawning.

"Will you do something for me?" says I.

"Yes-yes!" says he eagerly, as I pointed at the papers on the table.

"Will you take hold of these?"

"Yes-yes!"

"Taking a firm grip of them, mind!"

"Yes-yes!"

"Take a firm grip ... *and shove 'em up your arse!*"

I got up to leave but he grabbed my arm. He was pleading something pitiful for me to stay, so I shook him off. But then he turned nasty.

"You *must* do it!" says he. "We have Oakes and Pegg. They are pensioners at Greenwich."

"Oakes and Pegg?" says I, and those of you youngsters who've read my early memoirs will know that years ago, when pressed aboard ship, I was so brutally treated by one Boatswain Dixon, that I clubbed him and threw him over the side, which was murder, and two seamen saw me do it: Charlie Pegg and Solomon Oakes. For years I feared their testimony. But not any more. I'd risen too high. "Those two?" says I. "Scum of the lower deck! No court in the land would believe them." So I walked out. But I stopped dead in the middle of Horse Guards Parade, as something occurred to me. If I faced Oakes and Pegg in court, it wouldn't be a civil court with fair-minded English gentlemen for judge and jury. It'd be a court martial which would do whatever the Admiralty told it to do. Oh Hell and Damnation! They'd got me! They'd got my nuts in the crackers. But, my jolly boys, you must never give up. There's always a bargain to be made, so I went back, and got hold of the minion in the same room.

"Now see here," says I. "I might possibly do what you ask," and his eager little face gave him away. They really did want me, you see, and he was to be scapegoat if I said no. "I might do it, but I'll have your name, sir! I'll have it right now, or I'm out of the door!"

"Watford," says he, "Mr Earnest Watford, Leading Clerk."

162

"Right, Mr Watford, let's see that bloody map!"

At this point, you youngsters should get one and see how the Baltic Sea runs east into the Gulf of Finland, ending up at St Petersburg, just north of some poor little nations – Latvia, Lithuania, Karelia and Estonia – whose entire history is that of being raped and pillaged by each other, and by Russians, Swedes, Danes and everyone else, poor devils.

"This represents our latest information," says Watford, seeking to please. "It is complete with bearings, soundings and observations, as made by" – he paused – "Sir Edward Pellew and ... ahem ... his predecessors."

I studied the map and saw for the first time the words 'Ofrokaberg Castle'. It was ringed round in red ink, and it was at the eastern end of a lake five miles across, in a peninsula on the southern side of the Gulf of Finland. The lake and castle was joined to the Gulf by seven miles of the Ofrok river. It wound from one battery to another, all the batteries in different hands, and the river meeting the Gulf at the Straits of Ofrok, which, likewise, was thick with batteries. I looked at the minion.

"This Ofrokaberg Castle?" says I. "Is this where she's trapped? This Duchess?"

"Yes," says he.

"What sort of castle is it?"

"A fifteenth century construction of massive stone, rising from sheer cliffs over the Ofrok lake."

"And why can't the Duchess get out?"

"Because the castle has been under siege for two years, by a mixed force of Karelians and others, but it holds many years of supplies within its vaults."

"Why don't they take it? These Karelians?"

"Because it is so high above ground that guns cannot bear on the walls."

"Can't they build ramps? Bring up mortars?" He shrugged.

"I am not a military engineer," says he, "but other information is provided in your papers." Then he sat and stared at me, poor little grub.

"I'll do it," says I.

"Yes-yes!" says he.

"If!" says I, and his face fell, "if you give me what ships and men I might need."

163

"Yes-yes!"

"Including – to start with – a navigating officer who knows the Baltic."

"Yes-yes!"

"Especially the Straits of Ofrok!"

"Yes-yes!" says he, "you shall have it all!" He delved into his memory for even more. "And the secret password, sir, such that the Duchess shall know you come as a friend!"

"Oh?" says I.

"Florizal!" says he. It could have been *polly-wolly-doodle* for all I cared.

"Florizal," says I, "and now I'm off to see Pellew, for his best advice!"

"You're a bloody fool, Fletcher!" says Pellew in his London house. We sat in his library with his books, with port served by his butler, and we looked at the Ofrokaberg map. "I'll never go near that bloody castle again," says he, "and I can't imagine why you would!" I thought it best not to mention Boatswain Dixon, so I concentrated on practicalities.

"But if you did go back," says I, "what ships and men would you take?"

"Not ships," says he. "No ship can pass the batteries. Your only chance is boats, at night, and it's hard going against the current, which is fierce. You'll need boats, and light infantry not red-coats."

"Why?"

"So as to creep up quietly: no drums and bugles."

"So the business must be done ashore?"

"Mostly," says he. "And may God help you! But if God's busy that day and you're set on doing this?" I nodded. "Then go and see this rogue, whom I met in the American war." He scribbled on a paper and handed it to me. "Go and see him," says he, "and tell him the river Ofrok is thick pine forest on either bank. Tell him that because he'll like it." I looked at the paper. It was a short letter: very short.

Captain Gideon Starkey,
North Bridge House,
138 New Bridge Road,
By Hyde Park.

Dear Gideon,

This comes in the hand of a mad bugger, damn near as mad as you are, and who won't listen to reason. So, I ask you in the name of our friendship, to see if you can save him from quite entirely jumping down the bog-hole and slamming the lid on himself.

Ever yours,
Ed Pellew

CHAPTER 28

Ofrokaberg Castle,
Lake Ofrok,
Estonia.
(Dawn, Monday April 16th 1804)

"My Lady would not listen. She will never listen. She dreams of Cossack armies."
(From the diary of Sofia Petrykha. Translated from Ukranian.)

The Cossack officer ran into the bedroom, swept off his lambskin cap, and bowed such that the single plaited lock on his shaven head slid down beside his long moustaches. He bowed with much style, one hand on the hilt of his Shashka sabre, the other sweeping back his long coat with the cartridge-loops on the breast.

"Little Mother?" he said. "We've got one for you! Be quick!" But a fat woman shoved him out of the room, with all her considerable weight. She was Sofia Petrykha, a Cossack matriarch from her Kichka headdress to scarlet boots.

"Get out, you *peasant!*" she said. "She's not dressed!" But the officer just grinned. So did his men in the corridor behind him.

"Quick, Little Mother!" he said, "before someone tells him!"

The Grand Duchess Ekaterina Michailovna leapt out of a bed all furnished in silk: sheets, drapes, curtains. She was naked and did not care. She was thirty years old, tall and blonde and beautiful, and the Cossacks cheered because her mother had been just the same, and her grandmother before. Now she was *Little Mother* and she ruled the house, since her husband, the Grand Duke, had died in Siberia for supporting the wrong faction at Court.

"Robe!" she said. "Quick-quick-quick Sofia Petrykha!"

"Bah!" said Sofia Petrykha. She found the robe and threw it round Ekaterina Michailovna, trying to keep up as her mistress ran after the Cossacks, down corridors and up stairs, and out on to the battlements, where men stamped to attention. A cold wind came hard over the lake, and Ekaterina Michailovna hadn't even put on her shoes, but she ran with the robe streaming open. She ran right round to the land-facing side, with the Cossack officer beckoning, and his men beckoning.

"This one, Little Mother!" said the officer.

"Stand back!" said Ekaterina, leaping up onto the firing platform where a long, heavy firearm was mounted on a swivel, fixed between the crenelations of the battlements. It was a wheel-lock wall-piece, a hundred years old, by Herman Muller of Augsberg: lavishly engraved, and inlaid with ivory. The rifled barrel was six feet long, taking a ball an inch in diameter, rammed down over the powder charge with a steel rod and hammer. Loading was slow but the weapon was deadly at great range. There were others like it on the battlements, but this was the best, and a spotter was standing beside it with his telescope.

"Is it loaded?" said Ekaterina.

"Yes, Little Mother!" said the officer, "but left for you to judge the range."

"Good!" she said. She sat in the chair behind the rifle, pressed her cheek against the stock and reached for the first trigger. "Where is he?" she said to the spotter, who looked through his telescope.

"Little Mother?" he said. "Do you see the line of trees by their entrenchments?"

"Yes!"

"And do you see where the cart has gone over? And ..."

"Ah!" she said, "I see him. He's looking at *us* with a telescope."

"Yes, Little Mother!" said the spotter. "Your eyesight is a gift of God!"

"Look at the idiot! He's on a ladder, raised up over their barricade."

"Perhaps he's new, Little Mother?" said the spotter, "and nobody's told him to keep down?" "Shhh!" said Ekaterina. She adjusted the sights to her liking, and drew back the first trigger. *Click!* That meant the second trigger – the hair trigger – now set. Just a touch now ... just a touch ... she breathed slow and deep ... she felt her own heartbeat.

Sofia Petrykha came up and looked at the lovely, clever, creature twined round the rifle, so consumed with the game, she neither cared nor understood that her shooting killed living men. It was always like this. Everyone loved Ekaterina. The serfs loved her, Sofia Petrykha loved her and her parents had adored her. But Ekaterina saw human people as gifts of entitlement: hers to use as she pleased.

Woof-bang! The rifle fired, smoke rolled; Ekaterina leapt up as the ball flew, then clapped hands with delight.

"Got him!" said the spotter, "three hundred yards at least. What a shot!" The Cossacks cheered and Sofia Petrykha stepped forward with a silk wrap.

"Mistress?" she said and Ekaterina allowed herself to be cosseted in the arms of the woman who'd been her nurse. Sofia Petrykha led her back towards the bedroom, taking advantage of the moment.

"Little Katty," she said, "this can't go on. There are many others of us within these walls besides the Cossack guards. We are your serfs and servants. We are your responsibility. If you keep shooting the Karelians, then if ever they do get in, they'll slaughter us all."

"They won't get in," said Ekaterina Michailovna. "The castle's too strong."

"Then they'll just wait till we starve."

"No. The Cossack Army will come. They'll rescue us."

"But they're ordered to keep away."

"They'll come! Either that or the English prince will send another fleet."

"But he's tried three times and failed."

It was the same old argument, running down the same old path. But Sofia Petrykha had to go on, though Ekaterina merely shook her head, such that even Sofia Petrykha – who'd known her from birth – didn't know if Little Katty truly understood that so many lives were at risk, including her own.

"You must write to Prince Fyodor," she said.

"No."

"The Karelians are here by order of the Tsar."

"So?"

"If we pass a letter to them under flag of truce, it will reach Prince Fyodor."

"No." Ekaterina Michailovna laughed. She kissed Sofia Petrykha and all argument was ended: again.

CHAPTER 29

I went to Captain Starkey's house. I went in one of our nice new, rented cabs which was pleasing, because they were all over London. But Starkey wasn't there. An old servant answered the door.

"The Master's gone, sir," says he. "Gone to Shorncliff Camp."

"Shorncliff Camp?" says I, "with the Light Division?"

"Yes, sir," says he. I was impressed, because the Shorncliff Camp was famous in those days. It was where the Army was training up a new kind of soldier: one who thought for himself, and skirmished in open order armed with the new Baker rifles, and note that I said rifles: not smooth-bore muskets.

That was interesting but difficult. I couldn't sail into such a camp as Shorncliff and swagger round asking for Starkey, because the Army didn't like the Navy any more than we liked them. So, I got back in the cab and went to the Admiralty, grabbed Mr *Minion* Watford again, and demanded some authority to get me into Shorncliff.

"Leave it with me, Commodore," says he, and, by Jove, a package arrived by courier at my hotel that same day, and inside of it was a letter of best paper, elaborately drafted by Army scribes, and heavily sealed and stamped. It was addressed '*To whom it may concern at Shorncliff Camp*'. It required that '*every help and assistance be rendered unto Commodore Sir Jacob Fletcher*', and God wreck and sink me if it wasn't signed by Frederick, Duke of York, the King's second oldest son, the commander-in-chief of the entire British Army!

That's when I guessed that Prinny really and truly was behind all this. His name kept coming up, and the Duke of York was his younger brother. I *guessed* that it was him, until the occasion when it became proven truth, as was the name of the creature behind even Prinny.

[Here Fletcher refers to the notorious incident of Grosvenor Square - widely reported in the press - when he single-handedly overturned Lady Sarah Coignwood's carriage, pummelled her servants, and pursued her down Brook Street where members of the Moorditch Master Blacksmith's Guild – taking dinner in the Rose and Crown Inn – heard her cries for help and rushed out in the attempt to restrain Fletcher. These unfortunate and worthy tradesmen were likewise pummelled, but their efforts enabled Lady Sarah to escape. The entire matter was silenced with money, but the well-known reason for Fletcher's violence is the fact that, on passing him in the square, Lady Sarah had leaned from her carriage and said, "Fletcher! Know that it was myself that had you sent to Ireland, and myself that made Prinny send you to the Baltic." S.P.]

It was eighty miles in a hired post-chaise, from my hotel, down into Kent to the Shorncliff Camp: a long day's journey with nine changes of horse-flesh, which got me to the camp entrance in the late afternoon. I wore uniform and waved the Duke of York's signature at everyone, and everyone presented arms and saluted. I was a commodore, after all, ranking equal with a general of brigade.

The Camp was hundreds of acres of rolling green, with a fort, battery, a hospital, some big wooden mess huts and lines of tents, and hundreds of soldiers drilling, some in red and some in rifle green. There was a fine view over a beach to the sea, and it reminded me of the giant fort I'd seen in Cork, except the mood was different. The Army of Ireland always felt threatened, while at Shorncliff they thought they could conquer the world.

As in Cork I was escorted to Headquarters – another wooden hut – and presented to the red-coat, gold-laced officer in charge. He was Major General Sir John Moore who was later so famous in Spain. He puffed and blowed in amazement at the Duke of York's letter and sent for Captain Starkey who was out in the field. Then I was given a tent and a servant for an overnight stay, and they took care of my chaise and horses, while my driver got a tent among the sergeants.

I soon met Starkey, and note of the manner of his arrival. I was sitting at a table outside the Headquarters hut, with Moore and a couple of colonels. Wine and food was served, and there were men marching, officers yelling, and distant volleys of musketry and smoke.

"See there, Sir Jacob," says Moore. "That's your man!" I looked and saw a column of fifty men coming on at a steady trot, led by a tall man and every one of them in drab-coloured shirts, trousers, and round hats with wide brims. They held their firelocks in their right hands, and each had a powder horn slung over the shoulder, and a bullet-bag, knife and hatchet in his belt. There were no cartridge pouches, no bayonets, nor even boots: just soft leather shoes.

They approached our table, and the leader raised his hand. They stamped feet, stopped and took firelocks in both hands, then looked around, ready for action. The leader saluted Moore with a touch to his hat, then looked at me. I was an oddity in Navy blue. He was gristle and bone, weather-beaten, and any age up to sixty. But he was nothing compared to the three right behind him. I guessed them on sight as American Indians: dark, hook-nosed, and not a flicker of expression in their black eyes. The rest were plain Englishmen, but these three were something special.

"Captain Starkey," says Moore, "here's Commodore Fletcher of the Sea Service, who wishes to speak with you. Will you join us?"

"A pleasure, sir," says Starkey, and gave a nod to his men such that the three Indians sat down cross-legged some way from the table, while the others went off at a trot towards the mess huts. Starkey looked at me. "Here I am, sir," says he, sitting down, "and what does the Sea Service want of me?" His voice had a Yankee twang.

"Pellew sent me," says I. "Sir Edward Pellew."

"Ah!" says Starkey, and grinned, "that damned rogue? How is he?"

"He is well, sir," says I, "and sends his compliments." I did show him Pellew's note later, and he laughed. But I didn't need it. He was helpful at once because I told him everything, and all the others too, because nobody had said the Baltic duty was secret and I was fed up with being worked by hidden strings. So, I took out minion Watford's papers – brought along in a satchel – and spread them out, including the map, and explained that I was the fourth man sent to get Duchess Ekaterina out of Ofrokaberg Castle.

"It's a deathtrap!" says Moore.

"And political madness!" says one of the colonels.

"We're supposed to be at peace with Russia," says the other.

"And the Swedes," says Moore. "We need them against Napoleon."

"And who are all these others?" says the first colonel.

"Latvians, Estonians, Karelians and Lithuanians," says I, "and Cossacks."

"Is that all?" says Moore, all sarcastic. "No others? Not the hordes of Genghis Khan perhaps?"

"And in any case, it can't be done," says the other two. But Starkey spoke up.

"Can I see the map?" says he. I pushed it to him and he studied it, then looked at me. "What's the ground like, along this river Ofrok?"

"It's pine forest," says I. "Pellew said to tell you that." He smiled.

"Three cheers for Pellew," says he, "and some more questions. How old is this duchess? Is she fit and nimble? And what's the current like along this river?"

"What?" says Moore, wondering where this might lead.

"She's young," says I. "She shoots and rides, and Pellew says the current is strong, coming downriver."

"In that case, gentlemen," says Starkey, "serve this sailorman some rum, because the business can be done!" which sparked a most interesting argument.

"Rubbish!" says the first colonel.

"Rot!" says the other.

"Y'r talking out y'r asses again, boys," says Starkey, all Yankee.

So, they went at it something hard. They banged the table and shouted, although it was a pure professional disagreement on how light infantry should work. Here's just a flavour of it:

"You won't use bayonets," says the first colonel, "so how will you face cavalry?"

"Won't need to," says Starkey. "Cavalry don't go in the woods."

"You won't use rifles," says the other colonel, "so you won't have long-range fire!"

"Don't need it in the woods," says Starkey. "It's all short range."

"Your men don't even wear boots!"

"You've no bugles!"

"No uniforms!"

"No sergeants!"

"No discipline!"

Finally, Moore brought it to an end.

172

"Gentlemen," says he. "As you very well know, I have every confidence in Captain Starkey's methods, which is why I brought him here, provided those methods are confined to woodland warfare! I agree that his methods won't work in open country, but Commodore Fletcher's proposal seems to require a march through woodlands, and, therefore" – he smiled – "and since the Duke of York commands our assistance" – he looked at Starkey – "go forth, Captain, taking such men and gear as you may need." He looked at me. "And may you be lucky ... lucky Jack Flash!" They all laughed. I suppose my name was known.

After that, I was two days at Shorncliff, because Starkey wanted to show me how *he* worked, and find out how *I* worked, because he was measuring me up, just as I was measuring him. So he took me down to the beach with his three Indians and his men. The beach was all pebbles and our feet crunched loudly as we walked. There we stopped; the waves hissed and rolled; the gulls called, and it was all nice and quiet apart from some popping of musketry up at the camp.

"Give the Commodore a musket," says Starkey to one of his men, and I was handed a firelock, which wasn't a Brown Bess musket but a fusil: something neat, light and expensive, usually carried by officers. They were much like a gentleman's sporting gun and, similarly, had no fittings for a bayonet. But all Starkey's men had them. "Now Sir Jacob," says Starkey, "will you be a sentry? Will you look out to sea, but turn around so soon as you hear someone creep up behind you?" He pointed to one of his Indians. "Okwaho here, is gonna creep up with his noisy feet on all these noisy stones." Everyone grinned at that, except the Indians.

So, I did what he said, stood with the firelock and listened hard ... and not a damn thing did I hear, until Okwaho put the blunt edge of his knife to my throat.

"That's one way with sentries, but there's others," says Starkey, beckoning the other two of his Indians: Shawatis and Tier. "*Gabble-gabble*," says Starkey in some Indian language, and each of them produced the most beautiful and wicked war club you ever saw. I looked at them. Each was slightly different, being handmade, and each looked superbly fit for purpose. They were about eighteen inches long, made of dense, polished wood, with a hand-grip and a curved shaft ending in a ball the size of a man's fist.

"May I?" says I, reaching out to take one, for the feel of it. But the three Indians stepped back.

"Don't touch!" says Starkey. "They're personal. Handed down from the ancestors. They're very old. Full of spirit: what the white man calls *religion*. Even I don't have one, not being of the blood, but only adopted."

"I see," says I. "It's only your ... er ..." I sought a word to describe his Indians. "... only your servants that have these?"

"Not servants!" says he. "They are my blood brothers. We are equals." That made me think. That and him saying, "What the white man calls," as if he wasn't one himself. It made me wonder what went on inside him. It was only these blood brothers that carried the clubs while the rest had hatchets. They were ordinary wood-chopping hatchets, bought in some ironmonger's shop. But they were neat and handy, and not the encumbrance that a sword would have been in the woods. Later, Starkey insisted that I should carry one. So I did. And I used it too.

On another occasion he arranged a competition. He got a company of red coats from the light company of the 35th regiment, and some green-coat riflemen from the 75th. They came with their subalterns and sergeants, under promise of a gold guinea to whichever company could get off five volleys the fastest, against a dozen of Starkey's men. I'm sure he relied on my Duke of York letter to get the 35th and 75th to take part, because everyone knew who'd win before a shot was fired. But Starkey had a roast dinner laid on from the cook-house, with tables in the sunshine, and enough drink to keep everyone happy without falling over.

Finally, all three companies were lined up, with firelocks grounded and waiting the signal.

"Five rounds rapid ... Fire!" cries Starkey.

All credit to the 35th and 75th, they followed their drill smart and swift. The 35th with Brown Bess, bit cartridge, primed lock with a pinch of powder, poured the rest down the barrel, then rammed ball and paper down on top. When all were ready, they gave synchronous volleys. The 75th with Baker rifles, primed lock, poured a measured charge down the barrel using a flask, then rammed home a bullet in leather patch to grip the rifling. After that, they cocked and fired, likewise giving volleys. But their drill took longer as the patched ball was hard to ram down the barrel. And all the time, the officers and sergeants of their regiments were cheering them on.

Meanwhile, Starkey's men were amazing the entire world. Using powder horns, they poured powder down barrels without measuring, spat a ball after the powder, thumped gun-butts on the ground, and cocked and fired! You wouldn't believe how fast they fired. Mind you, they didn't give volleys, they merely blazed away. Didn't they just, my jolly boys. They won outright, and the 35th and 75th had the grace to cheer. At the end of it, Starkey gave a guinea to each team, for the goodwill of it, and later he showed me how it was done.

"You keep the lead balls in your mouth," says he, "five of 'em."

"Yes," says I.

"And you judge the powder charge by experience, then spit a ball down the bore. And see here!" He showed me the lock of his own fusil. "Look at the touch-hole: drilled out bigger, d'you see?"

"Yes," says I.

"So, you don't have to prime the lock," says he. "You just thump the butt and some of the main charge falls through the touch-hole into the pan."

"Doesn't it weaken the force of the shot?" says I. "Isn't some of the powder-flash wasted, blowing out through the touch-hole?"

"Yes," says he, "and we use undersized balls so they go easy down the barrel, and *that* weakens the shot. But it don't matter in the woods, 'cos it's all close range, and there's enough force left to knock down a man. Especially if you shoot before he can!"

There were other demonstrations of tracking men and beasts in the woods, none of which I understood because I could see damn-all where Starkey's men said there were marks in the grass and bushes. Then there were bird calls from pursed lips to send signals; there were tricks to avoid losing direction in the woods; and there was the rule that nobody must go off to empty his bowels, but all must use one hole dug for that purpose, and the hole quickly filled in afterwards.

"You can smell a war party a mile off, should they leave a trail of shit," says Starkey. "A child wouldn't make that mistake among my people."

There it was again. *My people,* says he, and I learned the fullness of it one evening when we sat round a campfire: myself, Starkey and his blood brothers. We'd eaten and Starkey offered a bottle of rum, being convinced that sailors drank nothing else. I took a drop, and he pretended to but merely wet his lips, while the three Indians drank nothing and said nothing. I seldom heard them speak English though they followed it well enough.

"So, were you a loyalist in the American war?" says I to Starkey.

"Yes," says he, "but not in the way you mean."

"Not loyal to King George?"

"Yes and no," says he, and looked at me. "What do you know of the Six Nations?"

"Six nations?" says I, shaking my head.

"The six nations of the Iroquois: the Seneca, Cayuga, Onondaga, Oneida, Tuscarora and Mohawk. They held the land before the white man came." He looked at his three Indians. "We're Mohawk," says he, "my brothers and me, 'cos I ran off as a boy and joined them."

"So, what about the war?" says I, "the American war?"

"The nations were divided," says he. "Oneida and Tuscarora fought for the Americans; the rest of us fought for the English." He shook his head. "We were fools. It made no difference. But Pellew was kind. He took us into his ship when we'd have been killed. So, we came with him when the Americans won." He turned to his brothers. "Gabble, gabble, gabble, Pellew?" says he.

"Pellew!" says they in deep voices, placing hands to hearts.

"Now then, sailorman," says Starkey, "enough of that, because here's how it's gonna be with your duchess." I nodded. "I'll pick a dozen good men," says he. "That's enough! You get us ashore near the mouth of the River Ofrok, and we'll go through the woods at night. We'll get round the batteries, take a canoe across the lake, rescue the woman, and bring her downriver at night. That'll be fast and smooth and she won't have to march through the woods."

"Good," says I, "but how do we get a canoe up to the lake?"

"Carry it," says he. "They're light-built for that purpose." He leaned towards me. "I'm no sailorman, but I guess you won't need a big ship for this, but one that's fast and handy."

"Yes," says I.

"And we'll need some way to let the Duchess know we're on her side, a letter? Password? Can you get that?"

"Yes, I've got a password: it's Florizal."

"Good!" says he, and smiled so nice and easy that I began to think the job could be done all nice and easy too. And so, my jolly boys, as I've told you many times before: if ever you begin to think like that, then you must take the most tremendous care.

CHAPTER 30

The Karelian Entrenchments,
Around Ofrokaberg Castle,
Lake Ofrok,
Estonia.
(Morning, Monday April 16th 1804)

"Von Strunz was a good officer, but too proud of his rank as a Prussian Graf."
(From a letter of April 19th 1804, from Major Ernst Wagner to his father in Berlin. Translated from German.)

Von Strunz took off his shako: it would make him too obvious a target. He climbed the ladder and looked beyond the earthworks, towards the castle. Then he took out his telescope. It was a risk but necessary. He'd only just arrived, and, as an *Oberst* – a colonel – of Prussian Artillery, he had to make his own judgement of why the Karelians had failed to bring a gun to bear.

"Take care, Herr Oberst!" said Major Wagner, safely below, behind the entrenchments.

"Watch for smoke!" said the Karelian officer beside Wagner. Officer? Von Strunz wondered if the word applied? He hadn't seen a uniform or badge of rank among these amateurs. He took a good look through his telescope, becoming absorbed in the problem. Perhaps they weren't such amateurs? The castle was on rocks so high, that even elevating-carriages, or timber ramps wouldn't help the guns reach the walls. He looked down at Wagner and missed the silent white puff on the battlements.

"Mortars!" said Von Strunz. "It must be mortars!" He turned for another look, and the *crack* of sound arrived with the ball that blew the contents of his head all over Major Wagner and the Karelians.

178

When everyone was cleaned up, and Von Strunz carried off for burial, Major Wagner drank vodka with the Karelians in a nice, safe bunker because they all needed a drink.

"Mortars?" said Oskar Kivi, the senior Karelian, who called himself a colonel. "Can you get them?" He spoke French, because no foreigner spoke Karelian, and Wagner knew French.

"Possibly," said Wagner, "I'll write to the Arsenal of St Petersburg in Prince Fyodor's name. If he has as much influence as you say ..."

"Fyodor?" said Kivi. "The Tsarina adores him! Who knows why, but she does."

"Then they can send a couple of heavy mortars, with powder and bombs."

"Will they do that?" said Kivi.

"Yes!" said Wagner, "provided no Russians are here. Von Strunz and I were sent to do their dirty work. Moscow spoke to Berlin, and Berlin sent us here." He paused and held out his glass. "Can I have some more?" He looked at his sleeve. There were bits of Von Strunz's hair among the stains. He brushed them off. Kivi poured and Wagner drank. "So what's really going on here?" said Wagner. "There's you around the castle; there's other batteries all along the river; there's the British trying to get to the castle, and there's a Cossack army nearby that you're all afraid of." The Karelians said nothing. They just looked at one another, embarrassed. "Come on?" said Wagner. "What's going on? What's that damned woman doing with her gun? It *is* her that shoots at you, isn't it?"

"Yes," said Kivi. "She's a famous shot with a rifle. She's killed five of us: six, including Von Strunz."

"What's going on?" said Wagner. "I'm brand new. Arrived yesterday. What did she do to this prince, Fyodor." Wagner saw them look at one another again. This time some of them sniggered.

"Well," said Kivi, and he crossed himself, Russian Orthodox style, with three fingers to represent the Holy Trinity. Wagner saw that, remembering that the Karelians were ruled by their priests, and didn't talk about women. As boys they'd been beaten for it. But still they sniggered. Wagner smiled.

"Oh, go on," he said. "We're all men here."

"Well,' said Kivi, "it is said that Prince Fyodor has special require-ments within the marriage bed." Kivi crossed himself again. "He is not as other men are."

"Oh!" said Wagner. "Is it boys?"

"No!" said Kivi. "Everyone knows what it is, and it's not that."

"Then what is it?" said Wagner.

"Let me explain," said Kivi. "Prince Fyodor proposed marriage to the Duchess. He met her at the Summer Palace and was entranced."

"So?" said Wagner.

"She said no. He asked again over many days, until she lost patience."

"Did she?"

"Yes. And finally, in the Golden Hall of Icons, before the entire court, and in a loud and clear voice, she said, '*I shall not marry you because you* ...' and she said it! And everyone heard!"

"But you said everyone already knew?"

"Yes! But it's never spoken aloud."

"So?"

"The Tsarina commanded the Duchess to apologise, and say that she lied."

"And?"

"She wouldn't. So she was banished. That was two years ago."

Wagner struggled to understand.

"But why is she here?" he said. "The whole river's fortified! Is it to keep the British out?"

"No," said Kivi. "It's nothing to do with them. We were ordered to fire on *anyone* who comes upriver, so we did. We don't even know why the British came! They must be mad." Wagner still struggled.

"So what *is* going on?"

"Politics!" said Kivi, "you don't know the loyalties here! The Russians have the power, but some of us love the Duchess. So every battery here is manned by a different nationality so we don't combine, and there's a Cossack army to keep us in order, and *she* is here as an example to others. She's banished here with the serfs from her mansion, and her own Cossacks." Wagner frowned as he struggled to follow. "But now," said Kivi, "the *Tsar's* fed up, never mind the *Tsarina,* and it's apologise or die." Kivi nodded to Wagner. "That's why you're here. We don't know artillery. We don't know that stuff." Wagner was really struggling now: struggling to believe in all this.

"This is a fairy-tale," said Wagner. "It's mad. It's nonsense. A stupid cow duchess won't apologise to a stupid idiot prince, so another lot of stupid idiots can go back to pretending they *don't* know what they *do* know!"

"If you put it like that," said Kivi.

"So what did she say? About the Prince? What does he do with women?" The Karelians sniggered again.

"It's never spoken aloud," said Kivi. "I told you that."

"Look," said Wagner, "I'm a soldier. I've been in more tart-shops than you can count and I've done it frontways, sideways and backwards." He grinned. "So whisper in my ear and I promise not to blush." Kivi leaned forward. He whispered and all the Karelians looked at Wagner in expectation. It was a while before Wagner completely understood.

"*Gott in Himmel!*" he said, reverting to German in the profundity of his astonishment.

CHAPTER 31

"I hope there's some good reason for this," says Pellew. "Diplomatic or strategic!" Starkey and I nodded. We were in Pellew's library with charts on the table. "I hope it's not just Prinny," said Pellew, "not just his promise to that bloody woman when she was in London and he tried to get his leg across her!" He reached for the decanter. "More port?" says he. I took some but Starkey did not.

"Did he?" says Starkey. "Get across her?"

"No!" says Pellew. "Can't blame him for trying though. She's a stunner: tall and blonde."

"You met her then?" says I.

"Yes," says he, "very lovely and very Russian! They sit down without looking, do Russians, 'cos a servant will always have a chair ready."

"So?" says I.

"She did that at Carlton house, but the servant weren't quick enough, and down she went! But up she jumped, and laughed, and chattered at the servant in French. She said *'In Russia you'd be flogged for that! But here,'* she turned to one of the other Russians, *'give him a gold rouble.'*"

So we all laughed. Then Pellew showed us a new map. "Of all my officers," says he, "only the Sailing Master survived, and he's sick with wounds. But he made this chart of the mouth of the Ofrok." He looked up. "Because – believe me gentlemen – we surveyed every inch before we went in!" He shook his head. "We did what we could." He sighed. "Here's your best landing place, south of the coastal batteries and giving you a nice little cove to be recovered from when the job's done. And you've got cover of trees for your night march."

"Marches," says Starkey. "It'll take a few." He pointed at the map. "We'll be in sixty degrees of latitude, and that far north we'll get only two or three hours of darkness this time of year."

"So march fast!" says Pellew. "And have you still got your canoe? The one we brought from America, all those years ago?" Starkey smiled.

"Years don't matter," says he. "A canoe's easy to fix when broke."

There was little to discuss after that. Pellew had done his absolute best for us, and we were afloat less than a month later.

I got exactly what I wanted from the Admiralty: a lovely little brig. Yankee-style from bowsprit to taffrail: flush-decked, rake-masted, ten 6-pounders, and the fastest man-o'war I was ever in under sail. She ran fifteen knots the first day out of Portsmouth and we overhauled a squadron of frigates so fast, that our people were hanging ropes over the stern in the traditional mockery of offering a tow. She was HMS *Beamish,* of 150 tons, and if she had a fault, it was being so sharp-bowed for speed that she didn't ride the waves but cut them, thus drenching herself in spray. But there's no perfection in this wicked world, my jolly boys, and she was neat and nimble besides.

I was in her with Starkey and a dozen of his men, plus a Norwegian merchant skipper called Haljem who knew the Baltic, and someone else too: Mr Midshipman Bayley. The whole world seemed to know that I was going to sea again, and young Bayley had the cheek to get down to Portsmouth, have himself rowed out to *Beamish* and come aboard, in uniform and with his sea chest, begging me to take him! I growled a bit, but couldn't say no because it was in his nature to improvise and anticipate, and I liked that. It's handy in a seaman.

Aboard, we found Lieutenant-and-Commander Cummings the Captain, with Lieutenant Youngmark and fifty hands, and I went through my accustomed coming-aboard ceremonies. I read my commission, then faced their fisticuffs champion: a horrid little goblin that went at me like a madman, swinging wildly, and I could have downed him with one blow. But his mates were looking on, and I respected their feelings by making a fight of it. Which I did until I got bored. Then I turned to Cummings and Youngmark in the faded coats and tarnished lace that was 'Full Dress' in small ships where there's no ceremony. Because that's what it was like in those days, and you shouldn't believe the fancy, coloured prints of smart uniforms that pretend otherwise.

Cummings was young, in his twenties, and a proven seaman. But he was nervous of Jacky Flash, especially with the ship's people watching, and so many newcomers embarked. Also, he was broad and squat, and had to look up at me, which bothers a man.

"We'll beat to quarters by the clock, Sir Jacob," says he, touching his hat. "Knowing that to be your way."

"Proceed, Captain!" says I. So the drum rolled – just one in this ship – and the people tried, but it was a dismal performance. They were slow, and there was the look about them that they weren't used to the exercise. When they were done, and stood by their guns, Cummings looked glum – very glum – and all you youngsters should mark what I did next, because I wanted Cummings giving of his best and not ashamed. So I had him, Youngmark, Haljem, and Starkey come aft for private conversation: them and the midshipmen – three including Bayley – plus the Boatswain and Gunner,

"Gentlemen," says I, "this is how it shall be among us: I shall have last word in the directing of the ship's course and our duties." They all nodded. "But you, Captain," says I to Cummings, "shall have last word in the handling of this ship, in all matters of what canvas she might bear, and what sailing orders might be given to the hands." *That* stood him up straight, and he stood even straighter at my next words. "You shall be master in that respect, Captain, since I'm not such a fool as to believe I could come aboard your ship and instantly know her better than you!" That's God's truth. It takes weeks to know a ship, and I didn't have weeks. Then it was Haljem's turn. "Meanwhile I look to you, sir, to inform myself and this ship's officers of every peril or hazard that might lie before us, together with such advice as you can give on how best to secure our objectives." He nodded, but I wasn't done yet. "Likewise, Captain Starkey," says I, "once we're ashore and in the woods, you must regulate of the manner of our advance, since you are the expert in that respect."

Then I told them exactly what we were trying to do, regarding Duchess Ekaterina and Ofrokaberg Castle. I told them everything, sparing nothing and I told them to study all the papers and charts as I'd brought aboard. I did this because I'll have no secrets aboard ship nor dishonesty towards the people. So I ended with these words:

"Make sure the crew understand what we're doing, and make sure they understand ... *that the whole business looks bereft of sense!*" I nearly laughed at their surprised faces. "Tell 'em that!" says I. "But then tell 'em that we're not sailing into hazard because Prinny made a promise to some doxie, but because there must be some serious matter of policy behind all this, and, before all else, because we *Beamishes* are going to succeed where others – even Pellew – have failed!"

They cheered that. So did the crew later on. It's the sort of rot you have to say.

[**As ever, Fletcher's dismissive words are a sham. When he dictated the above, he did so with pride. Many times I heard from old seamen that he was a natural leader whom they trusted and would follow into any peril. S.P.**]

We set sail on Thursday April 12th, and I think Portsmouth knew what we were up to, because we got cheered by the ships we passed, and boats followed us out with folk waving. After that, it was a voyage of near two thousand miles, allowing for the detours we had to take because of local rivalries. Thus, in 1804, the Baltic powers were Russia, Sweden, Denmark and Norway and everyone had been hammering everyone else for years. Denmark and Norway had fought Sweden; Russia had fought all three; while we'd fought Denmark; the French were, likewise, in the Baltic, even if they didn't fly their own flag, and they'd fought both Sweden and Denmark in the past.

Eventually, Britannia stepped in and sent a fleet to keep order among the blighters and a good thing too. But when *Beamish* entered the Baltic, we had to assume that every ship was hostile. So we sailed around them, which *Beamish* could easily do, but it meant a wandering discourse and, on one occasion, back-tracking for two days to avoid a Russian squadron that fired on us, even with British colours flying and our nations supposedly at peace!

It was a fine voyage in any seafaring sense, because *Beamish* was an absolute joy. Cummings knew her inside out and, to my astonishment, Starkey's men fell into seafaring duties and made friends among the ship's people. Off came their shoes to run barefoot like the seamen, and they were hauling, splicing, holystoning, and even going aloft. I never saw the like from soldiers. I said that to Starkey, when some of his men were out along the mainyard, making sail.

"Ah," says he, "that's 'cos they ain't soldiers." He pointed. "See that one? He was a poacher." He grinned. "I like poachers. They're woodsmen." He pointed again. "And that one? A pick-pocket!"

"What?" says I.

"Oh yes," says he, "a good pick-pocket is small and fast, and thinks crafty, which is what I want! I get 'em from the County courts. I save 'em from transportation." So there never was a ship with so many hands for seamanly duties. Of course, I had them at gun-drill, and Starkey's rascals did that too: all except the Indians. They didn't go aloft or swab decks either. They kept close to Starkey: never more than a few paces from him.

So it's as well we weren't in a big ship, with ship's routine of gentlemen – commission officers – in the wardroom, separate messes for warrant officers, and the hands slinging hammocks between the guns. That would have been difficult because Starkey wasn't anyone's idea of a gentleman. His shabby clothes said that, even if they were practical for his profession. Also, his Indian brothers wouldn't have been welcome in the wardroom, and wouldn't have wanted it. They slept on deck under the stars, even if they did need a tarred canvas for the spray.

The only problem was drink. The Service ration was half a bottle of rum, per man, per day in two 'whacks': one with dinner at noon, and the other at tea. It came diluted one-to-four with water, and with lime juice against the scurvy. The tars were bred up to it, as were the ship's officers, while Starkey and his Indians never took their ration. But his men did and two of them got roaring drunk on the first day at sea, being unaccustomed to the strength of seaman's grog. So I was interested to see how Starkey kept discipline. He waited until the two had sobered up next day, then got them on the main deck, all full of headache and nausea, and personally beat the lights out of them. He made me smile. By Jove, it was the same excellent method that I used myself, and to prove it, none of his people ever got drunk again.

I should add that little Mr Bayley was his usual self, though he wasn't really little any more. He'd grown; he'd got a man's voice and the ship's people liked him. He was a fine seaman, a practised navigator, and forever active with his kites and getting the people to compete in building them. I'd warned him off big 'uns after our Irish experience, so he had them making ingenious kites: which one was most like a seagull, or a dragon, or which could flap wings the best? But for himself he mainly made his his bat-wing, Leonardo kites. He was always making them and testing them, trying to get them perfect. He made them as big as he dared, the little devil. Also, he spent a lot of time with Starkey's men and even sat with the three Indians, trying to get them to talk. They didn't say much, but he got a smile out of them, which nobody else did.

Finally, after eighteen days on a passage which *Beamish* should have run in eight, we sighted the straits of Ofrok, with some small merchantmen working in and out of the coastal batteries. We kept clear, took careful observation, and came in at night, showing no lights, and the leadsman in the fore chains so we shouldn't run aground. I left the business to Cummings and Haljem, while Starkey and his men stood ready in marching kit, and myself besides: dressed in their style and with soft shoes.

All was dark, the weather fine, and the seas fresh and cool after a hot day. It was an exciting moment as we closed the shore, because who knew what was waiting for us? Then Mr Arthur Bayley was beside me, and even in the dark I could see he wore a set of Starkey-clothes and held a fusil. What an improvising fellow he really was. He looked at me, but I spoke first.

"You will stay here!" says I. "I promised your grandpa to bring you home safe."

"I'd be useful, sir," says he. "I speak French, which all the Russians do."

"Sod the French and their sodding language!"

"And I'm good at all manner of things."

"You'll bloody well stay aboard!"

Then damn me, if Starkey's rascals didn't plead for him!

"Ah, go on, Cap'n," says one, in a murmur. Lucky for him I couldn't see who it was.

"Yeah," says another, "bring him along."

"Aye aye!" says even the bloody seamen.

I sighed. I couldn't shout *silence on the lower deck*, nor go round punching heads. Not with us creeping so quiet and the shore full of ears.

"God help you if you get yourself killed!" says I.

"Does that mean I can come, sir?"

"Oh shut up," says I and changed the subject. "Captain Cummings?"

"Sir?"

"Repeat your orders, so that all shall know!"

"Aye aye, sir," says he, "I am to assume that once ashore, you shall reach the castle in four days, sending the Duchess downriver in the canoe on the fourth night. Thus, my ship must then be off the cove, awaiting a blue light from the shore, whereupon I shall send a boat to bring off the Duchess, and such of the shore party as are present. Then, since the canoe cannot embark the entire shore party, my ship must be offshore some nights thereafter, awaiting a blue light from those who must march to the cove."

You youngsters take note that *a blue light* was a firework tube a foot long, packed with nitre, sulphur, sulphide of arsenic and gunpowder. When lit, it gave an intense light which was in fact white, so don't ask your Uncle Jacob why it was called blue. But it was clear-visible for miles at night, and commonly used for signals at sea.

"Good!" says I, when Cummings was done, "but what if those beautiful plans don't work?"

"I must use initiative, sir," says he.

"So be it, Captain," says I.

After that, we were ashore in two trips of *Beamish's* launch, which hung on davits astern in the modern style, ready to be lowered. The oars were muffled, and I was aboard the first run with Starkey, with the canoe towed astern. We headed below the Ofrok and could see the lights of batteries to north of us, clustered around the mouth of the river. Then we were in the cove and grounding on a sandy beach with clumps of wiry plants. The pine forest was there too.

"Ah!" says Starkey, pointing to the trees, "there's our road to the castle!"

Out we got, drawing the canoe ashore, while the boat pulled back to the ship. The canoe was a little wonder: twelve feet of birch-bark, saplings and glue, with four thwarts, plus paddles and a bailer. I could easily lift it myself, but not on the march because Starkey took command, and read us the rule book.

"You shall go ahead, my brothers," says he to the Indians, who stood cuddling their firelocks, each with a feather in his hair and paint on his face, which was their custom on going into action. "The rest of you? Single file! Silence! Listen for my bird calls!" They all nodded. "Yourself in the middle, Captain," says he, "with Mr Bayley. Quiet as you can."

"Aye aye!" says I, "and we'll carry the canoe. We're seamen not woodsmen, so that'd be the best use of us in this venture."

"That's right good of you, sir," says Starkey, "and right true besides." He looked round at us all. "Not another word now!" says he, and he led the way with a small compass. So into the woods we went, where there was black dark, and I was hopeless lost in seconds, seeing only the man in front, and the canoe and Bayley behind. It was nervous work because my own breathing seemed loud as a hurricane, and I expected each moment to be discovered. But Starkey knew his business, keeping us out of trouble for three whole days, until we were almost at the castle. Then trouble found us in large degree.

CHAPTER 32

The St Petersburg Road,
North-East of Ofrokaberg Castle,
Estonia.
(Morning, Monday May 28th 1804)

"Of course we were loyal to Tsar Nicholas: totally loyal! But sometimes we wavered."

(From 'Recollections of a Cossack' by Dimitri Bukretov, published 1810 by Kushnir & Solvig of Odessa. Translated from Ukranian.)

General Bukretov reigned in his horse. The animal stood shivering, so close as it was to a sheer drop. All the horses were nervous. Bukretov and his bodyguard were on the edge of a mere track, looking down on heavy wagons lumbering along the Russian Military road a hundred feet below. Bukretov's men made a fine show: glossy horses, long lances, carbines and sabres and all the panache of a Cossack company, with fur caps and gleaming boots.

"What do you see?' said Bukretov, to his adjutant. "I'm an old man with bad eyes!"

"Never!" said the adjutant.

"Never!" said the entire company.

"You'll outlive us all!" said the adjutant.

"Very likely, but I still can't see distances," said Bukretov.

The adjutant looked down and described what he saw.

"They're coming, as expected," he said. "Seven big wagons, with six-horse teams of heavy draft horses." He chuckled. "Ah-ha! They've seen us. They're looking up at us: all the drivers and the cavalry." He studied the uniforms and headgear. "Looks like the Imperial Artillery-Mortar Regiment, with Lifeguards in escort. Lifeguards! Look at the fancy white uniforms! Let's give them a wave!" All the Cossacks laughed and waved at the Russians down below. The Russians looked up in stony silence. Imperial regiments didn't like Cossacks, which made the Cossacks laugh all the more.

"Stop it!" said Bukretov. "You're a disgrace to your mothers: those of you that have mothers." The Cossacks fell silent, because they always did what Bukretov told them ... usually. "What's in the wagons?"

"Mortars," said the adjutant. "Big ones. They look like twelve-inch mortars." He looked closer and saw thick, stunted barrels moulded in bronze. "There's two mortars: one wagon for each, and two other wagons for the carriages. Then there's three wagons for the bombs, fuses and powder. Those'll be 200-pound bombs." He shook his head. "It's Jesus Christ of a bang when *they* go off!" He paused as the officer commanding the Russians yelled an order and the wagons stopped; a group of horsemen came up the road towards the Russians.

"What's coming?" said Bukretov. "I can hear them."

"Karelians," said the adjutant, "what a mess! Look at 'em!"

He sneered at the band of Karelian irregulars, who wore every shade of peasant dress, and had every kind of skinny little horse, and they came on in a jumble, without ranks or files. Some didn't even have stirrups. They rode up in a cloud of dust, stopping just short of the Russian officer in his white uniform, polished helmet, and long jackboots. A couple of the Karelians half-heartedly drew swords and saluted the Russian, who waved his riding crop in return. The Karelians spoke to the Russian, which caused a lot of movement, with Russians getting down from wagons, and getting on to spare horses brought up by the Lifeguards.

"What are they doing?" said Bukretov.

"Just what we thought they'd do, General," said the adjutant. "The Russians are handing over to the Karelians. They don't want to be involved. They want someone to do it for them, yellow bastards. Holy Mary! Just tell me why – and for what reason – do we serve the Russians?"

"We don't serve the Russians," said Bukretov. "We serve the Tsar, God bless and keep him!" He crossed himself as he spoke.

"God bless and keep him!" said all the Cossacks, and crossed themselves, even though some glanced at each other and grinned.

The adjutant looked down as the Russian officer yelled more commands and all the Russians rode off towards St Petersburg; the Karelians wandered round the wagons, petting the horses, and staring at the heavy equipment. Then there was a lot of shouting among them, with their leader, shouting the most.

"What's happening?" said Bukretov.

"They're getting on with it, General," said the adjutant, "after their fashion." Whips cracked and the wagons lurched forward towards Ofrokaberg. "Yes! They're moving off. It's exactly what we'd heard. The Tsar's fed up with Little Mother Michailovna. So either she apologises to that piss-brain-dick of a prince, or she gets bombed out of the castle."

This caused an angry muttering among the Cossacks.

"God bless and keep the Little Mother!" said one.

"Aye!" said others.

"And God bless and keep the Cossacks in there with her!"

"Aye!" said all of them, and Bukretov spun his horse round and bellowed.

"Shut your mouths!" he cried. "We're ordered here by His Imperial Majesty the Tsar! Two thousand of us! Encamped and sending out patrols to keep the Baltic scum at their posts." He pointed towards Ofrokaberg. "Them!" he said, "them in the batteries and trenches! Karelians, Estonians and all the other little shits who won't do what they're told without a Cossack boot up 'em! And even she – Ekaterina Michailovna – must obey the Tsar, just as we do!" He drew sword and glared at them. "So!" he said, "does anyone argue with that? Does anyone want to face me?"

Nobody did. He could see perfectly well within a sword's length and he'd taken more heads than any man they knew. Nobody moved. And yet ...

"What about her Cossacks?" said someone.

"Who said that?" said Bukretov, and rode forward, looking left and right. But the someone kept silent. Bukretov sheathed his sword. "Anyway," he said, "they're not Durovi Cossacks like us, only Ural Cossacks."

"They're still Cossacks," said the someone, but he muttered it under his breath.

CHAPTER 33

Starkey was right. It took three marches – night marches – to cover ten miles along the south bank of the river, to reach Lake Ofrok and come within sight of the castle. That was because the nights were so short, and the need so great to avoid being seen by the men in the batteries that lined the shore. It was hard going for me, being so big. I got hot and bothered, stuck with pine needles, my shoes filled with stones, and I damn near poked my eyes out on twigs. God knows how Starkey's men managed. Finally, I just blundered along, head down to keep my eyes safe, staring at the ground and trying not to drop the canoe.

We slept in the day and moved at night counting seven batteries placed alternately on the north and south banks. The river itself was about two hundred yards wide, and the current fast. But there were no rapids nor cascades, so it looked like a swift passage downstream for the canoe, if things went well.

There were four batteries on our side of the river, and we had to keep well away from them during the day, and when we did move in the night, all the scouting ahead was done by Starkey's Indians, who moved like whispers and were supreme experts in finding out and reporting back, which they did in their own language to Starkey. So on the first night, we passed two batteries, one after another. We saw their campfires gleaming through the woods, and we heard their voices and their pots clattering, which was a pity because there were no fires and hot food for us. Not on the march.

Next day, with ourselves hidden among the pines well away from the river, I couldn't sleep and Starkey talked a bit, very soft and murmuring.

"We have to go specially slow and careful," says he, "and we have to go wide around the batteries and into the woods, because these folk don't keep in their camp. Not them! They wander about even beyond where their sentries are posted."

"Why?" says I, "what are they doing?"

"Going for a leak," says he, and grinned. "My brothers could chop 'em as they piddle, and they'd never know. Their sentries aren't much better. Lazy!"

"What are they?" says I. "Soldiers? Marines?"

"No!" says he. "Militia. No proper uniforms."

"What about the guns? What have they got?"

"A mixture of 12-pounders and 18-pounders. In earthworks."

"Are they proper gunners?"

"Proper enough for Pellew!" says he. "Enough talking. We have to be quiet."

It was like that until the fourth day, when we'd reached the lake and the castle. At dawn, Starkey led me through the trees to see it, with his Indians ahead, while everyone else stayed silent in our camp. He got me to just where I could use a telescope: a small one I'd brought along. The lake was about three miles across and I could see the castle clearly.

And, by Jove, what a masterwork it was! A masterwork of military engineering, even if it was four hundred years old. It was built on top of massive rocks that rose out of the eastern shore of the lake, and it looked impregnable. I could imagine some king of old arriving with his troops and siege engines, then taking one look and saying *'Oh bugger!'* and going home in despair.

There were grey towers and ring-walls rising out of solid granite, with conical roofs on the tower tops and banners in the wind, which blew strong from the west. A massive central keep rose up inside the ring-walls, with even bigger towers. It was all so high up that – just as Mr Minion Watford had said – it would be impossible to get heavy guns to bear on the walls to batter them with direct fire. I focussed at once on two towers facing west, with a couple of smaller towers in the middle, guarding a fortified jetty that stuck out into the lake.

"Ah!" says I, handing the telescope to Starkey. "See the jetty?"

"Yes," says he, "that could be useful. I'll get my brothers to have a look."

"They'll have to go careful," says I. "See there, to the south of the castle? There's an enemy camp. Biggest we've seen yet." He smiled.

"They'll be careful. You bet your white-man's Christian soul on it!"

We slept most of the day, and after dark the three Indians took the canoe and set out across the lake. They were gone all that night, the next day and most of the next night. When they came back, we all sat in a ring under the dark trees, and watched as they muttered away to Starkey, pointed back at the castle, and occasionally made throat-cutting signs, or laid hands on their war-clubs.

"Looks like there'll be fighting, sir," says Bayley.

"Yes," says I. Then Starkey had us all come in close.

"Here's the way of it," says he. "The enemy camp's a big 'un all right. Hundreds of men, with horses, guns and stores. Their sentries are properly on guard, and nobody's wandering out beyond them. They ain't so slack like the others, and they've got the castle surrounded by a double line of trenches, about three hundred yards from the castle walls, and there's little bastions dug at intervals to defend the trenches.

"Bastions?" says I.

"Little forts," says Starkey, "made of sandbags and raised up for a dozen men with muskets to fire along the trenches if anyone gets into them. Wouldn't be easy if we tried to cross the trenches, to get into the castle."

"Can't we go across the lake? says I. "To that jetty? Are there any boats on guard?"

"There's no boats," says he, "but the jetty's fallen into ruin, and it looks like them inside have given up on it."

"Then what do we do?" says I and Starkey looked unsure.

"Hard to say," says he, and he drew a picture in the dust. He drew a big cone shape, with a zig-zag line rising from the bottom to the top. At the top he drew the outline of the castle. "This here's the south-facing side of the castle. There's a winding road that goes up from ground level to the castle gateway, and the whole way up that road would be under fire from those inside should they think it's *us* that's the enemy! They wouldn't even need firelocks: they could drop stones. They'd be just as deadly. And as for the militiamen, their camp is placed for best sight of the winding road." He stared at me in the dark. "But it's the only way in." He leaned back and spread hands in a helpless gesture.

And now, in case you youngsters should think your Uncle Jacob very clever for seeing the way forward, just remember that this wasn't the first time I'd faced the impossible, with forts and guns and narrow ways. So, if the answer looked obvious to me, then it's because I'd been there before, in a manner of speaking.

"Right!" says I. "This is what we shall do," and I told them. They all nodded, including the Indians. Then we rested all that night, all except Bayley and one of the Indians who was good at craft work. We slept some of the next day and set out the following night, which placed us way beyond the four nights we'd agreed with Cummings aboard ship, but he'd just have to use his initiative.

So off we went, in the dark, in usual order of march, except that I was beside Starkey because hauling canoes might be the best use of me in the woods, but not when going into action. Bayley and one of Starkey's men had the canoe, and round the lake we went until we were just south of the enemy camp. We could see the light of their fires, and hear them easily. But they never heard us. Some of them never heard anything ever again, because – by my instruction – the Indians took little detours to find the sentries, and sent them to see Jesus. That was to focus the attention of the enemy in the wrong direction. Later on, we even heard the shouts of alarm as the bodies got discovered, because that's war, my jolly boys, and if you don't like it, then don't be a soldier. Or a seaman.

When the main body of us was completely round the enemy camp and marching towards the entrenchments, we heard the lively noise and fireworks let loose by five men left behind by my orders, to the south of the enemy camp, to make entirely sure that the enemy was looking the wrong way.

Bang-bang-bang! Bang-bang-bang! A rapid discharge of fire in the quiet night. It sounded like dozens of men, not just five. But that was Starkey's rapid-fire, you see. His men could do that. Then there was a flare of light as one of the blue light pyrotechnics was let off, and finally, a series of hideous whoops and howls. All manner of yelling came from the enemy camp, and drums and bugles sounded. There was a great rumble of boots, whinneys of horses, and a long rolling fight, as whatever militia it was inside that camp, grabbed their muskets, attempting a night fight against men who carried right on whooping and shrieking. Those were our men, and they fell back steadily, still returning fire against the hopeless volleys blazed away by militiamen who never even saw what they were shooting at. And all the time those militiamen were being led the wrong way.

"Go!" says Starkey to his Indians, and they led us through the night, leaving the enemy camp behind, with the dark mass of the castle rising ahead, and the lake gleaming to our left. We walked until we reached the first line of entrenchments where we got down into the trench line. I reached in a knapsack for some special devices that the ingenious little Mr Bayley had made to my instructions. There were three of them: powder horns with fuses taken from the blue lights, stuck into the narrow ends. I had those, and a length of thin line, smouldering nicely red at one end because it had been soaked in a thick solution of gunpowder in water, for the nitre in the powder, and then the line had been dried out.

So, I was a grenadier of old. I had three *grenadoes* and a match-cord to set them off! Three of them was all the powder horns we could spare, and they were my plan for the bastions, but no plan is ever perfect, and no reconnaissance either, because we ran straight into one of the small bastions of the entrenchments. The bastion was full of men, and they saw us first, and cried a challenge we couldn't answer. They gave a volley that split the night and dazzled our eyes, and the thunderclap deafened our ears. Four of us went down, including Starkey, though he got up at once. He did, but the others did not, and one of them was Okwaho, shot clean through the chest and coughing up his lungs.

"Oh no!" says Starkey. "No-no-no!" and more in the Indian language. He stretched a hand towards Okwaho, who clasped it. Then Okwaho drew his war club, touched it to his brow, and gave it to Starkey, who sobbed in grief as he took this infinitely precious gift. But we had to act, and at once.

"Stand by!" says I in a great shout, and lit the first powder horn, throwing it into the bastion. BOOOM! A great flash and roar, and shrieks from inside. I was scrambling up and over the six foot of sandbags, with men stumbling deaf and blinded inside, some already down, and all white faces and powder smoke. I swung my hatchet, and split one man through the brow, with Mr Bayley close behind, striking left and right. The rest of Starkey's men followed and we did for those militiamen in seconds, and stood panting and sweating, as you do when you've just killed men face-to-face.

But Starkey was yelling at one side of the bastion, where there was a way out facing the castle, right through the first line of trenches. So out we went, stumbling over the dead in the dark, and over some that weren't quite dead that still moved.

"This way!" says Starkey. "Quick-quick-quick! And bring the canoe!" He was staggering but showed the way, and we followed with three less woodmen now. I ran forward and grabbed a staggering Starkey before he could fall, and shoved him to one of his men, while one of the Indians put hand to lips for silence and beckoned me. We crept to the next bastion, and the Indian made a throwing gesture. I lit another powder horn and threw. BOOOM! Shrieks and screams!

"Come on you swabs!" says I in a shout, and the rest charged forward, up and over into that bastion, where it was hatchets and fists and boots. Then again, Starkey was calling, to lead us out of the bastion. We ran round to one side, which should have led to the plain beyond the trenches. But damn, damn, damn! There was a third line of trenches – one the Indians had missed – so we had it all to do again, charging to the next bastion, and myself throwing another powder horn before those inside could fire. But damn again, because they fired even as the powder horn exploded, and some more of our men went down.

But if it's true that no battle plan ever works in full, then it wasn't only ourselves that made mistakes, because there were only three men in that last bastion, and all were thrown over, stunned and helpless by the powder horn. We were quickly out by the side way, and we really were on the wide space between the entrenchments and the castle. I looked up at it, sweating and heaving with effort, and I saw lights on the battlements, so high up above me on the great black rocks. There was shouting too. So, they were awake, which is hardly surprising.

Fifteen of us had gone into the entrenchments, but now there was only myself, Bayley and Starkey, two Indians and four others. We'd lost six men, and Starkey was wounded.

"Can you go on?" says I to him, and he just laughed, while one of his Indians ran towards the castle, calling out like an owl, guiding us forward, and the other Indian hung on to Starkey. The canoe nearly got left behind, but Bayley and I grabbed it, even with a hole in the bottom where someone had trodden through it. So we ran with it just as the enemy behind finally realised they'd been chasing the wrong way. Bugles blew, and they came after us in great numbers. There was firing and a couple of musket balls went *whizz-whizz-smackety-smack*; the canoe jumped and there were more holes knocked in it. Bayley and I dropped it, then grabbed it again. Glancing back, I saw flaming torches, men running, bayonets gleaming and more muskets firing. Bang! Bang! Bang! They didn't hit anyone but, by Jove, it made us run faster.

Breathing heavily, we got to the zig-zag path that led up to the castle. We reached it before the pursuit, but they were coming on hard. Starkey was there, at the beginning of the path.

"Fletcher?" says he. "I'm no use. I'm hit bad. And my brother is dead. So me and them" – he looked at his two Indians – "we're going back to make trouble among the enemy, to give you your chance to get up there." He pointed to the gateway high above. He then looked at his surviving men. " I'm not asking anyone to go with us, but ..."

"I'm with you, Cap'n!" says one.

"Me too," says another. "They'd have sent me down to Australia but for you!"

"Thank you, boys," says Starkey, and grinned. "I take that right kindly from white men." He turned to me. "Get up there, Jacky Flash!" says he. "Knock on their door and give 'em the password! Run!"

So that's what we did: me and Bayley, hauling that blasted canoe all the way. We ran up the steep slope, with shouting coming from the ramparts above, and ourselves hoping that the castle folk wouldn't drop cold shot on our heads. We skidded round the bends, getting occasional sight of the battle raging down below. And take note, you youngsters, that a night fight with firelocks isn't like the same as in daylight where you notice the white powder smoke bursting out of the barrels. At night it's all bright flashes from the muzzles and priming pans, and instantaneous sight of the men nearby, as if they were frozen, and then it's dark again.

We couldn't see what was happening, except that there were no formed ranks nor rows of bayonets, and no volleys. It was a mad scramble of men blazing away at who knows what and churning in confusion. Knowing Starkey, I'd guess that he and his men would have got in among the militiamen and fired as opportunity presented, going after the officers first. That would have been his style. But whatever they did, there was a vast deal of shooting and shouting, and nobody came up the winding path after me and Bayley.

We reached the very top. We came gasping and groaning to a stone gatehouse in the enormous walls, with great towers on either side of the gatehouse, the towers full of loopholes from which we could be shot, and the gateway overhung with outworks full of loopholes and dropping ports. So we were standing in the most perfect deathtrap, and it was dark and hard to see, but in front of us we could make out that some thirty feet down a stone tunnel – again filled with loopholes and dropping ports – there was a big double gate of heavy timbers and square-headed bolts. The tunnel echoed as I gave my best mast-head bellow.

"Florizal! Florizal! Florizal!" I yelled and nothing happened except that the firing down below got less. So I yelled again. "Florizal! Florizal! Florizal!" I kept right on yelling, and the firing below finally ceased; we could hear orders given below and boots clumping as the militiamen started up the winding path. They came slow and wary, and Bayley and I looked at one another, wondering if we'd be caught even now, right at the castle gates. Then we noticed a path running round the foot of the walls. We might still escape!

"Look, sir!" says Bayley, "shall we dump the canoe and run? It's full of holes anyway."

"No!" says I, as the clumping boots came faster. "The canoe's easy to mend: just a bit of tar and canvas. And it's not just for the Duchess. It's our only way home. We'd never get through the woods without Starkey. Not now everyone knows we're here."

In that very moment a door swung open. We'd not seen it in the dark. It was on one side of the tunnel. It swung open and outwards, big and heavy, and it slammed into the canoe, knocking it out of our hands and sending it sliding to the edge of the winding path. It went right to the edge where it hung for a second such that we rushed forward to grab it, which we very nearly did. But not quite. So over it went. It went over and down, smashing and splintering into ruin.

CHAPTER 34

The Karelian Mortar Emplacements,
North of Ofrokaberg Castle,
Lake Ofrok,
Estonia.
(Afternoon, Monday June 4th 1804)

"Preparations for the bombardment went well. But then we were attacked in the night."
   (From a letter of June 6th 1804, from Major Ernst Wagner to his father in Berlin. Translated from German.)

Wagner was both surprised and pleased. It was important that Prussia should not be too involved, so he and his superior – the late Oberst Von Strunz – had been sent with only six men: a sergeant, two corporals and three bombardiers. That was enough for technical expertise, but not enough to get a pair of 12-inch mortars bedded into the ground, bearing on target, and properly served in action.

Six was nowhere near enough! Not for the levelling and hammering of a base-platform of crushed stone; then the rigging of lifting tackles and the heaving and straining to get the carriages onto the platform; then the heaving and straining to get the mortars into their carriages. Six was nowhere near enough when each mortar was over three thousand pounds weight of solid bronze, and each carriage was three thousand pounds of oak, iron and brass.

Therefore, Wagner was surprised and pleased that the so-called 'Colonel' Kivi had mustered enough of his men to do the heavy work, and that they were well enough organised to do it well. In fact, Wagner was almost irritated that they had done it so well. A considerable part of him would have preferred these amateurs to do a worse job than Prussians would have done. But never mind. The job was done.

Even now, two large teams of militiamen were standing by with heavy levers. The rest were standing back, under reasonable discipline and not hooting or calling out nonsense, as often these half-trained peasants did. Meanwhile, Kivi was at Wagner's very elbow in his enthusiasm to understand how mortars worked. He was so keen that Wagner softened and gave explanation. He gave it in French as usual.

"See there," he said. "There's the castle, yes?"

"Yes," said Kivi, and looked southwards at the distant castle on its rocky base. There were trees in between, but the castle stood out over them all. Or at least its battlements and tower tops did.

"So," said Wagner, "we're way out of range of that woman and her rifle, and she couldn't see us anyway because we're in a forest clearing with trees all round. Yes?"

"Yes," said Kivi.

"So," said Wagner, "there are the mortars: there in front of us, ready for final adjustment. Yes?"

"Yes," said Kivi, looking at the mortars some ten yards off, with his men ready to heave the massive carriages round the final few inches to get them to bear on the castle.

"And this is a gunner's theodolite," said Wagner, resting a hand on the complex instrument on a three-legged stand: a brass telescope with spirit levels, and scales for elevation and training. The telescope was nicely at eye level. "Take a look," said Wagner. Kivi looked and saw the castle neatly caught in the cross hairs of the instrument.

"I see," said he, and stood back as Wagner pointed to a horizontal scale.

"Now! See where the castle bears a little *off* true south?" he said.

"Yes," said Kivi.

"I've marked out a true south line for each mortar with string and pegs, see?" Kivi nodded. "And now I'm going to mark out the bearing *off* true south, for each piece, and your men will shift the carriages just the final little bit to line them up on the castle. Understand?"

"Yes," said Kivi.

"Right," said Wagner, "now come and have a look at the bombs and fuses."

"Oh yes," said Kivi, "I want to see them, but first: how do you adjust for range? You've said how you line up the mortars on target, but how do you get the range right, with mortars? They're solid in their carriages. You can't point them up and down." Wagner smiled.

"Easy!" he said. "We vary the powder charge. The more powder, the greater the range."

"Ahhh," said Kivi.

"Now come and see the bombs," said Wagner, leading the way to a timber and canvas shed, also put up by Kivi's men, and also put up with surprising efficiency. Wagner had to admit that. "This was well done," he said, looking round. "The weather's fine but we can't have the bombs and fuses getting wet if it rains."

"Thank you, Herr Major," said Kivi, acknowledging the first praise that had emerged from the Prussian's mouth.

"Right!" said Wagner, "these are twelve-inch bombs. That's twelve inches in diameter, and two hundred pounds weight when filled." Kivi looked at the rows of black globes sat in a long timber framework. Each one had a tube a few inches long, sticking out of the top.

"They're empty now," said Wagner. "We don't fill them until just before action. We fill them with black powder, and then each one gets one of these." He went to a chest, opened it, and took out a short wooden tube. "See this?" said Wagner. "This is a fuse. See the hole drilled down the length? That's filled with a paste of black powder and gum." Kivi nodded. "And see the scale marked down the length?" Wagner tapped a finger on one of the tubes sticking out of a bomb. "We hammer a fuse in here, cut to a judged length so that the bomb will burst when it drops on the target."

"Do you have to light the fuse?' said Kivi.

"No!" said Wagner, "the flash of the propellant charge does that."

"What if you cut the fuse too long or too short?'

"We try again. It's trial and error till we get it right."

"I see, and can you really reach the castle from here?"

"Come outside," said Wagner. Out they went and Wagner pointed at the castle. "A mortar fires in a great arc, not a straight line like a long gun. It throws its bomb a thousand feet or more into the air, and then the bomb falls on the target and bursts." He smiled. "Oh yes, we can reach the target. We can reach the target and blow her drawers right over her head, that bitch of a Duchess."

Kivi didn't laugh at that, and Wagner knew he'd never understand these people, because he was fairly sure that Kivi didn't really want to attack the castle. Not if it hurt the precious Duchess! Wagner thought that was amusing.

But it wasn't amusing when he was woken up in the middle of the night from a peaceful sleep. He was an old campaigner so he was dressed in seconds and outside the tent with sword and pistols. Men were rushing about shouting, and bugles were blowing. His sergeant and corporals ran up.

"Where's Kivi?" he said.

"This way, Herr Major," said the sergeant. They found Kivi with some of his men, all looking grim, chattering in their language, and pointing out to the edges of the camp.

"What is it?" said Wagner.

"Someone's murdered five of our sentries!" said Kivi.

"Who?" said Wagner.

"We don't know, but I've roused the camp."

"Good!" said Wagner. "I'll go to the mortars and stand guard. I'll need help."

"I'll send a company to go with you," said Kivi.

After that was done, everything was quiet a while. But as Wagner was posting men around the mortar site, there was the most tremendous firing in the night, with howling and yelling. Militiamen were rushing first one way, then the other, and finally there was firing coming from the direction of the castle itself! All Wagner's Prussian professional snobbery came right back.

"What's going on?" he said. "Are they mad, these people?"

"Jawohl, Herr Major!" said the sergeant, knowing better than to offer an opinion to an officer.

"They're probably fighting one another!"

"Jawohl, Herr Major!"

"There must be a regiment attacking, at least."

"Jawohl, Herr Major!"

In the morning, Wagner was even more mystified when, despite heavy casualties among the Karelians – sixty-three dead and wounded – the bodies of only nine attackers were found, and nobody knew who they were!

CHAPTER 35

Bayley and I stood horrified at the loss of the canoe, but we didn't stand gaping very long because the most remarkable woman appeared. She came out of the light that shone from the doorway. There were men behind her with flaming torches: every one of them with long moustaches, fur caps, pistols in his belt and a curve-bladed sword in his free hand. But we didn't look at them. We looked at her.

She was tall and slim. She wore a cap like the men, and damn me if she wasn't dressed as a man, with britches, long boots and a sort of blouse with loops for cartridges. She had pistols too, but she didn't draw. She just beckoned and spoke.

"Florizal?" she said.

"Florizal!" says I, then she gabbled away in some heathen tongue that we didn't understand.

"Huh!" says she and stamped a foot. I think she tried a couple of other languages, but one's the same as another to me, and all my life I've wondered why bloody foreigners can't speak English like sensible people.

[Note that this is a mere summary of one of Fletcher's favourite rants, wherein he claimed to believe that if English was good enough for Britain and America, then lesser folk should take note and do likewise. S.P.]

We just shook our heads, and then she switched to a heathen chatter that I *did* recognise, even if I'll be damned if I'd choose to understand it, because it was French.

"Ah!" says Bayley. He stepped forward and bowed, and gave her back gabble for gabble. He really could do it: speak French. She liked that. She smiled. He told me later that he'd said, '*My Captain and I are charmed to be in the presence of so beautiful and gracious a lady.*' Little devil! Would you believe it? I said he was resourceful and so he was. So she smiled, then spoke to the men with moustaches – Cossacks they were – and they sheathed their blades. She chattered at Bayley and he chattered back, and she laughed a lot. We were then led along a series of stony corridors, up and down a series of stony stairs, and out into the night, in the space between the ring-wall and the keep.

Bayley spoke as we went forward.

"She's the Duchess, sir," says he, "the one we've come to save." He looked at me. "I've told her who we are, and she knows we were sent by Prinny, because Florizal is the name he uses to ladies: special ladies that he likes. She says he's a fat idiot, because he has ... er ... *desires* ... for her and she thinks that's ridiculous. But she heard you yelling Florizal, sir, and so they let us in."

Finally, we went up another stony stair into what I supposed to be the Great Hall of the castle because it was furnished with a massive oak table, with massive chairs, and a raised platform at one end. There was an enormous fireplace; enormous chandeliers hung from the ceiling, with rows of spears and halberds on the wall. That, and gold and silver plate, whole suits of armour, and pieces of armour. It was like going back to the Middle Ages.

Which is what you might see in an English castle, but there was also something different. It was something Russian, or perhaps Karelian? It was a wooden balustrade with a rail at the far end of the hall, and behind it there was a great mass of people. There were men, women, children all standing silent, in peasant smocks, with their hats in their hands, the men with beards, and the women with embroidered scarves on their heads. It was odd. Very odd.

Then it got odder. The Duchess led Bayley and me up some stairs to the raised platform, but the Cossacks stayed put, looking up just the same as the peasants. A servant held a Frenchified gilt chair for the Duchess to sit on, and she motioned me and Bayley to do the same, clapping her hands. More servants brought gold goblets and a gold jug, and poured wine and scuttled off backwards, bowing as they went, except for a formidable woman in her sixties, with folded arms, grim face, and elaborately embroidered clothes. She wore boots as well, and she stood right behind the Duchess. Meanwhile, the Duchess looked me up and down and chattered with Bayley translating.

As I've said it before in these memoirs, speaking through a translator isn't at all bad, because you can study the look on the speaker's face before you hear what's said, and that's an advantage. So here's what we said, the Duchess Ekaterina and myself, leaving out Bayley's part.

"You are an officer of the English Navy?" says she.

"Yes, Ma'am," says I.

"No!" says she. "I am addressed as *Your Grace*."

She said that with the smile that you give to an idiot who doesn't know that London is the capital of England. She wasn't annoyed, just amused at my ignorance. She was the most self-assured little madam I ever met in all my life, except that *little madams* are usually spiteful, and she wasn't. She just knew that she was better than anyone else.

Now, as you've read earlier, the late Sir Joshua Walton of the 27th Light Dragoons – him that got so very well chopped – *he* too thought he was better than everyone else. But he was nasty with it and the Grand Duchess Ekaterina wasn't. She knew she was above us all, and smiled easily in the knowing of it. You could see it in the way she sat: rocked back on her chair, one hand lounging down, one twirling her fur cap on a finger, and booted foot stretched out on a second chair. She was a knowing, urbane creature, and very lovely if you like 'em long, pale and slender, with blonde hair, blue eyes, and a sharp, straight nose. Bayley goggled at her, and she looked at him and laughed.

"So, tell me how you came here," says she to me, "and how you will propose to make good your Prince's promise."

"Yes, Your Grace," says I and I told her. I told her everything.

"But this *canoe*," says she, "is now lost?"

"I'm afraid so, Your Grace," says I, and she shrugged. .

"No matter," says she. "I could not have gone in your canoe."

"What?" says I, taken totally aback, considering the efforts we'd made to bring the damned thing. "May I ask why, Your Grace?" She waved a hand at the Cossacks below, and the peasants behind the railings.

"Because these are mine," says she. "I cannot leave without them." She shrugged. "I am responsible for them." She didn't even call them my *people* or my *folk*: just *mine*. She said that as if it was the most obvious thing in the world.

"But doesn't the Prince know you can't leave without them," says I. "Prince George?"

"How should *I* know what *he* knows?" says she. "On the one occasion when I met him, the only thing I saw in his eyes was lust!" Bayley laughed aloud at that. She saw that and said something to him. He blushed.

"What did she say?" says I.

"Er ..." says he. "She said: *you are a pretty boy.*"

"Are you now?" says I. "Are you, indeed? So just ask her – pretty boy – how many people has she got here that can't be left behind? And ask her if she has any bloody damned idea how to get them out!"

"Aye aye, sir," says he, and off he went in French.

"Two hundred and fifty serfs," says she, looking squarely at me, "and sixty of my own Cossacks."

"Ahem!" said the big woman behind her, and the Duchess shrugged and said something that Bayley again translated.

"Sixty-one including my nurse. As for making them free, that is easy! There is a Cossack brigade close by. Once they are persuaded that I am in peril, they will ride out and clear away the Karelian traitors. Then I shall be free, and I will take them." She waved at the peasants and the Cossacks in the hall. "I shall take them with me."

"A Cossack brigade?" says I.

"Thousands of them," says she.

"Good!" says I, "But they have to be persuaded that you're in peril?"

"Of course!" says she.

"And how do we do that, Your Grace?"

"Huh!" says she. "That is a matter for you: isn't that why you are here?"

We didn't get much more out of her after that, and I remark here that at no time in that discussion did she so much as mention why she had all her serfs in the hall. They were there, and then they were gone. We never saw them again, not all together like that.

After that first audience with Madame, she went off with her nurse – the big woman – the pair of them gabbling in French. Bayley and I were given a room up in a tower, which was all hung with tapestry and had a big fire going, even in June, since the whole castle was stony cold. There was one enormous bed for the pair of us, and basins to wash, hot water in cans, and a pot under the bed. All very neat and nice. Then we were shown over the castle by the officer of Madam's Cossacks, who spoke no language we understood.

The only thing we did understand, up on the battlements of the Keep, was him pointing over the trees to where we could just see a big camp, a couple of miles off.

"*Cossacky!*" says he. "*Cossacky! Cossacky!*" He made gestures with his hands, indicating something big.

"D'you think that's them, sir?" says Bayley, "this Cossack brigade?"

"I do," says I. "So why don't they come here and raise the siege?"

"I'll see if he knows, sir," says he, and he tried French on the officer, who just shook his head. After that, he showed us everything, including the fact that the castle had no proper artillery, only German rifles for sharp-shooters, and a great store of heavy stones for dropping off the battlements. But you couldn't fault the place for stores. There was endless fresh water from a well, and vast cellars packed high with grain, salt-meat, pickles and the like. There was also a room crammed with oriental art: pots and statues, bales of silk and bundles of bamboo sticks and poles. It was the Duchess's father's collection: him being obsessed with all things Chinese. We learned that later.

We were given a formal dinner that night, in the Great Hall, with the Duchess in a silk gown looking sleek, and pale as a lily. Not quite my style, but Bayley was knocked sideways. He just gazed at her, which made her laugh. The food wasn't good, but what can you expect under siege? And the conversation was worse. There was just the three of us, apart from a dozen or more servants, and Madame wouldn't talk about anything other than music, art and architecture. By God I was bored, but Bayley wasn't.

"Did you hear her, sir?" says he, later, on the way up to our tower room. "She likes Mozart, and Palladian domes ..." There was a lot more of that, but there was a knock on our door soon after we got into the room. It was the nurse-woman; she bowed at me, then looked at Bayley and spoke French.

"Oh?" says Bayley, and he looked at me, blinking a lot.

"What is it?" says I, and the nurse-woman frowned at the delay, and beckoned at Bayley.

"Hum ... er ..." says Bayley. "It's the Duchess, sir."

"Gabble-gabble!" says the nurse, and stamped a foot and beckoned again.

"She's sent for me, sir," says Bayley, and I laughed and laughed and laughed. So did the nurse. She cracked her stone face and laughed.

"Well, my lad," says I, "off you go, and be sure to aim low and fire on the upward roll."

So I had the bed to myself. But they delivered up Mr Bayley to me next morning, for the pair of us to be fed and watered: breakfast in our room, where he poured out words, all awestruck, thunderstruck, and spellbound.

"It was wonderful, sir," says he. "She's wonderful, sir. I never knew it was like this because Grandpa said I mustn't. But it was wonderful, sir, it was all silk, sir, and the nurse made me have a bath. And she took me into the bedroom, naked wearing a towel, and she – Ekaterina – had nothing on either, sir! And she was gorgeous, and she grabbed hold of me, and pulled off the towel, and took hold of me and kissed me, and we got into bed, sir, and she showed me what to do and it was wonderful … "

I'll let you guess the rest, because we all have to start somewhere. With me it was a juicy trollop called Polly Grimshaw aboard the good ship *Phiandra*, anchored off Portsmouth, while with him it was a Grand Duchess. So good luck to him, say I! Indeed I do, and all you jolly boys should do the same if chance presents. In fact, I was so greatly tickled by Bayley's adventures that I didn't grasp some of the sense in his chatter. It went like this:

"It *is* just Prinny, sir," says he. "You said it couldn't just be him. Aboard *Beamish* you said it had to be something of policy, and it's not, sir."

"What d'you mean?" says I.

"It's Prince Fyodor, sir, who wants to marry Ekaterina, and she said something about him. She wouldn't say what, but she got banished and she called on Prinny by writing to him, special courier. And so here we are." I smiled at that. He was so earnest and so swept away with his sleep-less night that I just laughed.

"No," says I. "It can't be just insults and promises. Not with wars all over Europe. There's got to be more to it than that." But then we were interrupted.

THUD! THUD!

Two deep explosions. Gunfire. Something special. The flat, dull sound of heavy ordnance, but not long guns: not 24-pounders or 32-pounders. Then a loud whistling sound and a couple of terrific crashes from within the castle. Then bugles and shouting and boots rumbling.

We were out of that room in seconds and running to the Keep battle-ments. The Cossack guards were there and so was the Duchess. Some of the serfs were looking up from tents between the ring-walls and the Keep. They were looking at a scar down the side of the Keep wall, and a crater in flagstones beneath, while we on the Keep were looking at something in the battlements. We all ran towards it and I saw what it was.

210

"Get back!" says I in a great shout. "Everybody down!" They all looked at me, not understanding. They looked at me, while I looked at a damned great mortar bomb, sticking into the stones of the battlements and ready to explode at any second.

CHAPTER 36

The Karelian Mortar Emplacements,
North of Ofrokaberg Castle,
Lake Ofrok,
Estonia.
(Morning, Tuesday June 5th 1804)

"It was their fault: the St Petersburg Arsenal, and as for the Castle folk, no wonder the Karelians can't forgive them."
(From a letter of June 6th 1804, from Major Ernst Wagner to his father in Berlin. Translated from German.)

Wagner was angry: very angry. So was his sergeant. They went through the box of fuses, with Kivi and his militiamen watching. The Prussians did it as a drill. The corporals and the bombardiers kept everyone at safe distance, while the Sergeant brought out fuses from the munitions shed, one at a time, passing them to Wagner who laid them on the ground, and lit one end of each fuse with a slow match. Or at least he tried to.

"*Gottverdammt!*" said Wagner, looking up at the Sergeant. "This one won't even take light, and all the rest wouldn't burn properly. The whole box of them are duds!"

"Jawohl, Herr Major," said the sergeant.

"It'll be the gum, probably. Or perhaps they just didn't test them?"

"Jawohl, Herr Major."

Wagner sighed. He cursed the St Petersburgers in German, French and a few other languages. Then he stood up, straightening his uniform.

"Drill them out," he said, "all of them. Then make up some gum, mix it fresh with powder, and refill 'em."

"Jawohl, Herr Major."

"Make it quick," said Wagner. "Get it done by tomorrow or the day after! And make sure you test some of them! I don't want the bombs to fail again in front of them!" He looked at Kivi and his men.

"Jawohl, Herr Major!"

Wagner walked over to Kivi and pointed at the mortars.

"We were on target," he said, in French. "You saw that for yourself."

"I did!" said Kivi. He'd stood behind the mortars and seen the bombs in flight: a thin, black line against the sky, rising up then down. "You hit the castle," said Kivi. "So it was the Russians' fault if the bombs didn't explode. But it must have been people from the castle that attacked us last night, because who else could it be?"

"Who else?" said Wagner.

"So, you can blow the hell out of them for all I care," said Kivi. Wagner nodded. "As soon as the fuses are dry," he said.

"Good!" said Kivi, "because I've had men killed: good men! Killed in the night by treachery! And I blame that castle, and I'm sick of all this."

Later on, a party came out of the castle waving a white flag. They wanted to parlay, and Wagner – a professional – would have received them. But Kivi and his men were amateurs and they were angry. They fired on the white flag and drove it back into the castle.

CHAPTER 37

Duchess Ekaterina was astounded. She didn't know what to say. She was so upset that her nurse stepped forward and embraced her. We were on the battlements of the Keep again: her, me, Bayley, the Cossack officer and the nurse. The rest of the Cossacks were looking on from a distance. Then the Duchess pulled away from the nurse and spoke to me. It was French again with Bayley translating.

"I made the great concession," says she. "I would have apologised to the Tsarina. But the Karelians won't take my letter. They won't even speak to us."

"Hmm," says I, still mystified by these court politics. But I'd seen the Karelians fire at the Cossacks, even with their white flag. I saw that for myself. They even hit one of them and killed him.

"I made the great concession," says she, "because I am responsible for my people, and the Cossacks have not come, and because" – she looked hard at me – "because you say that these bombs can destroy the castle." She pointed to the one stuck in the battlements.

"Yes," says I. "They've stopped firing, because their bombs didn't burst, which is probably because the fuses were bad. But they'll fix that and try again. Then they'll open fire and destroy this castle with us in it." She stamped her foot.

"The Cossacks must come!" says she. "They must!"

"Are you sure they know you're here?" says I.

"Of course, the Tsar has told everyone."

"Then why don't the Cossacks come?"

"Because they are ordered not to. They are ordered by the Tsar."

"But you say they'll come if you ask them?"

"Oh yes. A letter might do it. But certainly if I spoke to them."

214

I nearly laughed at that. I'd given up on their politics and now she was saying the Cossacks would get her out, *if we could get her out.* Meanwhile, here we were, waiting to be blown to pieces. It was nonsensical. But then Bayley tugged at my arm.

"Sir?" says he, "Sir Jacob?"

"What?" says I.

"I've had an idea, sir. To get her out, sir. Her and me."

Perhaps I was less than enthusiastic.

"The canoe's gone," says I. "Starkey's gone. All the batteries are alert. What do you want to do? Fly?"

"Yes, sir," says he, "with a kite."

I did laugh that time. I laughed and everyone looked at me. But Bayley started talking, his words pouring out.

"Let me show you, sir. Give me time. I've been thinking." He said a lot more, and some of it in French to the Duchess, who threw her arms round him and kissed him. "She'll do it, sir! She loves it!" But then she looked at me and chattered, and Bayley's face fell. "Oh," says he, "She says it can't be with me."

"What?" says I, and the Duchess nodded, reached up and pinched my nose, and chattered some more.

"She says it has to be a man, not a boy," says Bayley. "A big man to impress the Cossack brigade."

I was deep lost in mystery by then, but it all came clear in the end. Bayley explained, then went off with the nurse, found a workshop and soon came back with one of his Leonardo kites. It was about three feet long, with a lead weight beneath for balance. He led us to the lake side of the castle, and launched it off the battlements into the west wind, and up it shot: up and up beyond sight! The Duchess clapped hands in joy; the nurse looked glum; the Cossacks cheered. I looked at the sheer drop below, and turned to Bayley.

"So, you'll make one full-size, will you?" says I.

"Yes, sir," says he, "they've got silk here, and bamboo which is ideal, and I've been working on the Leonardos for ages. They're far better than the things that Grandpa and I made. The wind'll take you straight up, then all you've got to do is turn, and it'll be a long glide down to the Cossack camp! You and the Duchess. It's only a couple of miles, and I've made all the calculations."

That's what he said, bless his innocent heart. But what else could I do? Sit and wait for the mortars to open fire?

"Go on then, Mr Bayley," says I, "but make it good!"

"Aye aye, sir!" says he, and off he went with the nurse, getting all the tools and materials he wanted, and help from women to sew the silk for the kite. Meanwhile, I was given a complete set of Cossack clothes, since the Duchess sneered at my woodman's gear, and because, apart from being her kite-driver – God help me – I was going along to impress the Cossacks.

It all happened fast. Bayley was a whole day making the big kite, and on the dawn of the second day ... THUD-THUD! Then the shriek of the bombs falling. Two colossal explosions followed: one in the air over the castle, and one blowing a great crater between the walls and the Keep. All credit to the castle's Cossacks. They sounded the alarm, got the people down into the cellars, cleared the dead and wounded, and tried to return fire with their German rifles, aiming hopefully into the trees where the battery must be. But it was no good because, ten minutes later ... THUD-THUD! This time both bombs burst in the air, but only just, and they scoured the battlements with iron fragments, killing one of our riflemen and wounding others.

Meanwhile, all hands were bringing Bayley's full-size kite up to the lake-facing battlements and the west wind. I was in my new clothes complete with boots, and the Duchess in unbelievable colours of fancy Cossack britches and blouse, and a white fur cap. She laughed and chattered all the while, completely fearless, and the nurse gabbling warnings in her ear. Then with us hauling up the kite on a line, since it was too big for the stairs ... THUD-THUD! Shrieeeek! Two huge explosions and everyone was knocked over by two direct hits on the Keep, with dust, smoke and rubble heaved into the air, and falling like deadly hail. Some of the Cossacks went down, but others came forward to make ready the kite.

"Not that way!" says Bayley, "the other!" That was in English but the Cossacks understood, and there was the kite, ready to go: two pairs of giant bat wings one above the other - wings of silk and bent bamboo - and underneath there was a transverse tiller-bar with which I was supposed to steer the bloody thing, and a harness of straps to secure myself and the Duchess. Oh Jesus! Oh God and all the angels!

"Get aboard, sir!" says Bayley. "And Ekaterina!"

She laughed without a drop of fear and kissed him, and kissed me, and kissed the nurse. "Bloody get aboard!" cries Bayley but it took time to get us both strapped in, what with fumbling fingers and strange gear. THUD-THUD! Down we all went again, one bomb blowing a hole in the land-side walls, one knocking out a corner tower of the Keep. More rubble came down, with something smashing into one of the kite's poles and breaking it. "Shite and buggery!" says Bayley – now fluent in more than French – and he leapt forward with a length of line and whipped it round, like a top-man securing a sprung spar. "Get aboard! Get aboard!" says he, lifting one of the poles to raise the kite; the Cossacks lifted the rest and turned it into the wind, keeping the nose down. Bayley pushed me forward, with the Duchess beside me, and I was wondering how to get over the crenelations when Bayley ran round and shoved up the nose of the kite ... and damn my soul! The wind caught the kite, the sail filled, and up we went with the Duchess screaming, and our legs dangling. Up, and up, and up, with all the world tiny below, and the trees and lakes and hills like a map. I could see everything, even the mortars firing. Puffs of smoke, then thud-thud, then two more explosions, one on the Keep, and one a total miss outside the castle.

We were facing completely in the wrong direction so it was up to me to come about, by hauling on the tiller-bar as Bayley had told me. But it was never me that turned the kite. It was the mortar bombs bursting below, the shock of which hit us like a squall and the kite rose sickening fast. It staggered and twisted, and – oh bloody hell fire – the kite dropped then filled again, and it turned round all by itself. It was luck – pure luck, and down we went on a long, smooth glide, over the Karelian trenches with tiny faces gaping, hands pointing, and down over the trees right towards the camp of the Cossack brigade.

The Camp of Bukretov's Brigade,
North-East of Ofrokaberg Castle
(Morning, Thursday June 7th 1804)

"It was a miracle. In later years the Archbishop of Odessa assured me of this."
(From 'Recollections of a Cossack' by Dimitri Bukretov. Translated from Ukranian)

Bukretov was facing a mutiny the moment the mortars fired. Every man in the camp knew why the mortars were there, and what they were shooting at. Therefore, every man in the camp was now crammed outside Bukretov's tent: two thousand of them, led by their officers. Bukretov faced them alone, with a hand on his sword-hilt, and his wolfhound beside him.

"They'll kill the Little Mother!" cried the senior colonel. "And you said we must let 'em do it!"

"I did not!" said Bukretov. "I said only that we must obey the Tsar, God bless him!" Bukretov crossed himself but nobody else did.

"If we do nothing, my General," said the colonel, "then these scum of Karelians and their Prussians, will ... "

THUD-THUD! Again it came from the Karelian battery, causing a huge roar of anger, and a surging forward of men. Even the horses on the picket lines were stamping in fury and the wolfhound howled. But Bukretov was a veteran. He'd seen everything before, even mutiny. He took a breath, and raised a hand, and such was his reputation that they listened.

"Are we Cossacks or traitors?" he cried, and there was silence. "Are we traitors to the Church and the Tsar?" There was a surly murmur; the murmur grew, and for the first time in his career, Dimitry Bukretov was in doubt. Could he control his men? Would his head find itself on a lance carried round the camp? That could happen to Cossack leaders. It could happen to him. So Bukretov wavered, in profound doubt.

Then the miracle happened. A voice yelled from the back of the great crowd. Then more voices, followed by a great turning around of men, and a deep and awestruck sigh. Men were falling to their feet and pressing crucifixes to their lips, raising them on high. Bukretov looked with all the rest and saw a huge flying thing that was not a bird but a pale and sinister bat, with wings that reached out like the devil's claws, and which flew down towards the camp with two living beings beneath it. Down it came, with all the Cossacks groaning in religious passion. There was a huge and united gasp as the flying thing landed. It tumbled and broke, and yet those it carried arose, freed themselves and stepped forward to the most enormous thunder of cheering, and to reverence and worship and joy. Men were pressing forward in hordes to fall on their knees and kiss the hand of the Little Mother, and gape at the magnificent giant who came with her.

"Saint George! Saint George!" cried the simplest, and even the cleverest wondered if this huge man was indeed the Patron Saint of the Durovi Cossacks, come down from the sky to move among them, and they bowed to him in awe. Bukretov ran forward, his men stood aside, and he fell on his knees before the Duchess Ekaterina Michailovna.

"Bukretov!" she said in Ukranian. "You rascal! Why are you here and not rescuing my people?" A huge laughter arose from the Cossacks. Bukretov shook his head.

"I am yours to command, Little Mother," he said, kissing her hand.

"Then persuade the Karelians to cease firing," she said, "and raise the siege, so that my people may join me here."

"Yes, Little Mother." She nodded and glanced at the giant.

"He has served me well," she said. "You will treat him with respect."

The pair of us went arse over tit as the kite came down, and I'm told that all the Cossacks thought it was a miracle, which it bloody well was: a miracle that we weren't killed. But the Duchess threw off straps and scrambled clear even before I did.

"Gabble-gabble!" says she sharply to me, putting on her white fur cap that had fallen off. She pointed at mine, on the ground among the wreckage.

"Oh!" says I. I stuck it on my head as she stood forward, stamped a foot and stood heroic and magnificent, chin up, staring at the huge mass of Cossacks running forward, in all their military gear. They were cheering and grovelling, falling on their knees, and kissing her hand, and damn me if they didn't grovel all round *me*! They thought I was a saint! Saint George! The cheeky blighters think he's *their* patron saint not ours! I'll never understand foreigners, poor devils that they are.

Then some sort of general came forward, and he grovelled before her; she gave him his orders in quick time, because she was utterly correct that all she had to do was face them, and they were hers.

So, two great masses of horsemen rode out of the camp: one to the mortar battery, one to the Karelian camp and entrenchments. We heard pistols popping, and some yelling, even as the Duchess and I took wine at the General's table outside his tent. Bukretov his name was, who looked an utter pirate, with his guards and officers stood like good boys all around. They all looked like pirates if you ask me. That's Cossacks.

The Karelian Mortar Emplacements
(Afternoon, Thursday June 7th 1804)

"I will never understand these people"
(From a letter of June 11th 1804, from Major Ernst Wagner
to his father in Berlin.)

At first Wagner and his men stood to arms as the Cossacks charged in
among the mortars, firing in the air. It looked like certain death, with
hundreds of horsemen, and them so adept at their business. But Kivi and
his militiaman made no attempt to take up muskets or make a defence.

"Don't!" said Kivi to Wagner, as Wagner made to draw his pistols.

"Why not?" said Wagner.

"Wait and see," said Kivi, as a Cossack officer rode forward and stopped
nearby, looking down on the Prussians, and the militiamen gunners. The
horse shuffled; dust settled; the officer leaned forward and spoke to Kivi
in Ukranian.

"Ahhhh!" said Kivi, and smiled.

"What is it?" said Wagner.

"That flying thing that we saw," he said.

"Amazing!" said Wagner. "Beyond belief."

"Yes, I know!" said Kivi. "Incredible, incredible. But that was the
Duchess. She's got out and reached the Cossack brigade."

"So?"

"So they'd lick the dirt off her boots! She's the Little Mother. The
Cossack general is raising the siege and sending us all home. All of us: all
the batteries." Wagner took a breath and sighed.

"But you were all ordered here by the Tsar," he said, "and the Cossacks
ordered to keep you here."

"That's right," said Kivi. "But now she's out, and everything's different."

"What about the Tsar? Won't he mind?"

Kivi considered that. "He'll come round. Now she's actually out. Half
the aristocracy are on her side and he has politics to consider." He shrugged.
"You don't understand our politics."

"As God is my judge, I don't!" said Wagner.

Which was the end of it: my Baltic adventure. The Cossacks brought the

Duchess's people out, and she herself was free, while Bayley and I had a cavalry escort all the way back to the cove where we'd planned to signal to *Beamish* with blue lights. But we didn't need to. The Cossacks spoke to the local folk, who went out in a fishing boat to find *Beamish*, which ship they knew, having seen her cruising off the coast. They took a letter from me to Commander Cummings and a few days later, Bayley and I were in *Beamish's* launch, pulling for the ship.

All hands turned out to cheer as we came over the side, and we met those of Starkey's men who'd survived. There were just six, already aboard, having reached the cove through the woods. Sadly, they confirmed that Starkey and all the rest had fallen in action and were dead.

Then it was a smooth passage to Portsmouth, with nothing to report other than Bayley's repeated insistence, based on what he'd been told by the Duchess, that the whole affair really was based on stupidity. He made that clear on our first dinner at sea, with Cummings and his First Lieutenant in company.

"Prince Fyodor wanted to marry her," says he, "and she said no, and told him why, which was something to do with women. Something so awful that she wouldn't tell me."

"What?" says I, "even when you'd had your wicked way with her?" Everyone laughed except Bayley.

"No, sir," says he, "and she had to apologise for what she'd said, but she wouldn't, so she got banished, and called on Prinny to get her out." He paused and looked at me. "I did try to tell you that before, sir."

He had too, and I hadn't listened, which I should have done because he was a very clever lad who went on to a fine career in the Service. But there were no more kites for him, because his younger brother, Edward, was nearly killed in an accident aboard one of Grandpa Sir David Bayley's flying machines, while we were away in the Baltic. Edward lay unconscious for two days before recovering and Grandpa took it as a warning. So, he gave up aerial navigation and begged his grandsons to do the same.

Back in England, I found myself very much worried that men had died, and ships been sunk because of two blockhead buffoons of princes. It was madness. Such a waste of lives. Here we were in the middle of a world-wide war, with fleets at sea, and armies in the field, while I'd been sent out on a piece of nonsense that had only to do with stupidity.

I'm not prone to depression, my jolly boys, but it left me depressed: deep depressed.

Ah well. At least I was back with my family and back in trade. That soon cheered me up, and I resolved never again to become involved in such futile affairs, when there was no sound sense in any of it.

EPILOGUE

To:
Joachim Murat,
Grand Admiral of France,
Hôtel de La Marine,
Paris.

Following recent events at Ofrokaberg Castle, and especially the destruction caused by mortar fire, all plans and preparations to gain possession of such fortifications in the Baltic, including even those plans and preparations which are at an advanced stage of readiness, are cancelled with immediate effect.

Napoleon
Emperor of the French.

Given this day at the Military and Naval Office of His Imperial and Royal Majesty,
The Palace of the Tuileries,
Paris.
12 Messidor an XII
(July 1st 1804)

(Letter without date, address or signature, believed to be from William Pitt,

My Dear M,

I confess to laughter, upon reading your account of W's determination to resign his post rather than, ever again, be obliged to deal with F. Please reassure him that he shall be kept free of such duty. Poor fellow: F is such a monster!

None the less, F has rendered great service to the Nation. As you know it has long been our policy that these Baltic castles should be demonstrated as vulnerable to modern artillery, since the French intended to seize one and hold it, as part of their plan to deny us access to the Baltic, with its indispensable supplies of masts, spars and other naval stores without which our Fleet could not sail, leaving the Kingdom at risk of invasion.

Thus, the ludicrous promise of 'A Certain Person' to the Duchess was a precious gift of fortune, enabling us to pretend to act on his orders, where otherwise we were held impotent by fears within Parliament of offending the Russians. Therefore – thanks to F – we have finally achieved a great and important objective of maritime strategy, at the cost of a few ships and men.

Furthermore, we are reminded that F is a creature of astounding improvisation and of irresistible determination to get things done, such that, however strong may be his dislike of covert actions, he remains our ideal choice for these in future.

Cordially, P.